PRAISE FOR ELIZ

"In the glittering world of influencers, perfection is the currency and authenticity is just another hashtag. But behind the curated feeds and polished captions lies a chaotic battleground where every post is a skirmish in the war for relevance. *Follow Me* is a wickedly funny, heart-wrenching tale that peels back the Instagram filter to reveal the messy reality of modern motherhood. With biting humor and searing insight, Elizabeth Rose Quinn holds a mirror up to society that simultaneously deifies and condemns mothers. It's a splashy beach-read thriller that's low-key a treatise on how capitalism and influencer culture have co-opted women's agency and identity in the pursuit of an unattainable ideal. This novel is a must-read for anyone who is a mother or has lost someone to the all-consuming vortex of modern mommyhood."

—Adele Lim, screenwriter of *Crazy Rich Asians* and director of *Joy Ride*

"*Follow Me* is a hilarious takedown of mommy influencers and the mighty rule of algorithms. How far will someone go to stay at the top of your FYP? Elizabeth Rose Quinn's masterful mix of humor and sarcasm makes this *the* book to read about #momlife. Especially if you secretly hate Insta-mommies. A must-read . . . I found myself sucked in and couldn't wait to find out what happened."

—Amina Akhtar, critically acclaimed author of *Almost Surely Dead*

"Whip smart, cacklingly funny, surprisingly gutting, and wholly original—this book embodies the very essence of contemporary motherhood, its messy rage and questing hope set against the backdrop of its fraught pursuit of unattainable perfection. I frankly can't believe what Quinn has pulled off here. Comedic horror? Earnest satire? Anti-domestic thriller? Whatever it is, give me more and keep it coming."

—Julia Whelan, international bestselling author of *My Oxford Year* and *Thank You for Listening*

FOLLOW ME

FOLLOW ME

A THRILLER

ELIZABETH ROSE QUINN

This is a work of fiction. Names, characters, organizations, places, events, and incidents are either products of the author's imagination or are used fictitiously. Otherwise, any resemblance to actual persons, living or dead, is purely coincidental.

Published by Thomas & Mercer, Seattle

www.apub.com

ISBN-13: 9781662524813 (paperback)
ISBN-13: 9781662524806 (digital)

Cover design by Alicia Tatone
Cover image: © brickrena, © CSA Images, © Vasil_Onyskiv / Getty

Printed in the United States of America

For my family.
Especially Ryan.

Chapter 1

Americana Mama

Chiara rolled down her minivan window to better take in the Mendocino hills. Hot summer air billowed in, and for the first time since she gave birth to her two boys, she felt like herself—her actual full self. She tried to remember the last time she didn't feel like a chewed-up, spit-out sticky ball of motherhood. The memories were vague, and none were more recent than two years ago. But with the window down and music blasting, she could almost block out the two toddler car seats the size of parade floats and the smell of vomit from their last attempt at a family road trip (aborted: car sickness, pink eye). In fact, if she squinted just right in the rearview mirror, she could even pretend that her forehead wrinkles were gone and the graying hair at her temples were actually sun streaks.

Chiara wasn't naive; she'd known motherhood was going to be hard. Especially when she'd found out she was having twins—or "Hell's Jackpot," according to her own twin, Adrienne. ("But at least they're not identical," Adrienne had quipped, echoing their mother's oft-repeated gratitude for that small mercy.) Chiara was ready for late nights, piles of diapers, and missing anything fun that happened after 5:00 p.m. But she wasn't ready for the one-two punch of personal obliteration and her new constant companion, hormone-fueled doom. That sneaky postpartum anxiety had her up all night, thinking of how exactly she would get her babies out of the car when the Richmond-San Rafael Bridge collapsed, plunging them into the dark gray-green San Francisco Bay water, and casually jotting down funeral arrangements in her Notes app when the twins caught the flu at four months and coughed until they threw up. Loud noises made her jump. The hideous cacophony of the garbage truck made her bones vibrate for two hours. Her internal monologue was just all the ways Death was beckoning her family to ruin: a car jumping the curb as the driver texted, flattening her double stroller; a grape grabbed too early off the cutting board getting lodged in a toddler's throat; drowning in the bathtub when she sprinted to grab an extra hooded baby towel. Her mind was a one-screen movie theater, the only film available was *Final Destination: Baby Edition*, and that horror show was playing on repeat.

Chiara remembered her mother's daily mantra when taking her own ineffectual antidepressants: "Better living through chemistry."

Chiara had thought her mother's turn of phrase was so clever and was crushed when, years later, Adrienne told her it was actually the tagline from a commercial.

But even with the unmanageable fear chewing away at her brain every second, Chiara had recently declined a Zoloft prescription. Her moods had been unpredictable, her patience as taut as a violin string. She could see outside her own body when she lost her temper, but she was powerless to stop it. Yet somehow she couldn't accept taking a medication while she was still breastfeeding.

The doctor had assured her it was safe for her boys. "A healthier mom *is* a healthier baby," her OB had said gently.

No dice. Instead of pills, she'd left the exam room with a pile of pamphlets on what to look for to prevent postpartum psychosis. Chiara tossed them in the garbage as soon as she was home, newly annoyed every time she thought of her doctor's earnest worry.

Chiara would take Zoloft, she had said. She just wanted to wait until the boys were properly weaned. She had a plan.

This was just the most recent example of her new emotional hierarchy. The boys always came first, even when it harmed her.

Therein was the irony: she couldn't see that the main culprit for her own obliteration wasn't her sons, but her.

That's what a good mother does, she thought. *Better living through self-sacrifice.*

So this trip to the mommy-influencer weekend was more than a treat—it was an aberration. While Chiara was sure a prescription wasn't right for her, a quick weekend away and two glorious nights of sleep would be crucial for her mental health. This weekend of rest would buy her the next six months of sanity. Then she could wean the boys.

(Does it ever occur to her that she can't undo years of exhaustion and bank six months of sleep in forty-eight hours? Of course not. Mommy logic is closer to a Zen koan than actual math.)

Chiara had never been much of a social media person. She posted infrequently and was always about three years behind whatever the new "It" app was. Born in '89, she had missed MySpace entirely, as she was slightly too young. Tumblr was a mystery. She was the last of her friends to join Facebook. She was only two years late to Instagram, which was early for her. By the time Snapchat came around, she declared that she was retired from all new media. Partially, this was laziness. But it was also due to a wish that when Instagram was no longer cool and perhaps even disappeared, so would her entire digital universe. Like when they closed the wave pool at the waterslide park when she was twelve, and she had not been in, nor sought out, another wave pool since. So the fact that Chiara became a tiny internet celebrity was implausible bordering on absurd.

Chiara had come to call it her "moment of cursed serendipity" when she posted a silly photo of her boys and had accidentally used the niche yet popular hashtag #ThankGodIMicrodosedToday to explain the glazed look of *I give up* in her eyes. The irony being that she hadn't microdosed that day—or any day, in many years. Not that anyone had asked her. Instead, one of the most highly trafficked mommy-meme accounts reposted her, and within what seemed like hours, Chiara had gone viral. Not only was her original post shared by several other accounts (using hashtags like #SoTrue, #ItMe, etc.), but her words were also superimposed on other people's posts. Posts about their dogs who'd eaten a large rock for the fifth day in a row, or their elderly parents' surprise hoarder homes that were supposed to have been packed up for the moving van by 4:00 p.m., or even one jilted bride at her wedding reception, *sans* groom.

While she struggled to retain any of the specific social media lingo (Stories vs. Reels? Hashtags vs. tags?), *viral* she experienced as the most intuitive word in the glossary. Her phone and life were overrun with unwanted dings, buzzes, and DMs. If her Instagram account was her quiet parcel of farmland, this viral moment was the once-in-a-generation flock of locusts coming to consume her.

Her Insta-inbox had flooded with offers for merch. But when she read the fine print, they weren't offering the wares for free—it was always for sale. And she didn't need any more stuff in her house. Stuff stuff stuff. Stuff was *everywhere*. Stuff piled up so high, in so many corners, that it was threatening to become sentient and smother her. Chiara hoped for a (small, controlled) house fire to cleanse her of all the detritus she had passively accumulated over the years. So the idea that random brands wanted to send her more crap, for the low, low price of using her face and her babies' faces in an ad for perpetuity? Hell no.

She was honestly waiting for the interest in her Instagram to dissipate, and even considered deleting her account for a bit to hasten the process. Then, about a week into her tiny internet fame, in a message she couldn't ever find again in the piles of DMs, someone had suggested this influencer weekend as something she should look into.

Even though Chiara didn't want to become an Instagram personality, the photos from the previous years looked so fun. More than fun—it looked like what she was needing: community. Or, as they called it, *coMOMunity*. She would pass on the cheap HGTV-knock-off home goods and expensive subscription Montessori-rip-off toy bundles that filled her targeted ads. She desperately needed other mom friends, and this weekend seemed like a good way to meet some.

She had tried meeting moms at the park or at mommy-and-me classes. But having twins meant that, more often than not, one of them was always napping, so she would go weeks without ever leaving the house. She couldn't even make it to the grocery store, and instead had to order things to be delivered, or walked out to her car while she held up a sign saying BABY SLEEPING, PLEASE PUT TARGET ORDER IN THE BACK! She felt like the entire world was happening on the other side of a pane of glass that was one thousand square miles, and no amount of planning could get her through the partition.

Her husband would come home from work and ask her, "How's nap jail?" The first time he'd said it, Chiara laughed hysterically, which then came close to actual hysteria. Then she'd dissolved into uncontrollable tears for thirty minutes as her husband lovingly held her, even though he was so confused that he was afraid to speak for fear of making it worse.

So no, she did not want a sustainable-bamboo spice rack with little vintage-style jars and the tiny pen to label the jars with the special spices that would be delivered monthly to her house. She did not need the rotating seasonal doormats that go in the washing machine. She did not covet the ethical-linen duvet set that matched the shower curtain that aesthetically tied to the carpet, which came with a complimentary set of furry poofs no one would ever sit on.

But this mommy-influencer weekend . . .

It was the Annual Style Summit for Instagram Moms, held at queen influencer Thea McCorckle's ranch in Northern California. It boasted spa treatments, crafting ideas, and most of all, coMOMunity! Chiara had wanted to ignore it. She told herself she had bookmarked the post so she could show it to her sister and make fun of it. *A style summit?* she'd planned to say to Adrienne. *What the hell is that?* Oh, they would laugh. They would feel so superior.

But that never happened.

Instead, Chiara found herself going back again and again to pore over the photos. Everyone looked so happy! The comment section was so supportive! Mothers were counting down the days until the event. In other posts, moms were asking for support on sleep training, on finding time for themselves, on making their husbands help out more with the kids. Chiara saw herself in this online world. Finally, the partition was gone. She posted, she tagged, she commented, she voted in polls, and she clicked every *Link in Bio*. Finally, she wasn't alone.

Chiara had even done something that a previous iteration of herself would have never, ever have done: she entered a contest to win a ticket to the summit. Chiara, who hadn't even once called a radio station to request a song, and who found the exhibitionism of *Wheel of Fortune* stomach churning, followed the multistep directions to enter her name in the Thea Summit Sweepstakes. She knew it was a long shot, as they were only giving away one spot out of two hundred, but the tickets were so expensive that winning was the only way she would get to go.

And then . . . she won.

Chiara had read the DM again and again, unable to comprehend that, for the first time in her life, she'd won something! The message was so generic that she almost deleted it, not realizing it wasn't yet another piece of marketing spam.

> Hello, Mini Mom! Welcome to your new home away from home—the CoMOMunity Style Summit! Your ticket is below. Can't wait to meet you! —Yours, the Mom Squad

Chiara was elated! However, she suddenly had a new problem: How would she tell her husband that she was going to leave him with the babies for a weekend to join an online world she hadn't yet told him anything about? This summit was going to seem completely out of the blue, possibly on par with a psychotic break. To be fair, she had been teetering close to a mental health episode for months, so she wouldn't blame him if he thought it was all a fever dream brought on by POW levels of sleep deprivation. Nevertheless, the promise of respite, the promise of sleep, the promise of life with adults—it all lifted her mood more than the Zoloft that her doctor kept suggesting.

Apparently, this emotional shift was obvious, because two days later her husband said timidly over dinner, "You seem happier. Are you?"

Chiara sheepishly told him about the Instagram accounts she was following.

Before she had even realized how much she wanted it, Chiara was halfway through her pitch on how she had won a ticket to the weekend, and why she needed to go, and how she could preplan everything so it wouldn't impact him or the kids too much.

Even now, Chiara could feel the strange mix of embarrassment and uncontrolled yearning she'd had during that dinner. Once her words had tumbled out, she braced herself for her husband to dismiss the idea.

Instead, he was on board immediately. "Chiara, I think this is a great idea!"

Her breath caught in her chest. "Really?"

"Really."

"You don't think it's dumb? It might be so dumb. I'll sleep on it. Maybe circle back in a couple days, see if it's really something I actually want to do."

He started shaking his head. "No, no, no. You are not going to talk yourself out of it." He pulled out his phone and started typing. "In fact, I am going to check . . ." Chiara heard the whoosh of a text message being sent, and then his phone chimed. "Yup, my mom is free that weekend. She will come help me with the kids. You're going."

Chiara laughed. "Why do you care so much? Think my mothering is that terrible? That I need a craft crash course?"

"Of course not!" Her husband paused and bit the corner of his mouth—the sure tell that he was debating the cost of honesty. Choosing his words carefully, he took Chiara's hand and looked at her with palpable compassion. "I just feel like this is the first time in a long time I have seen the old carefree you. I miss her."

Chiara's eyes welled with tears. "I miss her, too."

Now, finally, the summit was here.

Chiara felt lighter with every mile she drove. Her hand out the window, hair blowing in her face, she relished the feeling of being alone. Truly alone. Not the *hiding in the bathroom while small baby fingers smushed cereal under the door* alone that she was used to. She stopped at a farm stand and spent way too long perusing a variety of dried fruits—and why not? There was no rush! No nap to time out! No diaper that was in need of changing! Chiara's cheeks flushed with the sheer luxury of thinking *What would I like to do right now? What would I like to listen to? What snack sounds good to me and only me?*

She settled on dried apricots and a giant bag of mixed nuts, two things that were essentially outlawed in her home for being choking hazards. Chiara even did the unthinkable: she took a detour to a viewpoint on the map. She parked her slate-gray minivan under a large oak tree and took in the panorama. Big puffy clouds floated above her, and she watched as they slowly hit the cold marine layer and spread into a thin fog. Dappled sunlight caught her eye as she reclined in her seat, eating her bag of allergens and windpipe blockers. A nut rolled out of the bag, and she smiled ear to ear knowing she didn't have to immediately locate it before small hands did. The only sound was the oak tree's leaves rustling in a soft breeze and a lone dove cooing. If this was the high point of the weekend, Chiara would be more than satisfied.

Her mother-in-law had arrived the night before to help for the weekend. Chiara definitely got a perverse pleasure out of the fact that her husband had immediately recognized that he couldn't handle one single weekend alone with the kids. She hadn't had any experience with babies when she left the hospital with two newborns, but no one had seemed to think twice about her.

"You'll figure it out" was the only response she'd gotten when she shared her apprehension.

"Nature will kick in," the nurses had said as they ushered her out of her L&D room.

No one said that meaningless treacle to her husband, though. Everyone knew that this was too hard for one person to handle, as long as that one person was anyone but Chiara.

She even hoped quietly that the weekend was extra hard so he would really, truly know. But then she immediately felt guilty for such thoughts, because she knew if it was a hard weekend for her husband, then more than likely, it was also a hard weekend for her babies. She wanted them to be fine without her. She really, really did. After this little break, she could come back and be better than ever. More loving, more patient, more present.

Parenthood was a trip. As if she were seeing a monsoon moving across a plain, Chiara could feel the heart-shaking moments coming, soak them in, and then commit them to memory as they happened. Even if she missed it, the wildest part was that she knew another magic moment was coming. She just had to wait.

Her twenties, of course, had been filled with joy. Core memories of dancing in gay bars with Adrienne in the Castro District. Of that sunrise they spent on the beach in Mexico. Of a certain dinner party where the lighting was perfect. But she had been drugged out for so much of it that she never saw it in the moment. She saw it later, sometimes a day, or a month, or a year passing before she realized how special that time was, and by then the details had faded and she wasn't sure if what she was remembering was even true.

Parenthood for Chiara was having this higher power to see the past, present, and future all at once.

Holy shit. It's happening, she would think, and she would open herself up to the joy, the soul-rendering bliss. Sure, minutes later it would be followed by tantrums, or lost shoes, or, more often than not, vomit. But those were made oh-so tolerable by the happiness.

Everyone says parenthood is both so incredible and so damn hard. What people don't talk about is the awareness of it all. Chiara was unsure if this was her unique experience or if it was just too hard to describe until it was lived firsthand.

It felt so whole and wholesome, she could die at any second and never need more. Weekend pancakes. Lounging in the grass at the park. The first time the boys realized they could put bubble bath on their heads and they laughed until they both got hiccups, and then they laughed even more. The perfect five minutes of quiet after the babies fell asleep. This was to know contentment in its truest form.

Often, especially when the kids were crying and everyone's patience had left the building, she would take her husband's hand and say, "We are in it."

And he would say back, "We *are* in it."

It wasn't a rallying cry or a way to vent their frustration. It was a call to stay present in this chaotic moment. This was it. No other childhood was coming. They wanted to sink into it like a warm bath and never get out.

Her sister, Adrienne, wasn't there for these moments. She didn't see it. This was actual love. Actual romance. Someone who could sit in a used midsize SUV with an interest rate one point shy of loan shark territory and think, *I choose you.* Someone who could collapse into bed at 7:00 p.m. after a single trip to the market, the faint whiff of diaper cream embedded in all their clothes, and say, "This is all I have ever wanted."

More than *I love you*, "We are in it" meant "I would only do this with you."

As much as Chiara wanted to be angry with Adrienne for not understanding her new life in marriage and motherhood, she knew her sister had good reason to be skeptical. Chiara cringed in embarrassment for herself and flushed with deepest gratitude for Adrienne when she thought back to her very long, very subpar dating history. Chiara had had a real talent for picking losers with a mean streak. When the men would eventually shed their meek presentation to viciously cut her down, Chiara had always taken it. She accepted the inconsistent affection and the brazen lying, and quietly waited for more.

It was hard to choose the Top 3 Worst Boyfriends, but a few stood out. There was the bartender who would berate her if she tried to contact him more than once per day, even though they lived together and shared a car. Meanwhile, his expectation was that she was always available to him no matter what, and would be furious if she didn't drop everything to ferry him to and from wherever he needed to go. Even if that meant her waking up at 3:00 a.m. to pick him up from his shift, or her being forced to run for the bus at the last second because he was too hung over to drop her at her job. There was the boyfriend who "didn't like labels," and when he went on monthly business trips, he would always stay at "friends' houses" instead of hotels. It turned out, by *friends* he meant *women he was sleeping with on the side*. Not to mention his business trips were already suspicious as hell, as he did not have a job beyond selling pot to college students. Another boyfriend asked Chiara to marry him after they had been dating for eight months. Part of his romantic proposal was that his other girlfriend was three months pregnant, and he thought Chiara would make a great stepmom. He somehow didn't anticipate the math of *Help me raise the baby I conceived while cheating on you* as a downside. But all this bad behavior from every man had seemed acceptable to Chiara—expected, even. In every instance, it was only when she reported these things to Adrienne and her sister would blow a gasket that Chiara realized she deserved infinitely better.

Adrienne demanded respect for Chiara. On multiple occasions, she came to move Chiara out of apartments with men who were mistreating her. Boyfriend 1 came home to an empty apartment, changed locks, and a book of bus tickets taped to the front door. Boyfriend 2 arrived at one of his "business trips" only to find out that Adrienne had emailed every single one of his side trysts on a group email introducing them to each other, effectively detonating his carefully constructed web of lies. (The email subject: A Storm in Every Port.) Afterward, he had left voicemails for months threatening violence, and even tried to break into Chiara's apartment as revenge. But Adrienne smashed his hands with a baseball bat, called the cops, and got Chiara a new cell number all in one day. Boyfriend 3 was her opus. Adrienne bought a four-month supply of diapers, plus all the requisite baby-changing paraphernalia (as per the saleswoman) and sent it all to the mother-to-be with a card reading *When you throw out a dirty diaper, throw out that cheating asshole too*, along with copies of his texts to Chiara begging her to marry him.

It was Chiara's lifelong pattern: she fell in love with potential and promises. Even when the potential never actualized and the promises became a road map of broken trust, Chiara was ever hopeful that it would all work out. Adrienne tethered her back to reality, where these men weren't worth her time or attention. But it wasn't just hollow romances that Adrienne rejected for her sister—Ade also refused to accept Chiara's low self-regard in all its forms. When Chiara made a passing gibe at her own expense about wanting to try community college but being too dumb, Adrienne marched her ass to the Laney Junior College admissions desk and made her enroll.

"Chiara, you are smart as hell. Don't let anyone tell you that you aren't."

When Adrienne said it, Chiara believed her.

A year later Chiara was late to the lecture when her final paper was due at the start of class. She called Adrienne, heaving tears. "The professor won't accept it now! Without that paper in, I'll fail!"

"How many people are in the class?"

Chiara was confused how this was salient information, but she answered, "I don't know. It's a big lecture, so maybe one hundred?"

"Great. Don't move."

Adrienne drove to campus like a bat out of hell, double-parked in a loading zone, and found Chiara in the hallway outside the lecture hall. Adrienne took Chiara's paper and then waited next to the classroom door. When the professor exited, Adrienne pretended to slip, knocking him down with her. As she helped him gather his things, she slipped Chiara's paper into the professor's pile without him seeing.

Chiara passed the class. And the next. And the next. Adrienne was always helping pay for books, always reading the syllabus, too, so Chiara could bounce ideas off her and feel prepared in class. When Chiara eventually transferred and then graduated from Cal State East Bay, Adrienne brought an air horn and screamed, "That's my sister!" when Chiara got her diploma. The first college graduate in their family. Chiara sincerely wished she could give half her degree to Adrienne; it was only because of her twin's belief in her that Chiara had made it all the way to a bachelor's. It felt disingenuous that only her name was on the diploma.

So, as exhausted as Chiara was now with Adrienne's attitude, she couldn't blame her, either. When she assured Adrienne that her husband was good and that they loved their boring domesticity, Chiara could hear how it all sounded exactly like the denials from her past—that the crappy boyfriend was really sweet when no one was around, and it was totally fine that the newest jerk on the scene let his hard-core punk band use her studio apartment as a crash pad and a rehearsal space, and whatever menial job her GED got her was the best she could hope for. Except now it was Chiara defending a man who loved canonizing Friday Night Pizza Night (a.k.a. weekly frozen pizza dinner) and trying to sell Ade on the joys of the very specific Raffi playlist she had made ("'Bananaphone' is actually really catchy!"). She felt like a sane person trying to convince the mental hospital staff she was ready to go home. The more she pushed, the less convincing she got.

Ade is still waiting to save me, Chiara realized. *Just like how she has saved me a thousand times before, even when*—especially *when—I didn't see the danger I was in or when I thought I deserved for life to fall apart again.*

Maybe this was the key to the whole mess. Instead of trying to convince Adrienne that her life was good, she would invite Adrienne in to "kick the tires," as it were. She would thank her for every time she swooped in in the past and tell her, "It's because you did that *then* that I see how good this is *now*."

After many hours of driving, and a GPS that dropped out too often, Chiara finally arrived at Thea's ranch deep in Mendocino County. Highway 101 stretched up from the Golden Gate Bridge, with Route 128 first and then Route 20 farther north, cutting both west to the Pacific, creating a rambling square. Thea's ranch was in the center of this square. This was the type of area where directions like *Turn left at the fire station* and *If you see the gas station, you've gone too far* made sense because there were only one of each of those for fifty miles in any direction.

As Chiara pulled onto the property, joining a long line of mommy vehicles, it smelled like wild fennel but more intense somehow. Nature, augmented. She realized the scent was being pumped out of the misters, along with French lavender. The wholesome equivalent of pink lights in the supermarket produce section and oxygen in casinos. Better living through chemistry once again.

Across the perfect ranch gate stretched a banner: WELCOME TO CoMOMUNITY™. In case anyone didn't know who she was, there was a life-size photo of Thea in a faux-Instagram frame, which women were ecstatically posing with. There were rolling golden hills, no neighbors, and women women women as far as Chiara could see.

The Ranch presented as #Rustic, but anyone could tell every splinter had been sanded off and the cedar was imported from Italy. But no one was here for realism. All the Mini Moms™ flocked into the CoMOMunity™ perfect Instagram world ready to take it down like an expired quaalude. Chiara included. She had had enough of real life. She was ready for escape.

After Chiara parked, she pulled a little photo off the sun visor—her two boys lying on a blanket, looking absolutely adorable. The photo had been laminated, and the edges were soft with wear. This was one of the only habits she had brought into her current life from her own mother. A sweet Polaroid of Chiara and Adrienne had lived in her mom's purse for decades and was slipped into the broken AC vent of her car during drives. They had found the photo still on her nightstand when she died.

Chiara stared at her picture lovingly, then slipped it into her pocket as she got out of the car. She grabbed her suitcase and joined a group of women in line at the check-in table.

Once she was near the front of the check-in line, Chiara took in a woman whose name tag read *Opal Winslow*. Opal stood rigidly straight, with an iPad at the ready, like a sentinel from Hobby Lobby, and despite her big grin and can-do attitude, she had all the warmth of a built-in Sub-Zero fridge (#SponCon). "Welcome, Mini Moms! Who's ready to create a cohesive-content approach for Independence Day!"

All the women let out a big "Woo!" and Chiara jumped a bit, her nerves still frayed from the drive and from . . . well, life.

Another woman with an iPad and a glazed look of joy on her face that gave Chiara the heebie-jeebies waved Chiara forward. When she got closer Chiara recognized her—this was Ashleigh. Her blond braid glinted in the sun, and her lace nap dress fluttered in the breeze. "Welcome to the CoMOMunity Style Summit, Mini Mom. I'm Ashleigh. Tell me your name, how many babies you have, and your top post."

"I'm Chiara Shaw, I have twin boys, and my top post is, um . . ."

She showed the #ThankGodIMicrodosedToday post on her phone to Ashleigh, whose eyes went wide. She took Chiara's phone and started typing.

Chiara was startled. "Whoa, what are you—"

Ashleigh waved her off. "Don't worry, Mom. It's a surprise for later. Please scan this." Ashleigh handed Chiara her phone back and then held out a QR code. Chiara complied. Ashleigh looked to her iPad again. "Okay, you're on Wi-Fi and your personal devices are all synced up."

Chiara looked at her phone and Apple Watch; a new CoMOMunity app had opened up on both.

"You can find the weekend itinerary and site map and get reminders for your preferred events all through the app. We will also suggest meetups that we think complement your mommy style."

Chiara was impressed. "Wow. So if I click here . . ." She pressed a few keys on her phone.

Ashleigh smiled. "Yep. You just booked a massage. Time to relax, Mom. You are in Cabin 8."

A few minutes later Chiara entered her one-room cabin, which was identical to the rows of other little cedar duplexes lining the edge of the field. It was like a cozy Coachella summer camp, except instead of EDM and STDs, there was shiplap and crisp cottons.

Chiara tossed her bag on the leather club chair (#PotteryBarn) and lay face down on the bed like only an exhausted mother away from her twins can. Just from being there, her stress had already gone down ten notches.

There was a quiet knock at the door, and a voice gently called, "Cabin 8, your massage service is here."

Chiara rolled over and grinned. *Hell yes.*

Night came quickly, and Chiara was locking her cabin door to go to dinner. It was that particular hour in which the air around her face was still warm, but the grass underfoot was cooling rapidly. The contrast made her acutely aware of her body in a way she had forgotten was possible, beyond anxiety over her shredded pelvic floor. She wore a linen romper, little cowboy boots, and a cute Stetson-style hat with a feather. She felt good. *Still got it.* Nothing said *Woman on Her Own* like an outfit with no easy breastfeeding access. She'd been alone for most of the day—massage, nap, bath—so she was excited for the big welcome dinner. A night with only adults? Where people talk in complete sentences? And sociopathic YouTube Kids songs aren't playing in the background at full volume? Heaven.

Chiara entered the massive barn with legitimate pep in her step, where she saw long salvaged-wood dinner tables set for the two hundred moms in attendance. A giant brass pendant light twinkled above between the rustic beams. Garlands of eucalyptus, lavender, and sage mingled with tiny American flags and hand-stamped tin stars.

Everything was perfect. Everything was themed. Everything was #InstaWorthy.

Then Chiara immediately saw five other women wearing her exact same outfit. Right down to the damn feather. Chiara realized in that instant she wasn't a cool city mom on a glamorous night out—she just looked the worst in a generic outfit from the mall. Her confidence was shattered. Chiara's shoulders rounded forward, and her hands tightened into anxious fists. If she wasn't staying here, if this was just a dinner near her house, she would have left on the spot.

A woman in her outfit entered and yelled, "Oh my God, Lauren!"

Eighteen women turned around. Yes, they were all named Lauren. Yes, they all did that high-pitched lady scream that made Chiara jump in her skin.

Suddenly, Chiara felt like this weekend was a big mistake and no amount of hot-stone massages would make up for it. She winced at the steadily increasing noise level as more women arrived. The temperature in the room was rising, too. Chiara's romper suddenly felt too tight around her hips, and the linen fibers were making her itch all over. Feeling hot, she wanted to take her hat off but knew that her hair was a sweaty mess underneath. Besides, what would she do with the hat once she took it off? Carry it? Pop it on top of a centerpiece during dinner? She grabbed a napkin off a side table and dabbed at her temples, then shoved the wadded-up paper into her pocket.

Chiara went to the closest empty seat she could find. But when she pulled the chair out, the woman next to her grabbed it.

"Sorry. This seat is saved," the woman said, possessively draping her arm over the back of the chair.

Chiara gulped out an apology and walked over to the next open seat. But when she got closer she saw that a napkin had been laid on it in a clear signal of *Not Available*.

She tried a third seat, but just as she was about to sit, another woman kindly said, "Sorry, I'm sitting there. I was just in the bathroom."

Chiara awkwardly backed away. "No worries."

Except, all worries.

Chiara finally saw a seat that had no napkin and no possessive neighbor, and made a beeline for it. She was relieved to at last be sitting down, as sitting felt less exposed than standing. However, she had chosen a chair between separate groups of friends, and so, instead of meeting peers like she had imagined, she was stuck between two women who had turned their backs to her and were turned toward their own people. Chiara had all the social cache of a mop.

To escape her awkwardness, Chiara pulled out her phone and scrolled through the nostalgia album of the day from her photo stream. Normally it was all cute pictures of her boys, which always made her happy, but today it was old, scanned pictures of her and Adrienne. One indie sleaze–era picture from the Elbo Room made her laugh, and suddenly she wished Adrienne was there. They had argued again before she left for the summit, and Chiara just wanted to make it right. She took a truly hideous selfie on purpose and texted it to her sister.

Horrid welcome dinner. If I try to come back next year, tie me to a chair, she typed. (No emoji. Adrienne hated emojis.)

Things had been rocky between them for several years, ever since Chiara started dating her now husband. As the new relationship had progressed, a novel feeling entered Chiara's life: calm. It was such a foreign concept that it had taken Chiara several months to even identify the feeling by name. Before, the constant emotions in her life had been more of the anxiety, franticness, and insecurity varieties. Along with this centered, relaxed vibe came other changes: Chiara got a regular day job at last and was shocked at how much she liked it. She started grocery shopping and stopped returning calls from scumbag exes whom she had previously always gone back to. She only partied with Adrienne on the weekends instead of every night. And even then, those weekends grew further apart. In short, she felt like she was growing up.

Meanwhile, as her entire life seemed to be coming together, Chiara's relationship with Adrienne was fraying.

Chiara had hoped that as she lessened her drug use, Adrienne would follow suit. Instead, when they hung out Adrienne seemed compelled to do all the drugs that Chiara was leaving behind. Every pill, puff, tab, and baggie Chiara declined, she watched Adrienne take as if to punish Chiara for her new habits. If Chiara passed on a shot, Adrienne took it *and* her own, plus a beer back for good measure. More often than not, by the end of the night a sober Chiara would drag a stumbling Adrienne out of a weird warehouse party and then pour her into bed. After a while every minute they spent together just seemed to exacerbate the distance between them. The second most painful thing in the world for Chiara was missing her sister. The first most painful thing was being in the same room as her.

After a year, this tension boiled over during an awkward lunch at a cheap Tex-Mex place on the marina.

Over unlimited chips and salsa, Adrienne had been taking jab after jab at Chiara's new habits, at Chiara's new job, and most of all, at Chiara's relationship. Chiara's attempts to speed the lunch along—ready to order, no starters, no drinks—were slowed by Adrienne at every turn.

"Of course we should get chips and salsa! What do you mean, you aren't getting a margarita? Do you guys have flan today? Yes, please do check what the specials are; we can wait."

Nearly an hour into the passive-aggressive emotion emporium, Chiara was shredding her napkin in her lap and desperately trying not to take the bait. She took deep, measured breaths like she had learned in her new yoga class, and visualized this lunch ending as soon as the sizzling fajita plate was cleared.

Then Adrienne went too far.

"Oh my God, Chi, I saw the funniest thing online. Did you know that when moms post stuff online, they do it in this code? Like *DD* means *Dear Daughter* and *DS* is *Dear Son*. It's so sad. Like, wow, amazing encryption, Karen. Plus, all the stories are just the worst." Adrienne put on a mocking tone. "'DD won't bring grandkids to my house to trick-or-treat, says an hour is too far to drive on a school night.' Or 'DS insists on sharing Christmas with in-laws, but Christmas is MY thing.' On and on."

Chiara took a deep yoga breath and shredded a little more of her napkin. "Just sounds like women trying to make their families work."

Adrienne blew past her. "Don't even get me started on the *Dear Husband* posts. 'DH won't sort raked leaves for our decorative Fall Festival wreath.' 'DH doesn't know how to change a diaper.' 'DH thinks I need to spend less money crafting.' It's so cringe."

Chiara's breathing was speeding up, and her napkin was confetti. "Then don't read the posts."

Adrienne plowed on. "And I was dying because all that DH stuff is so your boyfriend. He is one hundred percent a future DH. Really captures that whole khaki-coated vibe."

Adrienne laughed too loud at her little joke to notice that Chiara didn't laugh at all. In fact, Chiara had absolutely had it.

"How about you be a grown-up and say what this is really about?" Chiara hissed through her teeth. She felt a flash of satisfaction when she saw Adrienne's smile falter.

"What are you talking about? I'm just joking. You're so serious now. What, does your *DH* not like jokes and now *you* don't like jokes?"

Chiara's nostrils flared, and the flush from her chest rose to her cheeks as she spoke. "He has a name."

Adrienne waved her away. "Let's order more margaritas. You need tequila so bad."

Chiara's anger modulated in a matter of seconds into a cool detachment she had never once felt toward Adrienne. It was as if all the chaotic strife of the last year had suddenly come into perfect focus. "Our entire lives you have pushed me to want better, to be with someone kind, to be with someone who would protect me and care for me like you do. And now I am with that person. And you hate him."

"I don't hate him. He's too boring to hate."

But it was Chiara's turn to ignore her sister and plow on. "I think you resent me for growing up. You liked when I was a mess, and you got to be the center of my life, always saving me. But I'm not her anymore. And I don't understand why, after a lifetime of being in lockstep, this new healthy, sober phase is the single one where you won't follow me even a little bit?"

Adrienne sputtered for a second, and again tried to get out of the conversation. "You have totally lost the plot. I'm fine. I am who I have always been. You've changed."

Chiara's voice rose, carrying to every ear in the immediate vicinity. "Yeah! That's the point! I am growing—why can't you? You think I don't see you using more? Spending time with the sketchy people we used to avoid even when we were at our lowest? Buying pills from dealers you don't know? This is dangerous stuff you're doing, and I know you know it! It's like you're hurting yourself to punish me!"

"I have to use more to drown out what an absolute bore you've become. I don't even know you anymore."

Chiara stood up from the shiny vinyl booth. She could feel the rest of the restaurant looking at her, but she didn't care. "Here's an idea: How about you stop being a selfish bitch and take some responsibility for your own mess?"

Adrienne stood up, too. "How about you admit that you bailed on me! On *us*!"

"'Bailed' how? I am living the life you always told me you wanted for me, and now you've disappeared. You say I left you, but I say you left me. Call me when you grow up."

At that, Chiara gathered her bag and stormed out.

She didn't speak to Adrienne for three months. The worst part was, she didn't really miss her. She was exhausted from the constant drama and the unpredictable anger she'd realized she had spent her whole life soothing. Adrienne's absence in her life wasn't a void—it was peace. Chiara loved her beyond measure, but she needed a break.

There was so much blame from both of them heaped onto the other, over and over, for everything. Weird unconscious emotional math was sprouting up in their once-unbreakable bond like poison oak.

But even with all the arguments, silent treatments, awkward reconciliations, and cooling-off periods that lasted too long, Adrienne was one of the most important people in Chiara's life. Anytime Chiara felt low, Adrienne knew the exact thing to say to boost her confidence—and tonight Chiara felt low as hell in this fancy barn. She would have paid any amount of money to have Adrienne here, at this weird weekend getaway, whispering snarky comments, stealing candlesticks from the centerpieces, and most of all, making Chiara feel special in this maternal monolith. She felt a pang of guilt for wanting her sister to be there for the sole purpose of uplifting her ego. Perhaps it was selfish, but maybe it wasn't.

Dinner finally began. An (apparently preselected) ensemble of mommies rose from their seats at the sound of a gong and efficiently headed toward a side kitchen behind a barn door designed to blend in with the wall, which Chiara had failed to see.

Chiara heard a mom whisper in an awed tone, "Incognito Barn is so hot this year."

In smooth, choreographed movements, the select mommies entered the kitchen, then exited ladened with food. They set platters (handmade pottery, no dishwasher) down at perfect intervals on every table, along with short menus propped up on tiny stands made from vintage wine corks.

Chiara read over the menu, partly because she was interested and partly to cover the fact that she was still in a social desert between two groups who continued to be oblivious to her presence. The meal was titled *#AmericanaMama*: BBQ chicken, corn (not on the cob, that's bad for pictures), Caesar salad (dressing on the side), biscuits with hot honey (#HotHoney was very on trend), and marinated jackfruit for the #HealthyGirlies. The word *organic* was listed so frequently that it started to look fake to Chiara's eyes.

Chiara ate her food and continued to read the menu over and over until one of the women next to her said, "Oh, hi, I didn't see you there."

Chiara smiled and replied in her best casual tone, "Oh, yeah. Just sat down." A lie she hoped she could pull off.

The woman smiled back and pointed to the menu. "Can I see that?"

Chiara handed it to her. "Of course!"

The woman took the menu, said thank you, and then immediately turned back to her friends, leaving Chiara alone again.

Chiara finished her dinner quickly and was plotting her exit when the gong sounded again. The twinkle lights sped up as the overhead lights went down. Women everywhere started wooing and clapping.

And then Thea came up to the stage, her mere presence hushing the crowd like a magic spell.

Chiara almost gasped when she saw her. Thea was, in a word, *magnetic*. She had long, brunette tresses that country songs were written about. She was beautiful in a way that felt accessible, avoiding all the fake lashes and lip filler that plagued other Insta-images. When she smiled out at the crowd, Chiara felt like it was a smile just for her. Her warmth wasn't a put-on. There was a reason why two hundred women had driven to the middle of nowhere for two days, and that reason was Thea. Chiara had spent hours poring over Thea's Instagram feed, and then her Pinterest page, and then her website, all while listening to any podcast in which she had made a guest appearance. Chiara could recite her story from memory now: a forty-year-old mom of three who built an empire by making motherhood feel less lonely. Raised in Topanga Canyon, she spent her early twenties doing design work in Manhattan, and she was one of the first bloggers to catch a following in the aughts.

Chiara had devoured the backdated blog like it was a long-lost friend's diary. She relished how natural and easy Thea's life seemed as she changed and grew post by post. First, her nights out at Bungalow 8 ("Great grilled cheese!") became nights in at her brownstone in Brooklyn ("I still miss Manhattan, though."). Then a mid-century DIY renovation in Santa Monica was documented in charming detail ("California girls always come home."). By the time she announced Baby #3 and their family moved to the country, she was a mommy-influencer powerhouse, and Chiara felt like she really *knew her*.

While their timelines had similarities, Chiara's transition from teenage dirtbag to suburban mom had been rocky at best. So many missteps, so many regrets. There were full calendar years Chiara wished she could forget. Meanwhile, Thea's growth was an organic progression that never felt forced. No awkward stages or terrible, universally hated boyfriends here. And her growth was always both personal and professional, with one informing the other, her internal yearnings feeding into her design work and coming out as a new way to see the world—or at least, a new way to see kitchen renovations. Whatever Thea posted was exactly what every white millennial mom wanted to wear, eat, *be*. Audrey Gelman might have put Millennial Pink all over the Wing, but it was Thea who first put plush dark-rose carpets in her bedroom. Posh and Becks named their daughter Harper *after* Thea did (her sons Finch and Radley came later). And even if someone remained unaware of Thea as a person, as Chiara had until recently, her love of kombucha, Cronuts, and Carrara marble reached far and wide. She'd even brought carnations back from the style dead.

But none of it—not even the Denny's-style carnations she dyed herself—was bullshit. Thea liked it all way before any sponsor paid for a spot on her grid, and she genuinely wanted to share it with whoever cared to listen, regardless of personal financial gain. And that casual *take it or leave it* vibe meant that everyone wanted to listen. In fact, Chiara was shocked to see how much of Thea's taste had already been present in her life. Millennial Pink–bath towels, kombucha in the fridge, and so much late-night googling for dupes of the expensive Italian marble she could maybe one day afford to put in her town house.

Chiara felt oddly breathless being in the same room as Thea. She had prepared to be let down when presented with the mere mortal.

Instead, this grounded individual was even more inviting than the curated media images.

Thea stood behind a tasteful podium with a small microphone that had been artistically tucked into a floral arrangement. "Welcome, Mini Moms!" she said like she was seeing her oldest friends for the first time in years.

Every mother there let out her best "WOO!"

Thea put on a coy tone. "I think you know who I am . . ."

Two hundred voices yelled out, "THEA!"

Thea winked, which actually somehow impossibly worked when she did it. "That's right! We have a great weekend planned. There are seminars on how to time the perfect family photo with fireworks, trend forecasting for #ToddlerMeals—can you say char-CUTE-erie? Plus, massages, facials, and wine tastings. #WineTime #MommyJuice."

This was met with the loudest "WOO!" yet.

Thea went on. "But first, we need to meet a few of our new Mini Moms. These are the moms who really made a social media splash this year, and they need their flowers. When I say your name, stand up. First is Becky Ackerman. She's a mom of six, living in Akron. Her top post is . . ."

Projected onto the screen behind Thea was Becky's top Instagram post: a Boomerang of all six of her kids lined up in personalized "pots of gold." A papier-mâché rainbow fluttered above their heads as the kids tossed out gold coins over and over and over.

This was met with a unanimous *Awwwww* from the crowd.

Thea touched her heart. "So cute! We still haven't picked our holiday for next year's CoMOMunity Summit. Maybe we should do Saint Patrick's Day? A little luck of the mommies?"

"WOO!" (So many *woo*s. Chiara wondered if the *woo*s would haunt her dreams.)

Thea continued, "Next, we have Shannon Trapps. She has triplets—two girls, one boy. And her top post is . . ."

Projected onto the screen was a photo of Shannon and her husband crouched on a lake dock with their three kids between them. Their teeth were so white you could see them from space. Chiara squinted. Did that small child have veneers?

Thea read the caption: "Life with you is always an adventure. #TRIPLETrapps."

More *awwws*.

"Follow that hashtag for daily joy, I am telling you. Next, we have Chiara Shaw, and her top post is . . ."

Projected onto the screen was Chiara's selfie as she stood over the bathtub. Her sons had smashed multiple tiles around the shower. Her caption read "#GoodbyeDeposit! #ThankGodIMicrodosedToday."

Chiara's post was . . . nothing like the others. Seeing it up on the big screen only made the stark divide worse. Her life was messy, and not in a cute way. The lighting in the windowless bathroom gave her and the kids' skin a grayish tinge. There was clearly a soap ring in the tub, with old bath crayon mixed in. The grout desperately needed a scrub.

It was . . . well, real life.

And apparently that was very bad.

A weird hush washed over the room.

Chiara felt every eye on her. The judgment was palpable, like a cold mist running down her back. Her eyes flitted around the room, and all she saw was a sea of derision, of whispers, of unmistakable anger.

Thea put on a gossipy tone. "Whose engagement numbers went down when this post hit the Explore page?" This was met with dead silence. Thea pressed a bit. "Come on, no need to be shy. If your engagement took a hit after this post went viral, put your hand up."

More silence. Then . . . Thea put her own hand up. There was a gasp from the crowd. And then, slowly, everyone else's hands went up.

"Oh yeah, it was this lady right here." Thea looked down to make sure she got the name right. "Chiara Shaw! She took the Gram by storm that month! My numbers dropped, too, ladies. No shame."

Chiara wished for a trapdoor to open beneath her chair so she could disappear from view. To be so judged, so singled out; to be mocked for her mothering—this was her hell.

Thea's tone turned chipper. "Here's what I've got to say, though. Social media is supposed to be just that: social. A way for us to connect! And real connection requires real vulnerability." Thea looked directly into Chiara's eyes. "Thanks for being real, Chiara. We moms all need that."

Thea was 100 percent genuine, and it made all Chiara's worries wash away. More than that, though, this comment from Thea seemed to act as a kind of blessing. Chiara could physically feel the other moms change their perception of her. She went from pariah to special in seconds flat, like a public opinion riptide that had happened to wash her ashore instead of out to sea.

"It's not all perfect—am I right, moms?" Thea called out. "Plus, this sassy post caught the eye of *Kristen Bell.* Yeah. Big deal."

The women around Chiara all murmured.

"Ahhhhhh!"

"She is so talented."

"I love those refrigerator commercials she does with her husband."

"WOO!"

(So. Many. *Woo*s.)

Thea shifted gears, making it clear that the getting-to-know-you portion of the night was over. "And now for a fun surprise . . ."

Thea made a motion to Opal, who pressed a few things on her iPad. Suddenly, there was a chorus of alerts from every cell phone and Apple Watch in the room.

Thea beamed. "That's right! Two hundred and fifty dollars off your next Target purchase from our sponsors!"

Every woman there went berserk.

In her best *You Get a Car!* Oprah impression, Thea called out, "Cupcake wine! Crest Whitestrips! *Joanna Gaines.* Yup! Two hundred and fifty dollars off for ALL of you!"

Chiara looked at her watch in disbelief. Two hundred and fifty dollars was a lot of money! Maybe between the dried apricots and this gift, she hadn't made a mistake in coming here. And after Thea's blessing, the moms on either side of her finally became aware of her existence.

The mom closest to her gushed, "Oh my God, I saw your post!"

The mom across from her nodded. "We didn't recognize you all cleaned up!"

Chiara shrugged, making the internal decision to ignore the insult. "That's me!" She put out her hand to shake theirs but just got a few limp waves back.

They opened their circle a bit, and Chiara leaned in to join. They were all named Emma, or Emily, or something else from a Jane Austen novel.

"We were just talking about school lunch," the mom closest to Chiara said. "I have to get up at five a.m. to cut all the fruit."

"Tell me about it!" a mom at the end of the table chimed in. "It's like Jenga to get all the aluminum containers to fit back into her Bento-To-Go-Kiddo."

"OMG, I love the Bento-To-Go-Kiddo!"

There was a chorus of "Me too," and Chiara found herself joining in. She had no idea what they were talking about, but the urge to be part of it made her feel like she was possessed.

The mom closest to her asked, "Which bento style do your kids like, Chiara?"

Chiara's mouth opened, but no words came out. She hadn't anticipated follow-up questions! Finally, she mustered, "They like the blue one."

There were some blank stares. Clearly she had answered incorrectly.

The mom said unconvincingly, "Nice."

Chiara breathed a sigh of relief when their eyes moved on from her.

There was something that felt a little off to Chiara the longer she listened. Every woman spoke in these little canned sound bites that invited no questions or discussion. A Greek chorus each coming to deliver their moment of plot to the group. Even when they allegedly opened up and complained about their lives, it was also a brag.

"Well, Stellen just got this huge, huge, huge promotion at work—so unexpected—so he's in Paris a lot now. Of course the forty-five percent increase in our budget is nice, but it's hard to find a nanny who can be flexible with our travel schedule."

Another mom commiserated. "Yes, it's so hard to find nannies who speak French. And we spend every summer in Aix. What are we supposed to do?"

"At least you two still get to travel somewhere warm. Eddison is one of the top skiers in the country. I feel like my entire year is taking him from event to event. I miss the beach, you know?"

"The thing about a beach house, though—the landscaping has to be redone every year. Such a chore."

Chiara couldn't tell who this was for. Nothing felt real or honest. There was a thick layer of impenetrable social lacquer she couldn't decipher. The only moment they seemed genuine was when they talked about Thea. How much they admired her, how much of an impact she'd had on them. They also all agreed that Chiara was lucky—so very lucky—because Thea knew who she was.

Chiara nodded and clutched her wineglass. "Yes, I am lucky."

The dinner conversation changed topics quickly, from one surface problem to the next. Besides tossing a few cursory questions her way, the group mostly went back to talking among themselves, with Chiara being a quiet observer. This felt okay, though. She didn't want the spotlight. The low-stakes chatter about who'd had the stomach bug versus who was doing a cleanse, and who was transferring from one private school to another was a balm to her exhausted social skills. She was delighted to have nothing to contribute to those hot topics and just be along for the ride. If she could be part of a mom group and not have to do much? Ideal. A toe back in the social waters was all she could do, but it felt like an accomplishment for night one.

A few hours later, as she walked through the fog to her little cabin, Chiara's mind swirled with everything she had seen today. CoMOMunity was truly delivering. Sure, she felt awkward being out in the world again—and no, she didn't think those moms at dinner were her new best friends forever. But Chiara was so starved for other adults that she would choose some personal discomfort if that was the price for socializing with other moms. Of course, being away from her children felt like having a phantom limb; she kept reaching out to see if she could feel them bobbing around her knees. The combination of relief and guilt when their chubby hands weren't there to take hers was heady. She couldn't tell whether she felt like she had been away from them for ten years or ten seconds. She never wanted to go home, and she was desperate to see their little faces again. How both things were true, she didn't quite know.

Missing her babies felt so sweet that she decided to savor it so she could remember this feeling the next time she needed to say, "We are in it."

After entering her quiet cabin, Chiara collapsed onto a bed that someone else had made and fell into a sleep so deep not even her post-partum anxiety could disturb her.

Chapter 2

Same Fog, Different City

Adrienne cursed both herself and the thick June fog that was slowly surrounding her parked car. On the one hand, she hadn't wanted to give this new dealer her address, and she definitely didn't want to go to his house, so meeting in a public spot had been Adrienne's idea. On the other hand, she was now sitting in the abandoned Berkeley Marina parking lot alone, no one knew where she was or who she was meeting, and with every passing minute her visibility and illusion of control went down. Her carefully chosen wide-open setting was now a claustrophobic mist that concealed the exits. No one more than three feet away would be able to see her if this deal went sideways. Adrienne almost had to laugh at plotting her own perfect murder.

Just when Adrienne thought it couldn't get worse, her heater gave out with a pathetic wheeze. She hit the vent a few times in a vain hope, but the warmth never came back on. Instead, she felt a steady push of cold air from the dashboard that smelled of radiator fluid. Admitting defeat, Adrienne turned the car off. She shivered in the driver's seat, craning her neck every which way. The sane part of her yelled to just leave, but the part of her that itched with craving made her stay put.

Finally, headlights glowed dimly at the entrance, and she gave her own lights a little flicker as a signal.

An old Charger made a long, unnecessary loop around the parking lot until it pulled up next to her. Whoever was inside was also wary.

Adrienne got out and took a breath to steady her nerves. She leaned down to the half-open passenger window and saw a gruff driver who refused to meet her eyes. "Hey."

He nodded, and then a small voice came from the back seat. "He doesn't like to talk to new people."

Adrienne turned and saw a girl who couldn't be more than eighteen years old and one hundred pounds, tucked into the back corner under a large Oakland A's fleece blanket Adrienne had seen at liquor stores. When the girl waved hello, Adrienne heard the cheap fabric crackle with static electricity. Her arms were scrawny, and Adrienne's eyes caught the remnants of a bruise on her delicate cheek.

"I'm Adrienne."

"I know." She let out a tiny giggle. "I'm Drew."

The man in the front seat shifted his weight—a message: *get to business.*

Adrienne was unsure what to do next, but Drew piped up again. "You can come sit in the back with me."

Adrienne opened the back door and quickly scanned to make sure the child lock wasn't on—a lesson hard learned when Chiara had once been locked in for a five-hour joyride with a scummy ex while Adrienne followed behind in a panic.

Adrienne slid into the back but didn't pull the door all the way shut, just in case. The dealer's car smelled like menthol cigarettes and stale Takis, scents that in isolation Adrienne didn't mind but in combination made her nose twitch with revulsion. She breathed in through her mouth, willing her gag reflex to relax, and did her best to address both the man in the front seat and the teen next to her. "Dennis said you would have—"

Drew eagerly pulled the blanket to the side, revealing a rusty muffin tin with a collection of baggies in each cup. Pointing, she listed, "Adderall are here. Benzos are in this row, in order of how strong they are, time release at the end. Oxys are here, dose increase left to right. MDMA is in the party corner. Normally, I put LSD here, but the Burning Man crew just wiped us out."

Adrienne saw the girl's pride in this little project, and her heart broke. By the looks of her—her delicate freckles, teeth that were still too big for her face—this kid should be organizing her school locker, not loose scripts.

Adrienne leaned over the pills and toward Drew, her voice as low as she could make it. "How old are"—she saw terror flash across Drew's face—"these Xanax?" *How old are you?* she had wanted to ask.

The girl answered quickly. "They aren't old. Maximum impact." Her eyes stole a glance at the man in the front seat, who hadn't said a word but whose presence loomed over them both like carbon monoxide.

Adrienne selected a baggie she recognized as a mix of Xanax and Ativan. She took a couple of loose Adderalls, too. Her eyes lingered on the Klonopin.

"Klonopin is more," Drew said.

"I'm good with what I got," Adrienne said quickly, the car's smell really starting to get to her.

Adrienne reached into her pocket, and at that moment her phone chimed. This tiny sound made the man in the front jump and, by extension, made Drew jump even higher.

His hulking frame turned to stare at Adrienne, his undivided attention menacing. But she knew her way around this energy. "It's all good. Just a text."

Drew's voice trembled as she delivered a practiced message. "He doesn't like phones in the car. You weren't supposed to bring your phone."

Adrienne moved slowly and used a voice for a spooked horse. "I get it. I didn't know. I'm reaching to get my money. Phone is staying in the pocket."

Adrienne took out the cash, fanning the bills out a little so he could count them before reaching out. But he didn't. His eyes flared, and

Adrienne got the message. She changed course and gingerly handed the money to Drew, who tucked it into her hoodie.

If this exchange was written up in a police report, the man would be clean and the girl would take the rap. *A bully* and *a coward,* Adrienne thought.

As Adrienne reached for the door handle, she wanted to somehow tell Drew to call her if she needed anything, to slip her phone number into that hoodie pocket, or telepathically lead her to the spare key if she ever had to get away quick. But Adrienne knew doing anything of the sort wouldn't save this small slip of a girl. To make a move like that, to destabilize the bully-and-the-bullied in this car, would put Drew in immediate danger.

So instead, Adrienne slid backward, opened the car door, and stepped out into the wet summer fog.

Adrienne drove the twenty miles home to Hayward with the windows down, trying to get that smell out of her nose and off her skin. Her cramped studio above the abandoned storefront was the holy trinity of real estate: cheap, month to month, and the landlord accepted cash. The mismatched furniture was definitely from the curb. There was a neon liquor store sign outside the window and another one across the street. Any sane person would get a tetanus shot after entering and check their socks for bedbugs. Besides a few family photos tacked onto the walls, there was nothing here Ade couldn't walk away from scot-free, and that was exactly what made it home.

Walking through her door safe and sound, Adrienne felt a wave of relief. Just like every other time she had met a sketchy dealer, she promised herself that *this* time would be the last time. After going over all the ways it could have gone wrong—the location, the unknowns, the girl in the car—Adrienne remembered the text message.

She pulled out her phone and saw the text was from Chiara.

Adrienne smiled a little, looking at the goofy picture. She started to type Hey, sorry about the other night but then immediately deleted it. Apologizing via text felt like a cop-out. She started typing again: Looks lame! See you when you get back. But she clenched her teeth a bit, knowing it sounded snarkier than she'd meant it to. Adrienne deleted that one, too. As she paused to think of exactly what she wanted to say, something else caught her attention: the baggie of white pills. She looked at her phone one more time but decided she would respond later when she knew what to say.

She took one of the Xanax pills, crushed it up, and then chopped it into smooth even lines with ease.

After this, she thought, she would know just what to text to Chiara to make it all okay again. There would be time after this.

Chapter 3

For Mamas, by Mamas

The next day Chiara woke up late—which, for a mother of small children, means 7:20 a.m. She dressed quickly, starving for some breakfast, and managed to catch the end of a posh matcha-latte bar and snag a croissant.

As she took her first sip of matcha, Chiara saw the moms she'd met last night looking for a table, and she waved to them, inviting them to sit. They waved, too, and then they kept right on walking, instead choosing a table just on the other side of the meditation yurt.

Chiara felt sick, and it wasn't the bitter matcha. She knew a brush-off when she saw one. There was a real sorority-sister energy of *You might be like us, but you aren't one of us.* And maybe they were right. The thought hit Chiara like a knife in the gut. They probably hadn't snorted drugs in a dirty bathroom stall or sold plasma to make rent on an illegal sublet with no running water. They had been nice girls who became nice moms who had always been on their way to this nice moment. How could Chiara be mad at them when she felt in her own bones that she didn't fit here?

Too embarrassed to stay, Chiara tried to play it off like she also had somewhere to go, checking her watch and gathering her plate quickly. But really, she just went back to her cabin to hide for a few minutes.

She checked her phone again. No text from Adrienne. She had assumed as much—assumed they wouldn't talk until Chiara was home.

Chiara looked at herself in the mirror, studied her eyes and her skin. She looked closely at her self-cut bangs and her inexpertly blow-dried hair. She took in her outfit and couldn't remember where she got it, or why. She didn't really recognize herself at all. She wasn't her old self, Adrienne's inseparable party pal, and she wasn't those moms, either. Somewhere along the maternal way, she had been flattened into a mommy facsimile, leaving her in an emotional nowhere land without any identity at all.

Chiara's head started to swim. Steady on her feet but dizzy inside.

She reached for her phone again and texted her husband: A bird can love a fish, but where will they live. A dirtbag can become a mommy, but who will sit with her at lunch. Miss you guys. Xx

He quickly sent a text back with a little photo. The boys were covered in paint. Uh oh, sad poet Chiara is here! 🙂 Day drinking already? Art class went well. Lol! Love you!

Chiara smiled and zoomed in on their little faces. And he was right: she was being Sad Poet Girl.

Chiara took a quick cold shower to shake off the Matcha Mean Girls and then headed out for the day's activities.

Chiara knew the schedule was on her phone and that she could lay here inside to read it, but she wanted to meet people. She went back to the breakfast area to see what she could glean.

Too shy to join a group directly, Chiara eavesdropped on some moms who were abuzz about the day's schedule. Apparently, each summit was run a little differently to keep it fresh for the returning mommies. Firstly, each summit was centered around a different holiday and held the month before for maximum impact. (Chiara was happy she had missed last year's Valentine's Day theme, because the summit had been held in January when it was freezing.)

Secondly, in previous years, every activity had been executed by Thea or a member of her designated Mom Squad. But in the run-up to this summit, there had been a lot made of the new For Mamas, by Mamas events. Over the past year, Thea had offered regular attendees a chance to pitch and, if selected, lead an activity on day two. The vibe among the rest of the attendees was both supportive and apprehensive. This was akin to buying a T-shirt outside the concert venue instead of at the merch booth inside. They knew the quality would be less; they just didn't know by how much. That said, if the experiment was a success, they could be one of the chosen few for the next year! Chiara could see the genius in this setup: everyone there had a vested interest in everyone else doing their very best, and therefore the likelihood of it all going well went up exponentially! If it takes a village to raise a child, it takes a coMOMunity to make a style summit evolve.

Even though the official holiday for this summit was Independence Day, America's popularity, both politically and as a basic concept, was decidedly mixed, even here. So the For Mamas, by Mamas block of crafts and activities seemed to have been selected by Thea to provide a wide spectrum of rah-rah-sis-boom-bah. On one end was "Only Here for the Fireworks," the middle was "Stars and Stripes Curious," and the furthest extreme was "Yankee Doodle Dandy Petting a Bald Eagle as He Shoots a Gun." The breadth of patriotism meant everyone got to turn their Pledge of Allegiance dial to just the right degree of Washingtonian.

Not really there for any activity called *Star-Spangled Baby Headbands* or something that she could only describe as a *Military-Industrial Complex Meet-Cute*, Chiara joined the *Tie-Dye Fourth* group. The sign over the tent was a photo of Nicole Kidman from the movie *To Die For*, but instead of gesturing to a sun like her weather-girl character, she was pointing to a tie-dyed baby onesie. Considering Nicole Kidman's character was murdered in the film, Chiara wondered if the woman who'd set up this activity had actually seen *To Die For* or if they just liked the clumsy pun. No one else seemed to be bothered, though, as the event was very popular. This included the mom who had checked her in—Ashleigh—who wasn't participating but was observing the activity like an SAT proctor.

Whoever had pitched this idea to Thea had clearly done their homework, as this setup looked akin to a wholesale-textile factory. There were streamlined sets of basins, hoses, electric kettles for boiling water, stacks of white cotton clothing to choose from, dye in both liquid and powder form, fabric pens, shibori sets, various types of string, rubber bands in every width, salt, vinegar, rubber gloves, and safety goggles. (Ashleigh nodded approvingly because #SafetyFirst.) Apparently, this was not enough, though, because the mind-boggling array of tie-dye accoutrements had also been arranged by difficulty, then cross-sectioned into appropriate age groups ranging from Baby to Teen. Likely Voter cross tabs during close elections wished they had this level of minute data. (Ashleigh *really* liked that because #Curated.)

Chiara joined the Toddler setup. Turned out the "oh so easy" baby technique involved the child wearing a rubber raincoat, surgical gloves, and a clear face visor while their mother stood behind them and held their uncoordinated baby hands around a spray bottle filled with permanent dye. All this was organized around a child mannequin sporting the recommended safety gear so the moms could practice their braced stance.

"This is a super-fun and easy weekday activity when you are home during the summer," the host mom assured everyone. "Take it from me and Poison Control: babies have to drink a lot of the dye before it's toxic. Like, *a lot* a lot. So have fun! Let loose!" She laughed a little too hard at her own joke, but when Ashleigh frowned, the host mom crushed her laughter and went back to Benevolent Mom Face.

For Chiara, this mom's lived experience with Poison Control did not bolster her faith in the process, and more importantly, Chiara felt like this was definitely an activity for people without twins. If she was doing tie-dye-rubber-coat goat rodeo with one of her sons, chances of her other son grabbing some errant dye and destroying the entire living room were 100 percent. Nevertheless, while she would not be able to replicate this activity at home, she enjoyed the simple pleasure of participating in something for herself and no one else.

Once everyone's masterpiece had been hung up on the clothesline to dry, Chiara had to find her next destination for the day, which felt like a herculean task. She had always been an introvert, and being a twin meant that even when she was alone, she was with Adrienne, who could (when she felt like it) talk to anyone. As a child Chiara had had a slight stutter when she spoke. It wasn't particularly noticeable, but it caused her such anxiety, particularly in new social situations. When she approached a word that troubled her, she would often freeze, unable to speak or pivot to a different, less troublesome letter. Adrienne knew this, and crucially she also knew if she said the difficult word first, it clicked something in Chiara's mind and she could repeat it without issue. One hundred times per day Adrienne would bridge that gap midsentence, midthought, even from across crowded rooms. Chiara felt like she was a tiny radio station and Adrienne always had her antenna pointed her way. When people asked if they had Twin ESP, Adrienne would laugh and say no, but secretly Chiara would think *yes*. Or at least, she thought Adrienne had it.

Chiara hadn't stuttered in years, but she felt the emotions of the stutter still. And she was most definitely feeling them now. How she wished Adrienne could be there to bridge the gap, to smooth out the first letter, to extrovert Chiara out of herself. But Chiara had to do this on her own. She had to end her isolation.

Chiara decided to walk the meditation maze, as something to do but also as a way to get a sense of where she should go next without looking lost. From what she could see, the activities at this hour were all sports-centric, and Chiara wasn't ready to tear her ACL by stepping into a gopher hole. Then, in a moment that seemed to be fated, her Apple Watch pinged.

The Summit app was showing her an alert: Hey Mini Mom! Based on your profile we think you would like the Multiples Event that is starting in 20 minutes! Go to Tent 2!

Chiara could have kissed the little app notification. This was exactly what she needed. She took some deep breaths. It was time to be brave; it was time to *join*.

Chiara entered Tent 2 to see a circle of cute retro, woven lawn chairs all arranged around a central area that was covered with a large gingham sheet. A little sign was pinned to the gingham with a novelty gold safety pin the size of an oven mitt; it read, in matching gold calligraphy, To Be Revealed!

Most of the chairs were taken, so Chiara's options for seatmates were limited. She scoped out the least intimidating duo and went to the edge of their group. "Mind if I join you?" she asked, pushing through the lump in her throat.

"Of course!" both women replied generously, turning their chairs a bit to include her.

Chiara took a seat and introduced herself.

"I'm Michelle," said the first woman, who had long, dark hair and a nose that twitched like a cat's.

"And I'm Andie," said the second, offering her hand. Her short, curly hair was tucked up in a bandanna and she wore overalls unironically.

"Do you guys know each other from home?" Chiara cringed a bit at her phrasing. *From home?* Were they children at sleepaway camp?

"Oh yeah. She's my sister-in-law," Michelle said, nudging Andie.

Andie asked, "Did you come by yourself?"

Chiara nodded.

"Good for you! I could never do that," Andie replied.

"Well, we have a renegade on our hands, Andie. This is the #MicrodoseMom!"

Chiara was shocked. "What? No! Is that what people are calling me?"

Michelle cracked a grin. "Girl, don't even worry about it. I absolutely loved that post and sent it to all my old college friends."

"Me too," Andie said. "Besides, the moms needed to be shaken up a bit. I mean, who has time to re-grout their tub when it gets used every single night?"

Chiara felt somewhat better. Somewhat.

Michelle pointed to the center of the circle. "She's here!"

A woman, whom Chiara vaguely recognized from Thea's posts, stood in the center, turning to take in everyone's faces. "Hey, y'all, I'm McKenna!"

"Woo!" the women all replied as McKenna ran around the circle to high-five everyone there. Chiara smiled—the feeling of connection was finally happening.

McKenna gave a little bow. "If you're here, that's because you have at least one set of multiples, am I right?"

Chiara gulped. *At least one set?* Was it possible to have more than one? She felt ill at the very thought.

McKenna nodded. "I've got my two sets of twins. Any triplet moms here?"

Two moms waved.

"Any quad moms?"

One mom stood up and took a little bow.

"Wowie! Quad mom, maybe you should lead this!" McKenna laughed. The quad mom laughed. Everyone laughed, even Chiara. "No, but really. You know what they say, Multiple Moms: Fuller hands mean . . ."

"Fuller hearts!" the group said in unison, completing the catchphrase.

McKenna put her hand behind her ear. "I'm sorry, what? Fuller hands mean . . ."

"Fuller hearts!" the group replied again, louder and with more enthusiasm.

"That's what I thought," McKenna said, satisfied.

Everyone giggled a little bit. The energy wasn't self-serious. It was more like the laughter that comes after escaping a car crash unscathed. A release of tension, and joy at survival.

"I think as moms of multiples, we are entitled to do something here that we could never do with our kids. Something . . ." She paused for effect. *"Dangerous."*

After another suspenseful beat, McKenna dramatically pulled off the gingham sheet, revealing an elaborate s'mores buffet and a portable gas firepit. Chiara recognized the entire setup from her Instagram targeted ads (#LavaRocks, #Sustainable, #FreeTradeChocolate).

McKenna did some cutesy pointing like she was in an IRL story post. "Open flames? Metal skewers that could poke out an eye? SUGAR? Oh yeah. We are going there, mamas!"

Chiara couldn't help but be charmed by this low-stakes danger. Except it wasn't low-stakes danger if there had been small kids—it was literally a death trap. And everyone in the tent felt the same. The glee at being able to do a simple decadent thing and not have to wrangle a *minimum* of four tiny hands washed over them like a rosé epidural.

As Chiara ate her perfect s'more, Michelle peeked at her marshmallow. "How did you get it gooey all the way through? Mine is golden on the outside but still cold in the middle."

"I told you, you hold it too far from the flame," Andie said, pushing her skewer in deeper—and at that second, her own marshmallow caught fire. "Oh, goddamnit."

Michelle laughed. "I'd rather have a chilly middle than a charcoal blob."

Chiara laughed, too. "I hold it right above the flame until it seems soft, then, at the last minute, move it a tiny bit closer to brown the outside."

Andie was trying to remove the shriveled, blackened marshmallow from her skewer and, in the process, covering her fingers with ashen goo. "Can you do that for me? I am not gifted at this."

McKenna, who was handing out round two of marshmallows, overheard Andie. "Oh my God, yesssss, mama, yesssss segue! Everyone, listen up! When you have a second, I want y'all to write down one part of being a multiples mom that is really hard for you. What's a logistical thing that you just cannot figure out? What's your pinch point in the day? I know showing our flaws can be scary and asking for help so, so hard, hence the secret ballot–style. But really think about what ails you. I bet a mama here knows a trick! Cards and pens are over there; put them in the box when you're done, y'all."

After toasting a marshmallow for Andie, Chiara went to the card table. She knew exactly what her pinch point was, and no amount of googling had helped her. She wrote down her need and was relieved to see a hefty stack of cards already in the box.

A bit later, when everyone had had their fill of sugar, McKenna opened the box. "Who is ready to get their problems solved by the power of MAMAS!"

Everyone *woo*'d at full volume. They were high on fructose and the promise of easier bedtime routines.

McKenna read the first card. "Okay, first pinch point is . . . 'Grocery shopping! If one kid is riding in the cart, where does the other kid go? My babies are two. Whoever isn't in the cart is too big for a baby carrier, too small to walk! Help!' Okay, mamas, any suggestions for this?"

One mom raised her hand. "I have a solution: Costco."

McKenna, with the warmth of a therapist leading her client to a breakthrough, said, "Yes, yes, say more."

"At Costco the carts are extra wide and have two seats!"

Everyone clapped like this was a noncompetitive *Family Feud*. Chiara was waiting for someone to say "Good answer! Good answer!" as the survey revealed the results.

Another mom stood up, nearly shaking with nervousness. "Okay, that's my card. And I live . . ." She gulped down some shame and her eyes welled up. "In an apartment."

McKenna took a dramatic breath. Apartments were bad, apparently.

The emotional mom continued, "I just don't have enough storage for Costco-sized items!"

The first mom stood up and put her arm around her in genuine support. "You got this, mama! Find another mom and go to Costco together. You can get the bulk prices but split the wares so you don't have to store forty-eight paper towel rolls and twenty-two Omaha steaks alone."

The emotional mom seemed comforted by this simple solution. "Wow. I hadn't thought about going with another person."

McKenna clapped like they had just brokered a Middle East peace deal. "Yes! YES! That's it. That's what I am talking about. Mommy power. Let's do this. Card Two. 'My babies are fourteen months. They are too big for the infant tubs over the sink, but they are too uncoordinated to be in the bathtub unassisted. They slip all over the place. But if I bathe them one by one, the baby out of the tub has a tantrum and then bedtime is totally screwed. How do I bathe them both at once when I am home alone?' Oooh, this is a good one. Who knows how to handle this?"

Chiara blushed. That was her card. She felt like a failure that something so basic—bathing—was so hard for her to manage as a mom. Keeping her children clean was necessary for their health and safety, right up there with keeping them fed and clothed. But she couldn't figure out how to do it without always feeling like one of them was seconds from drowning, or smashing their lip into the tub wall, or peeing into the heating vent while she tried to wash shampoo out of the other's eye. She was ashamed to say that many nights she just spritzed her sons with a water bottle during their diaper changes and tried to clean every crevice she could reach with a wipe. Chiara hoped her face didn't look as red as it felt.

Michelle waved her hand. "Oh! I got this! Fill up the regular tub with one to two inches of water, and then put the babies in the tub but have each of them sit inside their own laundry basket. It's like a little holey boat! Keeps them from drowning. Contains them. Water is still free-moving around their butts. Game changer. If they are small or extra squirrelly, you can roll up a bath towel around them or under the baskets to secure them."

McKenna was one excitement level away from doing the Arsenio arm pump. "Yes! Yes! YES! Love an easy solution with common household items we already own!"

Chiara couldn't believe it, either. This really was the answer she had been in desperate need of for months! The part of the day that was supposed to be the beginning of winding down for bed had become a source of total anxiety. Now she was so happy imagining all the relaxing bathtimes to come that she could have wept.

McKenna continued to read out cards, and no matter what the problem, another mom there had the solution. Too hard to get both twins looking cute at the same time in a photo? Use a professional photographer; they know how to make it happen! A lot of moms recommended day-in-the-life photo shoots instead of posed portraits for better luck. Babies never asleep at the same time? Here are five tips on how to sync their schedules and find the best wake windows depending on their age! How to feed both kids and pump breastmilk? A mom busted out an entire photo album on her phone of how to simultaneously breastfeed the babies via a certain hold/pillow combination and then use special cups to pump out excess. Chiara had never been so happy to see thirty pictures of a stranger's boob—from multiple angles, no less! The problems went on and on, but the solutions were even more plentiful.

Finally, McKenna turned over the box. It was empty. "Hey, mommies . . . what did we learn today?"

Andie cracked a joke. "Um, everything?"

The group laughed. It was true.

McKenna nodded. "Actually, yes. More than that, though—what I hope you learned was that we know everything when we work together as a coMOMunity. If you need an answer, chances are the mama next to you has it. Give yourselves a hand."

Even if Chiara had only encountered some of the problems listed so far, and even if a couple of the solutions didn't work perfectly for her, her biggest takeaway was that she was no longer alone. She had felt everything these mothers were feeling, and *they* had felt what *she* had been feeling. The partition of loneliness had finally shattered.

As the group wound down and exited the tent, Chiara felt like she had joined a sisterhood. Everyone was already nostalgic for the event they had barely just left.

Andie and Michelle started walking toward the barn.

Andie touched her stomach. "I'm starving."

Michelle's mouth dropped. "How? I just watched you eat eighteen marshmallows."

Andie waved her off. "Those don't count. They're like ninety percent air. Let's see if lunch started."

Chiara awkwardly murmured, "Oh, okay. See you later."

Michelle crinkled her nose. "Huh?"

Andie mimicked Michelle's tone. "Yeah, 'huh?' Are you one of those people who doesn't eat lunch?"

Chiara was flustered. "I eat lunch. I eat lunch every day. I just—" Her voice dropped a second. She wasn't sure if she wanted to say this next part. "I didn't know if you wanted to eat lunch with me."

Michelle's nose crinkled more. "What is happening right now?"

Andie's brows were knit together in confusion. "Why wouldn't we want to eat lunch with you?"

Chiara closed her eyes to try to reset her brain. "Sorry. I just had a super-weird thing last night and this morning. These moms I sat with seemed okay and then—"

Andie's brows unknit and went up in understanding. "Oh. Michelle, she got Mean-Mommied."

Michelle's eyes softened into something close to anime. "Oh no! You got Mean-Mommied? That's the worst!"

Chiara felt a rush of gratitude. "It was!" She fought back tears. "They literally walked by me this morning like I was nobody."

"Respectfully, screw them," Andie said, and she put her arm around Chiara. "Let's get lunch."

The rest of the day was one of the happiest Chiara had had in years. Andie and Michelle were fun—really fun. After lunch they went to a yoga class led by a human rubber band named Tamarind, but they had to leave because Michelle got a cramp and her toes were frozen in such a weird shape that Andie and Chiara had to carry her out, all while failing to suppress their giggles.

They heard Tamarind cue an extra-loud "Om!" from the class to drown them out, but that only made them laugh harder.

During a home repair crafting hour, they didn't even make the craft because Andie managed to immediately stick three glue guns together. The project leader, Opal, sweetly yet sternly told them to focus their efforts on un-melting the glue just enough to separate them. By the time they exited the tent, the glue guns had been separated, but they all had glitter, yarn, gingham, and a myriad of other craft ephemera stuck to their hands.

Through all this, Chiara felt fun, and silly, and light. In short, she felt like herself. Unlike the mean mommies, Andie and Michelle swore and made jokes that even Adrienne would laugh at, and they weren't ever trying to present life as anything other than what it was. On paper they had failed every coMOMunity class, but Chiara didn't care.

Best of all, the three of them talked in nitty-gritty detail about how hard those infant years were and how much harder toddlerhood was.

"I mean, yes, feeding two infants from my body was not a great time. But at least they were STATIONARY!" Michelle yelled, cackling. "I could put them down. Go pee. Come back. They would still be there."

Andie was also in stitches. "My girls are three months older than her twins, and when she sent me the first photo of her babies moving? I sent her a funeral wreath."

Chiara couldn't catch her breath, she was laughing so hard. "A funeral wreath? Why?"

"Because her life was OVER." Andie tipped out of her Adirondack, wheezing with laughter.

Michelle pointed at Chiara. "Why? That is exactly the question! I am over here freaking out. I put my baby down, come back a second later, and he had MOVED. Literally squirmed under the couch!"

At this, Andie let out another snort from the ground.

Michelle gave Andie a playful kick. "And this pill sends me a FUNERAL WREATH that said *Condolences*! I was looking for support!" She smiled at Chiara. "She was right, though. My life was one hundred percent over."

Chiara wiped away tears. "When my boys started moving, I made a pen out of baby fencing, with bungee cords and tape. I couldn't keep up! I needed to secure them. I felt like a jailer. It was like twenty years of therapy happened when I made that pen. I am a twin and I felt so bad for my mom in so many ways. I am barely making it with my husband. I have no idea how she did it on her own." She took a deep breath. She hadn't expected to take the conversation there. "Do you guys feel like . . ." She searched for the wording. "Do you ever feel like you are crashing up against your own childhood all the time now?"

Michelle nodded. "Oh yeah. It's a wild ride."

Chiara smiled. "Yeah. It is. Okay. Not going there." She laughed a little. "Not what this weekend is about! This is about *wine time*!"

Andie picked up the bit without missing a beat. "#MommyJuice!"

Chiara checked her watch. "I'm gonna change out of these glue-crusted clothes. Want to meet for dinner in twenty?"

Andie frowned. "We actually have to leave early."

Chiara was crushed. "What? Why?"

Michelle sighed. "Our mom's birthday is tomorrow."

Andie frowned even more. "Technically, she is only my mother-in-law. So I am extra pissed."

"But you guys are my only friends here!" Chiara lamented, hoping her joking tone covered up her genuine disappointment.

Andie put her arm around Chiara. "Go hang with the Multiple Moms! You know them!"

Michelle took Chiara's other arm. "Besides, you only have to survive one more night without us."

Chiara agreed, but made sure to get their contact information.

"Will you be back next year?" Chiara asked hopefully as she typed her phone number into their phones.

Andie answered, "If it's a summer holiday, then yes!"

"It's too complicated to leave during the school year," Michelle said. "We shipped our kids to sleepaway camp so we could come this week."

Chiara nodded. "Oh yeah, I hadn't thought about that. My kids aren't in school yet, so it's tricky no matter when the summit will be." She laughed.

Michelle smiled. "Hey, even if we don't come back next year, it doesn't matter! Because we can meet up outside of the summit!"

Chiara smiled back. "Yeah! We can!" With that one promise of friendship outside of the summit, the entire weekend was a success. She'd done it: she'd made mom friends.

As Chiara walked them to their cars—they had already packed up that morning—Michelle seemed emboldened. "So, Chiara, how did you go so viral?"

Chiara was a little embarrassed. "It was an accident."

Andie was shocked. "Shut up!"

Michelle shook her head. "Of course it was. I knew it. I bet you barely post, normally."

Chiara shrugged. "Kind of."

Andie laughed. "Oh my God. Everyone was freaking out about their numbers tanking, and meanwhile you're just raking in the sponsorships that people here would kill for. How many did you take?"

Michelle shook her head. "Andie, look at her. Look at her face. She took zero. You took zero partnerships, didn't you?"

Chiara nodded. Zero partnerships.

Andie was dying with laughter. "Oh my God. Honey, do not tell people here that! If they find out you tanked their algorithm for four months and you didn't even care? Didn't even mean to do it? They will go insane!"

Chiara was laughing now, too. "I didn't do it to make anyone mad!"

Andie said, "We know, babe. We know. But the drama you caused then? The money people lost? Don't make them feel stupid on top of it. You'll go from no friends to all enemies."

Chiara gave a little salute. "Noted."

Michelle pulled Chiara into a big hug. "Call us when you get home. We will all go to Costco together and buy eighty Omaha steaks."

Andie hugged Chiara, too, and then they got in Michelle's car and drove away.

At the last second, Andie leaned out the passenger window. "Chiara! You are a good mom! Now go have some fun for us! Rile those moms up!"

She blew Chiara a big kiss, and Michelle honked the horn.

As their taillights faded into the distance on the dark country road, Chiara thought she would feel like shrinking back to her cabin without her only buddies. Instead, she felt confident. Dinner was already well underway, and she knew a couple of moms' names.

As she entered the barn, she thought to herself, *I'm not going back into isolation.*

By the time Chiara had finished dinner, the party was in full swing and Chiara was having a ball. Everyone was all chardonnay'd up. Everyone had sparklers. There were Adirondack chairs and fringed hammocks arranged around firepits. Everywhere you looked, it was #CuteAF. Chiara was pulled into a group photo, and she smiled so hard her cheeks hurt.

Thea spoke into a sky-blue mini-megaphone. "Come on, Mini Moms. No one has an early bedtime tonight!"

Katy Perry's "Firework" started blasting over the sound system, asking every worn-out mom if they wanted to start again. Just as everyone loudly sang about letting their colors burst, the night sky filled with Fourth of July fireworks, and every single woman lost her mind. Without any city lights, the explosions seemed to drip glitter into the darkness longer than Chiara had ever seen a firework do before. Each giant *POW* was followed by a full minute of increasingly delicate shimmers until they mingled and merged with the farthest stars. Everyone danced beneath them, stretching their fingers up into the glow. These were the #InstaWorthy montage moments of women dancing together that gave everyone with a pulse some serious FOMO.

Chiara was in deep, dancing with her sparkler and already planning to return next year.

Who knows, she wondered as a mom topped off her wineglass, *maybe this solidarity and freedom is actually heaven.*

Several hours and way too many bottles of wine later, the grounds were dark and quiet. A cold fog had crept in over the hills from the Pacific, bringing with it the smell of salt and damp. Chiara had made it back to her cabin (barely) and was asleep in her romper. One boot on, one boot off. It had been a good night, apparently.

And then she heard something . . .

She pushed the pillow next to her. "Honey, can you get the baby?"

Wait. Not her husband. A pillow. She remembered where she was.

Chiara roused slowly as the crying got louder.

Her mind sluggishly corralled around the sound. *Is that . . . a baby crying?* All her motherly instincts pulled her from the deepest rest; the cries tugged her forward like a sonic hook in her belly button.

Chiara came out of her cabin, both boots on now and on high alert. The fog made her shiver as she pulled her jacket on (green anorak, Nordstrom). She followed the sound away from the rows of cabins and their sleeping occupants, stumbling several times in the darkness. They really were out in the middle of nowhere. Not a single light on the horizon. And the chardonnay sloshing around her brain wasn't helping matters.

Chiara followed the sound until she saw a small bundle tucked at the base of a split tree. The mangled tree—clearly once hit by lightning, dead branches reaching up from its hollowed-out center—cast strange shadows over the tiny muslin bundle.

The cries continued to ring out as Chiara bent down.

It was a swaddled baby. A rush of hormones made Chiara's heart break and her resolve to save the child harden. She picked it up gently, cooing, "Sweetie, what are you doing out here?"

She pulled the muslin away from the baby's face.

Wait.

Not a real baby.

Chiara unwrapped the muslin to reveal a swaddled doll with a baby monitor taped to its face.

Chiara was repulsed. "What the fuck?"

The monitor cut out, leaving Chiara in complete darkness. Her eyes struggled to readjust, but she couldn't make out anything, not even the decoy in her arms.

The charred tree limbs creaked ominously in the wind.

Suddenly, in a moment so surreal Chiara wondered if she was hallucinating, Katy Perry's voice slowly swelled again from speakers hidden in rocks, telling her to ignite, telling her she was a firework. And then . . .

SSSSSSSSSSTPOW!

A firework shot out of the darkness and straight into Chiara's torso.

Chiara looked down in horror. Her clothes were singed, and her skin sizzled around an open wound.

SSSSSSSSSSTPOW!

Another firework impaled her stomach. It was clear now that this wasn't an accident.

Chiara looked around helplessly. *Who? Why?*

With each Katy Perry lyric, another firework was launched into her body.

SSSSSSSSSSTPOW!

SSSSSSSSSSTPOW!

SSSSSSSSSSSTPOW!

On her knees now, Chiara clung to the dead tree, the bark cutting into her face and snagging on her clothes. Chiara's blood mixed with the sparkling burns. It was hypnotizing and disturbing. She was reminded of the fizzing glitter from earlier in the night when she felt like she had found heaven. The music, the moonlight, the smell of her own flesh. She was frozen for just a second, unable to make sense of any of it.

A snap of the bark snapped her back into herself. Chiara knew she had to go, had to get away from this spot.

She wrestled off her burning jacket, ripping her Apple Watch from her wrist, and coughing into the dirt. She slowly stood again. Hobbling at first but soon gaining speed, Chiara made a break for it.

Painfully, Chiara ran to her car and wrenched the door open. She sat in the driver's seat, her breath ragged. She retched from the smoky stench of her own body, but then steadied herself.

She reached into her pocket, wincing from the pain, and pulled out the photo of her twin boys. She put the photo of her sons back on the visor. Looking at them and her own eyes in the rearview mirror, she fortified herself.

She was gonna live.

As Chiara reached into the glove box for the valet key and fumbled it into the ignition, the driver door burst open again. There was someone there in the darkness, someone grabbing at her clothes. With all her strength, Chiara pulled the door closed, but it wasn't enough. Hands banged on the windows.

Chiara tried to turn the car on, but nothing happened. Not even a flicker of headlights. Then her bloody hand slipped off the key; she grasped at air, unable to find it again.

Her vision felt smaller, the pain further away.

She just had to find the key.

Turn the key, Chiara. You can do it, she told herself as the last light in her vision went dark.

Chapter 4

One Year Later

Adrienne's apartment in Hayward, California, was a million cultural miles from the Mendocino County ranch. Even in the bright midday sun, it was pitch dark inside—and thank God for that, as it was messy to the point of bordering on unhygienic.

The only sound was a color printer in the corner pumping out missing flyers of Chiara.

Adrienne lay in bed, despondent. Although at this point her bed was closer to a rodent's nest, the crumbs and twists of worn cotton sheets one step above wood shavings and a running wheel. The sisters weren't identical, but the many photos of them on the walls showed their tight bond. Adrienne had been staring at them for twelve long months—her days spent in bed, her nights spent in bed, none of that time spent sleeping in any sort of healthy way.

Last time Adrienne was in a depression this long, Chiara had known just the thing to prod her out of bed.

"Even Molly Bloom would say this was a bit much, Ade."

"Who makes a *Ulysses* reference?" Adrienne had replied from under a pile of laundry (some clean, some dirty, all musty and rodent adjacent).

"I do."

"I officially regret encouraging you to go to college."

"No you don't," Chiara had said, smirking.

"No, I don't."

"Come on, it looks like a D.A.R.E. ad in here."

"No it doesn't!" Adrienne yelled as she tucked herself back under her blanket.

Chiara tugged the blanket down, then pointed around the room to a pile of empty wine bottles in the corner, the overflowing beer cans in the trash, and the ashtray that was a hazmat site.

"It's fine. I'll get it later," Adrienne said as she pulled the blanket fully over her head.

Chiara pulled the blanket down again. "Get up. We're getting breakfast."

"Is it time for breakfast?" Adrienne had asked, trying to suss out the hour from the small crack in the shades.

"Let's not stand on ceremony when we both know you are ninety-nine percent pizza bagel right now."

"You know what they say: you put pizza on a bagel, you can have pizza anytime."

That was their shared twin language. A dialect closer to kitchen patois mixed with inside jokes, song lyrics, and long-gone commercial jingles from their years as latch-key kids.

But Chiara couldn't solve Adrienne's problems now because Chiara was the cause.

Last June Chiara had been missing for two days before stupid Dear Husband had called Adrienne. Sure, they weren't technically speaking at the time, but two days of keeping her in the dark seemed excessive. When he'd finally come to talk to her, all bound up in his own bullshit, Adrienne was furious.

She'd screamed, and yelled, and demanded to know what he had done so far to look for her. She wanted him to yell back, but instead he collapsed like a sad little tuft of cotton candy tossed into a puddle.

Through tears, DH said, "I called the police; they put out an alert. Her car is on some list or something. But they said with her past as a heavy drug user that they couldn't be sure she hadn't relapsed."

Adrienne's head spun. "Her past as a drug user? How did they know about that?"

DH looked at the ground and didn't answer.

"*You told them that?* Instead of leaning on the beautiful-missing-mother angle, you tag her as an addict?"

"I didn't mean to! I was trying to be honest!" he wailed back.

Adrienne felt like her head was going to explode. The stupidity was off the charts. She paced back and forth, focusing on triage. "Okay, fine. Who is overseeing the investigation? I'll call them."

"Well, no one knows which county she disappeared in—or when, within a five-day range—so it's been a little chaotic. I can't figure out who's leading the investigation."

"Wow. I am honestly impressed that you managed to derail this so quickly! If there was an award for efficiently ruining any hope of seeing Chiara again, you would win, hands down. Way to go."

"I'm sure the police are working hard."

Adrienne's voice was so sarcastic it felt like sludge coming out of her mouth. "Are you sure? How? Why? Why on earth would you be sure? You gave them a reason to ignore her—drugs—and haven't made anyone be responsible for the search efforts. Cops don't want a dead end with no clues on their docket. This is going to stay on the bottom of the pile forever. Congratulations. Good work."

As was her style, Adrienne had attacked her sister's disappearance with all the finesse of a deranged child mid–sugar crash. Nothing was off the table: threats sent via email to friends she suspected, soft bribes to police that were unanimously rejected, demands for media attention. She tried it all.

Adrienne winced now when she thought about her press conference. She had built it up so much in her own mind, sure that it would bust the case wide open. Some nurse would realize the coma patient who hadn't woken up yet was Chiara, and Adrienne would know where her sister was before the news vans had had a chance to pack up. Instead, it was one of the biggest mistakes of her life.

Adrienne had spent days writing what she thought was the perfect narrative, rehearsing it in the mirror and writing it on little index cards in her clearest penmanship. Right before she walked out with her prepared statement, Adrienne had downed a double shot of whiskey. She'd told herself it was necessary to steady her nerves. Only a couple of press members showed up, and it was all undercut by the obvious absence of DH and the (very few) friends who were sober enough to arrive on time. Even so, she had hoped it would lead to a new break.

She watched the footage later and cringed. Her speech was disjointed, scolding; even Stalin would have told her to take the fist-shaking down a peg. Surrounded by druggies who hadn't seen the midday sun in several months, Adrienne looked like the president of the Vampire HOA Board instead of the grieving sister of a sympathetic victim. Worst of all were her own glazed and unfocused eyes, which slid back and forth to the smattering of cameras. The whiskey "for her nerves" had made her physically sluggish, and midway she lost her place in her speech. The discord between her angry words and her half-in-the-bag physicality was apparent and viscerally off-putting. Most of the channels who had shown up didn't even broadcast it on the news. This was page three of the web-only Local Section at best.

Instead of being angry at her own failure, Adrienne drove to DH's house, careening in and out of lanes with a recklessness on par with a kamikaze's. After two short turns off the highway, Adrienne entered the picture-perfect subdivision where Chiara's town house was—a tract home indistinguishable from its neighbors. The exteriors were an uninterrupted line of prefab faux shingles in shiny plastic coating and unmovable shutters in one of three shades of navy blue.

Adrienne screeched to a halt, parking at an awkward angle across the driveway. She pounded on the vinyl front door with both fists until he opened it.

Adrienne didn't wait for him to speak; she was primed to rage at him again. "You are so spineless. The media needed a big white man to tell them to listen, and yet you are incapable."

He just held their sons and wept.

Adrienne couldn't stop the words pouring out of her. "God, you cry so much you're basically amphibious now—constantly slick with tears, glistening with weakness. I disliked you before because you are an interminable bore. Now I hate you for being the impediment to finding Chiara."

"An impediment?" he croaked out. "You think I don't want to find her?"

"Doesn't seem like it! You aren't doing anything to help."

"What are you talking about? I called the police—"

"Late. You called the police late."

"And I let them turn our house inside out."

"After you had cleaned it, I bet. Scrubbed her from it."

"You think I did this? You think I had anything to do with this?" His face was drained of color, and his voice was hoarse with a new timbre Adrienne didn't recognize. His body had gone rigid, right down to his fingertips.

For one second, Adrienne saw a dark cloud pass over his face, and she willed it to turn into a rage. She needed someone in this squalling hell with her.

Instead, he took a deep breath and said, "Don't make this about you, Adrienne. Chiara is not you."

And he calmly shut the front door in her face.

At that, Adrienne had picked up a flowerpot and smashed it on the front porch in response. But this was only partly directed at him. Months earlier, in that exact same spot, Adrienne and Chiara had had a similar argument.

Chiara had yelled, "You dominate everything with your moods. How is my marriage about you? How is my transition to motherhood about you? You were so angry at Mom for taking up all the oxygen, but now you do the same. When do I get time to breathe on my own?"

DH, Adrienne could happily dismiss. Chiara, though . . . not so much.

All her life, Adrienne had known how she looked from the outside. She couldn't help herself. Even on her best days, she presented as angry, explosive, and ready to strike. Only Chiara saw the true inside—the softness, the wounds, the deep desire for innocence. Adrienne loved her sister, of course, but another reason she was clawing so hard to find Chiara was because if she was gone, Adrienne feared she would lose access to that part of herself. That inner world of delicate hopes that could be bolstered or washed away with a single comment. The little emotional fractures that had never reset right but her sister could tenderly address. Chiara could always get to that place in Adrienne. In fact, Adrienne realized she had never been able to get there alone at all. How alienating to know there were parts of herself that only someone outside held the keys to. A locked door in her own heart.

Adrienne couldn't pound that door down, so she pounded the pavement instead. She had interrogated every slacker burnout from her circle whom Chiara might have gone to if she had truly backslid to her worst habits. That list was exceedingly short, and for better or worse, several of them had been in police custody at the time after a mass arrest at their drug squat. Once they realized Adrienne was (in their addled minds) "aligned with the cops," they avoided her completely. Chiara's boring suburban neighbors hadn't proven to be interesting suspects, as almost all had been accounted for at a local girl's lacrosse tournament or had been out of town for a summer holiday. It seemed Chiara had made two friends at the summit last year, Michelle and Andie, but they had been at a thoroughly documented family party for the rest of the weekend in question. They hadn't been helpful at all, but they did seem genuinely sad that Chiara was missing. After a while, though, they clearly tired of Adrienne and stopped returning her calls. How many times could they say *We don't know anything*?

Everywhere Adrienne looked she found the same dead ends as the police. Every rock she turned over yielded less than zero. The only lead she couldn't fully investigate was the summit itself. That was the last place Chiara had been seen alive. If everywhere else was coming up dry, then it stood to reason that someone who had been at the ranch with Chiara knew something.

Now it was a year later, and Adrienne had pushed and pulled and prodded and raged at every possible reason for Chiara to disappear; the summit was the only avenue left. Adrienne was nearly ash after burning through so much anger for so many months. A stiff wind was all she needed to complete her emotional cremation.

Adrienne picked up her phone and hit the speed dial button.

A voicemail answered after only one ring; a calm, authoritative woman's voice came through. "You have reached Detective Gabrielle Bautista with the Alameda County Sheriff's Department. If this is an emergency, call nine-one-one."

Adrienne put a stern note in her voice that didn't quite suit her. "Hello, Detective. It's me, Adrienne Shaw. Again. Just wanted to know if you're doing anything to find my sister. Anything at all. It's been a year."

She called again the next day, the stern note mixed with frustration. "Hello, Detective. Me again. Any leads? That one-year anniversary came and went, and nothing?"

A week later and frustration had center stage. "Bautista, what the hell. I'm a taxpayer some years, you know. Call me back."

Later, a midnight call inspired by gin and Lennie Briscoe went off the rails immediately. "Look, I get that you don't have jurisdiction up at the fancy lady ranch—yeah, I said 'jurisdiction.' I know stuff."

Adrienne knew she wasn't achieving anything with the messages, but they were the only thing that scratched the itch. Over the last year she had drank, and smoked, and screwed as much as she could, and even more than that, but yelling into this voicemail was her only approximation of peace. Besides, there was no one else left to call. No one else in her life who would pick up. And she couldn't take the silence anymore.

Nursing something between a headache and a mild buzz from the night before, Adrienne woke up midmorning and, without a second thought, packed her backpack with all the essentials: a thick stack of Missing flyers, a handheld packing-tape dispenser, a staple gun, and spray adhesive.

As she walked to her car, she put flyers up on every wall, pole, or bench with a near-religious fervor. She was methodical, her muscle memory finely honed over the last year. Swift, smooth motions laying the poster on whatever the available surface was; an immediate assessment of what adhesion was best, which was deployed in seconds. Old telephone pole? Staples first, then a wrap of tape. A bus bench? Tape making an *X* across the center, with an extra strip up top. A concrete streetlamp? Spray adhesive would momentarily gloss Chiara's face and then dry to a hardened sheen nearly impossible to remove without solvent.

In her own neighborhood, flyers stayed untouched for months until the salty fog slowly faded them to nothing. Adrienne had just refreshed most of those last week, so today she had a different destination.

She got in her old Corolla, which smelled of mildew, and first started driving north on the four-lane slingshot surrounded by redwoods known as Highway 13; then she veered onto Highway 24 East, through the Caldecott Tunnel, with its long lines of fluorescents along the ceiling. Underneath the Oakland Hills, Adrienne zoomed until the air and the tax bracket went up a few notches on the other side of the hill. This was Orinda.

The subdivision stood silent as Adrienne turned her car into the unnecessarily speed-bumped roads, all with names like Oak Lane Court, Oak Grove Place, or Oak View Way. She was sure this repetitive naming was a trick to get outsiders lost. Adrienne slowly rolled by Chiara's town house. Every time, it shocked her how ordinary it looked. Adrienne squinted, looking for a sign of disrepair to signal that the family inside was broken. Instead, the hedges had grown. The grass was edged. The welcome mat had no leaves clinging to its corners.

The first time Adrienne had come here was for a neighborhood welcome BBQ thrown by the nosiest woman on the block and her pedantic husband, who prefaced every sentence with "When I was a district judge downtown . . ." Chiara was thirty weeks pregnant, and even though she was nearly toppling over from the weight displacement, she breathlessly gave Adrienne a tour of the town house. A two-bedroom, two-bathroom that Adrienne thought had all the personality of a Kleenex. In every room there were bizarrely high windows topping thin walls, and awkward skylights in vaulted ceilings whose only purpose seemed to be to make every sound echo like a banshee. The bedrooms were dark, with more emphasis put on the closet shelving than the functionality of the space. The bathrooms were a study in beige, with cheap towel racks that had already fallen off the walls. Throughout the floors were the hideous gray-hardwood laminate that had infected the mid-tier home-design market like Ebola. At the end of the tour, Adrienne told DH the house was the style equivalent of black mold.

Chiara hadn't talked to her for a month after that.

Today Adrienne opted to park two doors down. Before she had even turned off her car, she saw the neighbor's curtains twitch. Everyone in this subdivision knew everyone else, and more importantly, it took less than a passing glance to identify an interloper when they saw one. She was neither a welcome guest nor an expected gardener. She was a feared stranger in a strange homogenous land.

Two women in their sixties passed by with their dog, barely containing their suspicion.

"Nice poodle," Adrienne said in her best suburban babble.

"It's a *doodle*," the older woman said with a sneer.

Adrienne knew her time was limited.

She put in her headphones and pressed play. The familiar sample kicked in: A reversed high-hat building up like a firecracker. A wah-wah guitar cord extending out into pleading. Then Tracey Thorn's velvety voice filled Adrienne's ears, saying she knew a girl who needed shelter.

This was Massive Attack's "Protection"—or, as Ade and Chi had called it, "Our song."

One freezing July night when Adrienne and Chiara were twelve, they had discovered the pirate radio station Free Radio Berkeley. Since it was broadcast from secret locations all over the East Bay, they felt like they had stumbled into a secret society, a doorway to a fantasy land. The program that night had been a heady mix of bands they had never heard of before—Air, Groove Armada, Zero 7, and the like. They quickly put a blank tape in their Salvation Army boom box and recorded three hours of the broadcast. That tape had then become one of their most prized possessions, played again and again, the cassette delicately repaired with a pencil over and over. No CD Walkmans in this house, Chiara and Adrienne would wander their childhood apartment complex sharing headphones, imagining that they weren't poor kids in a crappy neighborhood. They were living out a stylish Sofia Coppola dream sequence (not that they had ever seen a Sofia Coppola movie). They reenacted the radio DJ's patter, including his coughing fit halfway through side 2. They dramatically sang along with the lyrics, pledging to protect each other from the force of the blow, to have no fear, their voices rising and rising until someone in a neighboring apartment would yell at them to shut up, and the girls would scurry away in a fit of giggles.

For ten years the mixtape was passed back and forth like an emotional talisman, until it was stolen out of Chiara's car. They cursed themselves for never making extra copies.

A few years later, when Adrienne was particularly broke and unable to buy Chiara a birthday gift, she had meticulously researched and found every song that had been on that tape and created a digital copy in the exact order they had committed to memory as kids.

While the perfect sound quality and lack of DJ interjections couldn't be helped, Chiara nearly cried when the familiar music swelled, transporting them both back to their wildly unsupervised childhood defined by sheer freedom and no safety nets.

Since Chiara had gone missing, Adrienne had listened to this mix obsessively, and today was no exception. She cranked the music to max volume as she exited her car, drowning out the old man on the porch questioning her large backpack. With swooping European trip-hop flowing, Adrienne wasn't the lowlife besmirching their picture-perfect existence; she was the determined heroine living outside the lines.

Missing flyers in hand, Adrienne started with the community mailbox, using the spray adhesive to quickly plaster five Chiaras on the back side. Even with her music blasting in her ears, the boldness that came so naturally in her dodgy neighborhood was inaccessible here. Adrienne's hands shook a bit, and a small trickle of sweat went down her back. She gave her head a quick shake, hoping a rush of DGAF would come as she put another flyer over a cursive sign that read PLEASE NO POSTERS, HOA RULE 2, SECTION 4.

Adrienne jumped when she felt a strong tap on her shoulder, followed by a muffled, "Adrienne, what are you doing?"

Adrienne recognized DH's voice but set her chin, refusing to turn around. "I'm putting up Missing posters."

He sighed. "We talked about this. Everyone here knows what Chiara looks like."

Adrienne continued with her back to him, moving from the mailbox toward the community-pool gate. "Maybe someone has been on vacation and doesn't know she's still missing. People remember things later, you know." Adrienne bit her lip after confidently delivering this weak argument. "Or maybe you don't want people to remember? And if so, why is that? Why am I the only one putting up posters?"

She heard the crunch of gravel, and finally turned to see DH sitting on the ground. A baby monitor was next to him, a tiny screen showing two sleeping babies in adjacent cribs. She couldn't tell if DH was crying, but his shoulders were rounded and his head was nearly to his knees. A pose of pure defeat. Adrienne nearly felt jealous—defeat looked so calm and passive.

Adrienne revved up for another round, but as she opened her mouth, she heard the *whoop whoop* of a police car pulling up to the curb.

"You seriously called the police?" Adrienne clicked her teeth in sheer disgust.

DH couldn't even muster a verbal response, and instead flicked her a look of resignation before getting up and walking home in silence, his hands in his hair, baby monitor tucked into his pocket.

Detective Bautista got out of the cruiser, and Adrienne could read her exasperation from ten paces away—the downturned mouth, the knit brow, the slow walk to slightly delay the inevitable. Bautista, a Filipina woman whose face could oscillate from kindness to steel in seconds, was projecting compassion today. And that pissed Adrienne off.

"Bautista," Adrienne essentially coughed out.

"Ms. Shaw," Bautista replied. "My partner will drive your car back to your house. How about you come with me?"

"You're arresting me?"

Bautista sighed loudly. "No. I just want to talk."

Adrienne begrudgingly handed her keys to the other detective and then stomped over to the police cruiser with all the emotional regulation of a toddler.

Once they had pulled out and were headed back east on Highway 24, Bautista broke the silence. "Are you drunk?"

"Excuse me?"

"On most of your messages, you seem drunk."

Adrienne winced. On most of her messages to Bautista, she had been, in fact, quite drunk. Some people call ex-boyfriends when they are hammered. Adrienne left chaotic messages for Bautista. Nevertheless, in this precise moment, she was sober—or at least sober enough to muster offense. "I'm fine."

"I'm not judging; my dad had a problem." Bautista was genuine—caring, even—and it completely threw Adrienne off guard. Bautista continued, "I just don't want to have this conversation now if you aren't gonna remember it tomorrow."

"I'm sober. I swear. So, any leads on my sister?"

"We were able to search Ms. McCorckle's ranch"—Bautista seemed to brace herself for impact upon hearing Adrienne's excited intake of breath—"but we didn't find anything."

"Search it again!" Adrienne screamed.

"Ms. Shaw, the owner allowed local law enforcement to search her property as a courtesy. We didn't have probable cause. Hell, we didn't have *un*-probable cause."

Adrienne was frantic. "Her ranch is like one hundred thousand acres! Did you bring dogs? Or something?"

"The sheriff up there assured me they did a thorough search."

This answer only fueled Adrienne's anger. "And you believe him? I bet his whole department is in that lady's pocket!"

"I don't think being acquaintances means he's corrupt."

"'Acquaintances' my ass. That was the last place anyone saw her alive; there has to be something there!"

And here they were, back at the beginning of an argument they had been having for a year. But they both made their cases. Again. Talking past each other. Again.

"Ms. Shaw, by all accounts, your sister had a nice time at the event and then left. Her car isn't there. We found no body. No signs of foul play. No one knew her prior, so no motive."

"My sister didn't just disappear!"

"There are a lot of dark roads up there, a lot of dangerous roads. She could be anywhere between Mendocino County and the Bay Area."

"Here we go—the *Drove off the Road* theory. My sister would make three right turns to avoid one left turn. But you think she sped off a cliff."

"Her husband says she hadn't been sleeping."

"Ever wonder why he pushes the accident theory so much? Because *I* wonder that."

"He has an alibi. And an accident is possible. Especially if she was tired, if she had been drinking. And given your sister's past—"

"Her past drug use?" Adrienne's blood was boiling. "Are you seriously bringing that up again? Yes, she had a drug problem eight years ago, but so do a lot of people!"

Adrienne vowed again to never forgive DH for telling the police about Chiara's past. What an idiot, dooming his wife with his big stupid mouth and square attitude.

Bautista pushed on. "And she had been expressing frustration about her life—her marriage, her kids . . ."

"She was a stay-at-home mom for twins! Of course she was expressing frustration!"

"Her final text to him was very strange. I could read it as a goodbye."

"Oh God, that stupid text! A bird, a fish, a dirtbag, blah, blah. None of that means she drove off to Canada to start a new life! She would never abandon her children!"

So far this had been rote, but Bautista was working up to a new piece of information. "Chiara had been diagnosed with postpartum anxiety—recurrent intrusive thoughts of death, low self-worth, fear. Given your mom's mental health history, Chiara was flagged as high risk for postpartum psychosis. Her doctor urged her to take antidepressants, but Chiara refused multiple times. Did you know that?"

Adrienne had had no idea, and it stung so much she clutched her stomach.

Bautista went on, her tone almost tender. "Your sister was unwell."

"According to who? Her husband? That's suspicious!"

"No. According to her doctor. Directly from her doctor. We have her medical records."

Adrienne had a split second of doubt, but instead doubled down. "Okay, so first you ignore her because you think she's doing drugs, but now you ignore her because she *refused* to take drugs?"

Apparently, Bautista hadn't seen this perspective coming, and was caught on the back foot.

Adrienne took the moment of silence to keep pushing. "How can you stop looking for her? How is this possible? I thought missing white women were like Atlantis for you guys. Never stop searching!"

When they were nearly at Adrienne's apartment, Bautista decided to say the one thing she knew would make Adrienne leave the car by her own steam instead of by force. "I'm not saying you have to move on, but I am saying that after a year we do need to reallocate resources towards more recent cases. That's the unfortunate reality. Maybe it's time to call your brother-in-law."

As per their well-worn pattern, Adrienne hit the roof. "No! No, no, no. He's even more useless than you."

Bautista sighed in both frustration and relief—the end of this was in sight, as was Adrienne's front door. "He's just trying to put his life back together. And so should you."

Bautista guided the car to the curb in front of Adrienne's house.

Adrienne's anger was at an all-time high. She saw what this was: the final dispensation. "Fine. Quit. Buy the dumb theory that she drove off a cliff or fled to Canada if that makes your life easier. But my life will never be together if Chiara isn't in it. So I'll handle this myself."

Adrienne slammed the car door shut in a powerful rush and snatched the keys from the detective who had parked her Corolla behind them.

Adrienne's flood of emotion dissipated as soon as she locked the flimsy door to her apartment. She slid down to the floor in a dramatic heap, feeling more defeated than ever. She scrolled through over one hundred unanswered texts to her sister (Where are you? Hey, just let me know you are okay? Chiara, I'm getting scared, please answer me).

She scrolled all the way back a year to her sister's last text. The text she hadn't answered. A photo of Chiara at the ranch with the message If I try to come back here next year, tie me to a chair.

Suddenly, something clicked.

Come back next year?

Adrienne opened Instagram and found Thea's profile. It wasn't hard; she popped up instantly on the Explore page.

Thea's most recent grid post was a Boomerang of her throwing black and orange glitter in front of an expertly hand-painted banner that read HALLOWEEN! The caption: "Style Summit Holiday is Halloween! #TBT to The Big Reveal!" The glitter flew up and down, up and down, up and down, showering the pumpkins at Thea's feet.

Adrienne checked Thea's Stories.

Caption: "Getting ready for the next CoMOMunity Summit on October 1st. Hope to see you there, Mini Moms. Going to have a Spook-tacular time! #SwipeUpLinkInBio."

The rest were all reposts of reposts of her Story. Every comment and caption was some variation of OMG can't wait to go. Can't miss it! So ready!

She clicked the link, her pulse starting to speed up. She didn't realize the date of the summit moved each year—and that she could still make it to this one.

Adrienne read the website: CoMOMunity Summit: Halloween Edition! Only 3 months away! She found the ticketing page.

Damn. This thing is expensive, she thought.

Ticket Tier 1: Mini-Mom Squad (#MMS), ELITE ACCESS—WITH SPECIAL 3RD DAY PASS—$10,000—SOLD OUT

Ticket Tier 2: Mini-Mom Regular, $3,000—PLUS ACCESS—Two Day Pass—Available

Ticket Tier 3: Festive Friend, $1,500—BASIC ACCESS—Two Day Pass—Available

(And in tiiiiiiiny print: #Nonrefundable. Because of course it was.)

Adrienne didn't give it a second thought. At last she would have a chance to search the ranch herself—and better yet, have as many suspects from last year back in one place.

She grabbed her credit card.

Chapter 5

Arrival

October 1 came at last, with hot, dry days that seamlessly slipped into cold, misty nights. The beginning of #SpookySeason meant it was finally time for the CoMOMunity's Seasonal Style Summit at Thea's ranch. But now, instead of last year's Americana-Independence Flag-aganza, it was all about Halloween—a holiday cherished for its nondenominational safety and endless crafting opportunities. October 31 was the day when the Influencer and the Influenced did their very best to, as the internet said, "make childhood magic." The summit was to serve as the adult style springboard, a Pinterest page come to life and pumped full of steroids for every mom to replicate as soon as she got home.

In a rented minivan the size of a boat, Adrienne made her way north on Highway 101. Her hair was neat now, her makeup subdued. Adrienne had come to blend in, and curtain bangs with #DewyGlowySkinCare were the new mommy camo. When she stopped for gas before turning west on Route 128, Adrienne bought a box of Cheerios and a couple of cheap toys at the register. She emptied the entire cereal box around in the car, crushing the little *O*s into the upholstery, and tossed the toys into the back seat. Just in case anyone was checking. She couldn't quite re-create Chiara's van's slight scent of vomit, but she did leave some dirty socks on the dashboard to bake in the sun.

Adrienne hadn't eaten breakfast before she left, and soon her stomach was growling. She saw a fruit stand and pulled over. She passed over the dried fruit and instead bought a large cellophane bag of peanut brittle secured with a little sticker.

The woman behind the counter offered her phone with the card-swipe cube attached, but Adrienne paused. The woman smiled. "We also take Venmo!"

Adrienne wasn't sure why, but she didn't want a paper trail of her movements just yet. "Do you take cash?"

"As long as it's correct change," the woman responded.

Adrienne dug into her backpack and found the necessary crumpled dollars.

The woman smoothed out the money and said, "Thanks. This will be my tip for the day." She looked over at her daughter and playfully put her finger over her lips. "Don't tell Daddy."

The girl smiled at their little game and put her fingers over her lips, too.

Adrienne didn't feel like driving again just yet. Plus, she wanted to arrive in the throng, not stand out. She needed to stall for half an hour.

"Hey, is there a spot nearby to park for a little bit?"

"There's a great lookout a half mile up the road."

Adrienne was hoping for just a parking lot but instead, half a mile later, found herself pulling the minivan into a beautiful viewpoint.

She sat on the back of the van, her legs dangling over the bumper. The open cargo door overhead created a perfect patch of shade for her as she looked out at the tranquil vista. Golden hills. Oak trees. Sunlight. Gentle shadows. It was beautiful; Adrienne could objectively see that. But she felt nothing. Instead, she silently ate her bag of sugar and compulsively scanned every inch of hillside she could for Chiara's van, a crash site, or tire marks. A ridiculous task. She didn't even know where exactly she was in relationship to Thea's ranch or if this was the route Chiara had taken. But maybe it had been the route. Maybe, if Adrienne turned her head just right, she would find all the answers that had felt just outside her periphery since Chiara had disappeared.

The effort to get to this moment—this precipice—was immense. After the previous year, spent seesawing between bereaved catatonia and grief-fueled fury (both of which were accompanied by a full menu of mind-numbing substances), the past three months had felt like a *Rocky* training montage. Except instead of chasing chickens or running up the steps of the Philadelphia Museum of Art, Adrienne was dyeing the bleach streaks out of her hair and trying to figure out what exact outfits she needed to appear Peak Mommy but also cover her various tattoos. A blurry stick-and-poke tattoo given to her by a man named Needle was going to be a slight giveaway that she wasn't #MommyMaterial. That said, Needle owed her a favor and knew how to take out her septum ring, so it all evened out.

None of these tasks were remotely as daunting as what she knew was the most essential step: sobriety.

Adrienne had staggered into her first Alcoholics Anonymous meeting the day after Bautista drove her home. The group gathered in a community theater center that was currently putting on *South Pacific*, and Adrienne mixed powdered creamer into her instant coffee amid paper palm trees and a cardboard hospital.

A fellow addict asked, "So, what brings you here?"

"Spite," Adrienne said with a big smile.

"That works," they said, giving her Styrofoam cup a gentle cheers.

Adrienne sat in a metal folding chair on the side near the exit so she could bolt if it all became too much. She had been Anonymous adjacent enough times to know the lay of the land. She'd told herself that instead of the lame *one day of sobriety at a time*, her goal was much lower. Namely, slow down her drinking so that by the summit, she was one month sober—and then after that, who cares. It wasn't hopeful, but the realistic parameters made it seem doable. Like that time she'd had to stay off booze while taking antibiotics. Or when she didn't snort anything during a nasty sinus infection.

Adrienne assumed the God stuff would be the worst part of the program, because at no point in her entire life had she thought, *Wow, what this moment needs is more Jesus!* However, the light WASP vibe was fine because so many other people before her had found workarounds for the God Issue.

"Call it your 'Higher Power.'" (Same difference.)

"Call God 'She.'" (Same difference, but make it feminism.)

"Think of God as just the natural earth in balance." (Barf through a peace sign.)

A veritable candy land of annoying deity loopholes!

But not even a lifetime of spiritual skepticism could knock Adrienne off the program this time. She'd even gotten a sponsor—an older woman named Lisa who had been sober for thirty-two years. Lisa was the one who could get through to anyone. With waist-length salt-and-pepper hair and a permanent flip-flop tan, Lisa was so chill that Adrienne was sure she was going California Sober—no booze, no drugs, just pot.

Lisa had started their first meeting by matter-of-factly saying, "So, your life has become unmanageable."

Adrienne shrugged. "Not really."

Lisa's face didn't change. "That wasn't a question." Lisa took a long time to speak again, then pinned Adrienne like a butterfly to cardboard when she finally did. "The big issue you're gonna grapple with in recovery is your ego."

"What else is new?" Adrienne snorted.

Lisa didn't seem to think this was funny, and instead said, "You won't heal until you get rid of your ego. Pride will keep you in the dark."

Adrienne understood what Lisa meant; she could feel herself being in her own way. However, somehow her addiction and Chiara's disappearance had become a giant knot, and she couldn't see where Chiara ended and the bottle began. It was the same way her drug use had increased the longer Chiara was with DH. She had been punishing Chiara by hurting herself. After Chiara went missing, this one-sided pattern had increased fivefold, as if going on the bender to end all benders would conjure Chiara from wherever she was to drag Adrienne out of the pit once again.

That said, Adrienne's ego was the only piece of her that hadn't been completely shattered, and she was afraid if she shed her ego now that she would in effect be giving up on finding out what had happened to her sister. It was like driving a Ford Pinto to work. Sure, it might explode at any second, but it was the only way to put food on the table and, therefore, worth the risk.

Adrienne reached into her peanut brittle bag only to realize it was empty. Her cravings had been increasing with her stress, and this was only the latest clue.

Adrienne got back in the driver's seat and started the minivan.

The GPS chirped, "Please confirm your destination."

Adrienne read the ranch address on the screen, checked the little finish line flag on the map, and pressed Confirm with unnecessary force.

With still more than two miles to go, Adrienne came around a bend on the two-lane country road and almost rear-ended a caravan of cars. She craned her neck to see what the holdup was—a downed tree or maybe a stalled vehicle—but then she realized this was the beginning. On a longer straightaway, she saw a line of SUVs and tricked-out minivans lined up from every direction, all going to the same place: Thea's ranch.

Adrienne had wanted to arrive in the cover of the crowd, and she had succeeded. As the roads convened toward the long private driveway, Adrienne signaled and merged and waved *thank you*, mirroring what she saw everyone else doing, while inside her blood pressure rose.

Fake spiderwebs were draped over the ranch gate, and hundreds of pumpkins lined the driveway between a series of ten-foot-tall wicker arches woven with pampas grass, which blew dreamily in the hot afternoon air. Everything was Autumnal, all the details vibed Harvest, and every square inch was Cutesy-Spooky. Not a schlocky plastic ghost or rubber zombie mask in sight. If Eli Roth was at one end of the spectrum, this had leap-frogged Classy Martha Stewart to a new level of atmospheric, stylized *festive* as yet unseen by human eyes. Kitsch would be incinerated on sight.

As she drove onto the property, passing under a tunnel of pampas, Adrienne was floored by the sheer scope of this place. The land just seemed to extend for miles and miles in every direction. No neighbors, no streetlights—just this.

This lady was supposed to be #Relatable. Instead, she had a fiefdom.

The natural beauty was spectacular, but was it *actually natural*? Adrienne was curious—what had been cultivated? What had been imported? What had been trimmed into shapes never intended by evolution? Adrienne remembered learning that every inch of Central Park had been stringently plotted to feel wild. The paths deliberately curved to create the illusion of discovery. Even the exposed bedrock was a design choice. Once she knew that and, after further research, knew about the eviction of the Black citizens of Seneca Village to create this controlled, unnatural nature, the park lost some of its magic. Knowing that human hands had touched every curvature spoiled even the most innocent cherry blossom. She hadn't seen the blueprints to this ranch, but still she could sense the same invisible forces bending nature to their curated brand.

Adrienne pulled into the field that had been cleared for parking. There were multiple fields, in fact. She had to read the cedar sandwich board directions (chalkboard, calligraphy) like they were street-sweeping signs in San Francisco on a holiday weekend.

Adrienne tried to play it cool, but her anxiety was sky-high as she turned her thirty-day sobriety chip over in her hands. Alcoholics Anonymous had been a mixed bag so far, and she wasn't sure she was going to stick with it. She missed the release that only getting shit-faced afforded her. But she knew if she wanted to have any hope this weekend, she needed to have a clear head.

Hope. It felt dangerous to even think the word. Adrienne's vulnerability was like a sinkhole ready to bury her, and this summit was her skating close to the edge. It was safer to be angry, but anger wouldn't get her any answers here. She looked out at the sea of smiling faces and did her best impression in the rearview. When did she get so many teeth? And why hadn't she bleached them before she came? She rubbed at a coffee stain with the back of one knuckle and gave up after it made no change.

Adrienne took a deep breath. "Lord, grant me the serenity to accept the bitches I cannot change, the strength to punch the ones I can, and the wisdom to know the difference."

The difference being Chiara. That was why Adrienne was here. And for her sister, she would do anything.

She tucked her thirty-day chip into her purse, pulled out her phone, and saw the words No Signal on its screen.

What the hell?

Adrienne got out of her vehicle and called out to a group of women unpacking, "Hey, does your phone have a signal?"

They all shook their heads but seemed unbothered, which was almost weirder than not having a signal in the first place. Was this not news to them? Had Adrienne missed a note on the website?

A woman with an iPad walked over—her name tag read *Opal Winslow*, and she gave off major substitute-teacher-with-a-sadistic-streak vibes. Adrienne couldn't help but notice Opal's giant smile did not reach her eyes when she said, "No phones this weekend. New policy. The summit is not about the *posting*; it's about the *present*."

Creepy, Adrienne thought.

Opal flipped her iPad toward Adrienne. "And here's the NDA. Time to share all our secrets."

Double creepy.

Adrienne signed reluctantly and, therefore, deliberately made it an illegible scrawl. She had hoped to arrive a little more under the radar, but "under the radar" didn't seem to be an option here.

Opal squinted at the signature and asked, "Name?"

"Adrienne . . . Scott." She bit her lip, wishing her fake name had come out more smoothly.

Opal scanned the iPad, then said, "Here you are. Cabin 4."

She handed Adrienne a too-cute iron key tied with twine and a tiny gold spider. She also handed her a green rubber wristband.

"Wear your wristband at all times. It will get you into all our Basic- and Plus-Access events."

Adrienne figured if "under the radar" wasn't possible, she might as well get some intel. "I was hoping I could meet Thea?"

Opal replied in a *Sorry, not sorry* voice, "Meet and greets with Thea are only for Elite Access. Have a great time."

This might be harder than Adrienne thought. Although, to be fair, *get to the summit* had been the entirety of her plan.

Adrienne entered her cutesy cabin. Burnt-orange flannel, black velvet–accented duvets, and too many pumpkins to count, all painted white and gold, filled the space. She pulled the blinds closed (linen, taupe) and locked the door (dark-chocolate wood stain, seasonal washable welcome mat, #SponCon).

She allowed herself one big sigh and then spotted the gift basket. A comically large faux luggage tag read, in calligraphy, LOVE THE SKIN YOU'RE IN! Adrienne picked through the pile of swag. *Love the skin you're in, but also moisturize your armpits with this $28 natural deodorant, and fill those wrinkles with this retinol, and clip in these hair extensions.*

Adrienne draped the extensions on her head. "This is some raccoon-hat bullshit. And my armpits are fine, thank you very much," she said as she tossed the deodorant into the trash.

She slid all the decorative pumpkins into the trash, too. Then she stuffed the eight accent pillows and the cashmere throw (#Anthropologie) under the bed. Flowers: gone. Candy tray: gone. Besides just clearing out the space so she felt like she could think, this culling had a secondary goal: she was trying to push all her saltiness out now—here, in private—so when she opened that door, she could go perform as MOMMY. Smiling, harmless, neutral.

A voice punctured the silence. "Hey, you."

Adrienne jumped about a foot in the air. "What the fu—"

"We are so excited you're here."

Adrienne whipped around, looking for whoever had just noiselessly let themselves into her space; then she saw that the TV had been on this whole time, playing a welcome-orientation video.

Thea was smiling from the screen. "If you go into your welcome basket, you will find a map of the ranch and a schedule of events."

Adrienne found these items tucked inside the basket's organic-straw filler and looked them over. She spent the most time on the map—the lines of cabins, the parking area, the various event tents, the corn maze, the barn, the oak grove with little firepits . . . and over in the corner, *Thea's House.*

The itinerary was longer than a CVS receipt, with a big note: 3RD DAY IS FOR ELITE MOMS ONLY.

Adrienne rolled her eyes. She just got here and they were already excited to kick her ass out. She knew the type: *Welcome, welcome, welcome, sit anywhere but don't sit there, and take your shoes off and use a coaster, and no you can't smoke in the yard, and wow that was a nice visit but it's been a whole forty-five minutes and you probably need to be going, and here are the crackers you brought you can take them back we won't eat them, so I will get your coat and stand by the door until you get the hint.* Hospitality that you can count on like a semi-frozen pond.

Thea continued her welcome speech. "Of course, Halloween is our theme, but we have so much more to offer this weekend. Join us for sunrise yoga . . ." On the TV, a woman stood in Warrior Pose in the tall grass. "Check out our spa options . . ." A woman was mid–hot stone massage with crystals all over her face. "Or just bask in the friendship you can only have with other mothers." Moms drinking wine, lounging in hammocks.

Adrienne wasn't under the aspirational spell, though. "Jesus, it's like a Viagra commercial."

Thea went on. "If you need anything, just ask SARA. Hey, SARA!"

A little virtual-assistant smart speaker lit up next to the TV. "Yes, I'm SARA. Did you need something?"

Thea laughed. "Not now, SARA."

SARA replied, "Okay. Goodbye for now." Her light spun and then dimmed out.

The coordination was supposed to be cute. It was not.

Thea started wrapping it up. "Up first is our kick-off event, where we finally answer the question burning in all your hearts: What kind of mom are you? See you soon."

There was a beat, then . . .

Thea waved from the screen. "Hey, you. We are so excited you're here."

The video had looped back to the start.

Adrienne found the remote and turned off the TV. In its absence, she could hear the excited chatter of women outside and see her reflection in the black screen. In the dark flatness that blurred her face, she could find more of her resemblance to Chiara. Different chins, but the same wide cheekbones. Adrienne had a smaller, squatter forehead, but their ears poked out at nearly the same elfish angle. There wasn't much else they shared, so she cherished the warped seconds of likeness she could conjure. Seeing Chiara in her own face was the ultimate sweetness and an ice pick in her chest.

With the map and itinerary from the gift basket in hand, Adrienne went into the bathroom (white quartz with silver veining, brass fixtures) and started to unpack piles of printed Instagram photos from the last summit; photos of Chiara, including the last selfie she had sent from the welcome dinner; and a satellite Google Maps printout of the property. She taped it all up inside the shower. It wasn't quite conspiracy-theory-string-connecting-the-dots, but it was all she had so far to fill her command center. Adrienne took a last look and then pulled the shower curtain closed.

Adrienne peeked out the window at the moms who were already leaving for the welcome event. It seemed there was an unofficial uniform this weekend: expensive jeans; brown suede boots over the knee; a chunky sweater that still highlighted their boobs; and perfect, long hair in loose waves—points if you wore a cute felt hat.

Adrienne pulled her new clothes from her bag—she had done her research. She ripped the tags off and got dressed to infiltrate.

Once the outfit was settled, Adrienne needed to nail down the hair and makeup choices. She swiped through her iPad; still no signal, but she had a folder full of images she'd saved from social media. All the Instagram mothers started to coast across the screen. Cute, coordinated costumes, babies with bubble bath on their faces, holiday decorations that boggle the mind. Enough slouchy cream sweaters to suffocate Nancy Meyers five times over.

Again and again, she read the hashtags: #ChristianGirlAutumn, #LoveMyBabies, #BestJobEver, #Blessed. The photos began to bleed together. The cuteness wore thin and then stuck to her eyeballs like roadkill.

She zoomed in more and more on the mothers. On their perfect hair. On their talon grips around unruly toddlers. On their artificial white teeth poking through tense smiles. While she could see the value of these overly posed #PricelessMemories, there was one thing she could never quite gloss over—their dead eyes. The eyes of people who hadn't slept more than four hours in four years. For Adrienne, these women didn't exude "loving family." Quite the opposite. Those hollow eyes rang of all her memories of her drug friends. Late nights turning into gray mornings, looking for one more score, assuring each other that no one could tell they were on anything. Except everyone could tell. It was written all over their faces, in their bloated cheeks, saggy necks, and poorly brushed teeth. These perfect mommies were the same. No Dyson blow-dryer could cover up that they were on the brink.

These perfect mommies doth protest too damn much.

After a few more swipes, she saw the right #Inspo for the day and copied the hair and makeup as best she could. Lots of lip gloss. Lots of cheek highlighter. Gobs of shine serum on the hair. Then it was time for the final touch. She pulled out a little pile of costume jewelry. She selected a fake princess-cut diamond ring (because #WifeLife) and layered on necklaces with letter-initial charms (one per each fake baby) and faux birthstones to signal #Mommy. By the end, she was a sentient Nordstrom.

She was ready.

Chapter 6

Welcome, Mommies

Adrienne entered the Welcome, Mommies–event tent to find all two-hundred-plus moms sitting on cutesy hay bales with Pendleton-style blankets. It was so fall she could barf: Gourds of all shapes, pumpkins of different sizes, several statement walls of dried golden gingko to pose in front of. More pampas grass floating above them like an autumnal specter. She took a seat in the back. The mood was lively and full of anticipation.

Finally, the lights started to swirl, and the women began to cheer. Opal ran down the center aisle, Ellen DeGeneres–style. She stopped to dance, high-five, and wave to the returning moms.

Adrienne clapped along, waiting for the wink, the nod that this was all a bit much, but through a frozen smile, she realized, *Oh my God, they're actually serious.* She suddenly questioned if she would be able to keep up the act long enough to get the answers she craved. She also questioned why she'd thought getting bangs would be enough. She had underestimated the fervor and now didn't know how deep it went. Her stomach dropped, like when she'd tried to touch the bottom of a dark lake and instead her head went underwater.

Opal made it to the stage. Her dark hair was in a pin-tucked chignon, not a strand out of place. She wore loafers, trim cigarette pants, and a loose button-down oxford shirt. A green anorak broke up the business-wear, but just barely. You could tell she was one of those *Oh, I don't own sweatpants* mothers.

Opal took the mic. "Wow. I am supposed to be welcoming you, but you just welcomed *me*!"

All the moms in the audience yelled and whooped.

She went on. "The energy you just gave to me? The motivation? The drive to do my best? That came from you. Yes. Yes, it did."

The message was positive, with a little televangelist vibe thrown in for good measure.

Another mom with a mic stepped onto the stage in the most scripted "Who, me?" way possible. At the sight of her, a woman next to Adrienne shrieked, "It's McKenna!" Adrienne wished she had a note-pad to keep everyone's names straight. McKenna's deep-auburn hair was trussed up in a messy bun (that actually wasn't messy at all). She wore the jeans-and-high-boots uniform, but her twist on it was a perfect plaid button-down tied at her waist. She was hitting this impossible target of Flawless Casual.

"Um, Opal?" she said.

Opal turned. "What's up, McKenna?"

"I'm supposed to follow you, but I don't know how I can."

Opal made a show of being shocked. "McKenna, you are a Multiples Mom. You can do anything! Where are my Multiple Moms?" She turned back to the crowd, and many women stood up, pointing to themselves.

McKenna looked sheepish. "Sure, I have two sets of twins. But I think I need some of what you just got!" She looked to the crowd. "Can I get some of that, y'all?"

The moms went wild, and McKenna ran down through the crowd. She high-fived, she booty-bumped, there were even a couple of (very white, very off-beat) dance-offs. After a few minutes she returned to the stage.

"*Woo!* I needed that! You guys are the power here. Not us."

Opal nodded. "Not us. You, mamas. And on you is where we want this weekend to start." She clicked a remote in her hand, and the screen behind her lit up with a giant slogan: *What Kind of Mama Are You?*

McKenna hit her cue. "We don't want to make you like us."

Opal vigorously shook her head. "No. We want to help you be the best you."

McKenna placed a hand on her heart. "Just like we do for our babies."

This got a variety of sighs and shouts of "So true!" and "One hundred percent!" from the crowd.

Opal nodded. "Exactly, McKenna. So this year we are doing it *all differently*. No app. No QR codes."

McKenna mock-bit her nails. "No phones! Eek! But that's because this year, we want you to go inside and find out who you really are." She turned a little serious. "Now, we know there have been a lot of questions about continuing our For Mamas, by Mamas events, where you brilliant women get to share your gifts with the coMOMunity. Last year was a complete success."

Opal echoed, "A complete success. I mean, I'm *still* thinking about those star-spangled baby headbands."

"Me too," McKenna agreed. "So cute. Had to make one in my size."

Adrienne didn't know what they were talking about, but she could smell the spin. It seemed so did everyone else, as this was met with a rush of whispers and murmurs.

To quell the unrest, Opal dug deep for her most #Authentic tone. "But we felt like putting that pressure to achieve in this venue—it took away from what these weekends are really about."

McKenna made intense eye contact with Opal as she talked. "Well said, Opal. These weekends aren't about proving anything. Y'all do that all day, every day! Right, mamas? CoMOMunity is about slowing down and giving *you* the time to meet *you*." The crowd was with them now. "So let's all take some time to really turn inward. Reflect on who we are and what we've done."

At that last sentence, Adrienne felt a little shiver that no one else seemed to share.

Opal brought it home. "And to that end, we have made a little quiz for you. Just wish there was some way to pass them out . . ."

From behind the crowd came two voices in singsong unison: "Helloooo!"

Adrienne felt the rush of every eye turning to look, and she craned her neck to get a peek.

Two women popped into the tent, mics in hand. One was on the shorter side, her black hair cut into thick bangs with a perfect high ponytail and a body so toned Adrienne thought she could bounce a quarter off it. The other was tall, slim, and looked like she was almost floating due to her cotton nap dress; her impossibly long, blond hair was tied back with a single ribbon that matched the ribbon woven into her basket. Opal and McKenna reacted with shocked delight, even though this was obviously choreographed down to the second. The moms in the audience ate up the whole pantomime with a spoon and were vocally begging for more.

Opal was amazed. "Everyone, welcome Tamarind!" Tamarind did a little yoga bow. "And welcome Ashleigh!"

Ashleigh held up her wicker masterpiece with trailing silk ribbons. "I heard something about a basket of quizzes?"

Tamarind made a face that was half awe, half exasperation. "Ashleigh, did you weave that basket yourself?"

"Maybe . . ." Ashleigh winked, and the moms swooned.

Adrienne could not get a read on this. What exactly was happening? It was all Disneyland fakey-fake, and yet everyone had fallen for it hook, line, and sinker, reacting like nothing realer had ever unfolded before their eyes. It vibed so religious adjacent that Adrienne wouldn't have been surprised if someone asked to be cured of polio by the power of a glue-gun prayer.

Tamarind and Ashleigh walked the aisles, passing the baskets around for people to take the quiz.

The basket finally reached Adrienne. She scanned just the first page of multiple-choice questions, and every alarm bell in her head went off.

QUESTION 1: Do you want to make money for your family?

1. Yes. 2. Would be nice, but not my focus. 3. My husband provides for us outside the home, and I provide inside the home.

QUESTION 2: How would you feel about giving birth at home?

1. I already have! 2. Home-Birth Curious. 3. Eek! I'm scared!

QUESTION 3: How much baby weight do you still have?

1. Zero! 2. 5–10 lbs 3. I broke the scale. 🙁

QUESTION 4: How many affirmations do you say to yourself per day?

1. I love myself! 2. I like myself but forget. 3. I struggle with accepting love.

QUESTION 5: Do you agree with the statement "I feel relaxed when I am creative"?

1. 100%. Hobby Lobby is my happy place! 2. I like it but wish I could do better with the finished product. 3. Help me make Childhood Magic!

QUESTION 6: Do you agree that the husband is head of household?

1. Yes. 2. We are partners. 3. I have my role and he has his.

QUESTION 7: Homeschooling your children: Dream come true or nightmare?

1. Dream 2. Wish I could with teacher support. 3. Nightmare.

As the crowd read on, Opal called out, "Look over this quiz. And then look into your heart. There are no wrong answers."

"Bullshit," Adrienne muttered to herself.

As the foursome left the stage, McKenna waved like a pageant queen Adrienne once saw on TV. "See y'all in one hour, moms! Wear your athleisure!"

True to the schedule, one hour later Adrienne followed the crowd to the main event of the day.

She didn't know what to expect and was unenthused when she saw a low-ropes course set up in a grove of oak trees.

Opal, McKenna, Ashleigh, and Tamarind all stood at the starting point wearing adorable safety helmets that looked like witch hats.

Thea stood up on a little platform. Her helmet/witch hat was white and, somehow, against all odds, #CuteAF.

Thea lifted her golden paper megaphone. "Welcome, moms!"

When the moms saw Thea, they all started running like they were at a Taylor Swift concert. There were shrieks, and more than a little shoving. Suddenly, Thea's elevated platform made sense as not just for status but also an added level of safety.

Thea waved and smiled to the crowd like a politician working the rope line of undecided voters on Election Day. Finally, she addressed the group as a whole. "We promised this year's summit would be the best yet. Our Halloween theme is already a winner. But we wondered, what did that really mean—'best yet'? Did it mean more spa treatments? Gourmet meals? Giveaways? I mean . . . *yes*. Of course."

She laughed. Opal, Tamarind, McKenna, and Ashleigh laughed. Everyone was laughing. Ha ha ha. Ha. Holy shit, this was weird.

Thea turned serious. "But really . . . the summits are about more than merch, and sponcon. They are about you. So we decided to really kick it up a notch with . . . *a ropes course*! Please get a helmet and a harness."

More running, more (playful?) shoving.

Apparently, the cute witch helmets were for the stars only, because soon every woman there was wearing a giant orange safety helmet painted to look like a pumpkin.

Thea directed the group toward the starting line. "Okay, everyone, we are going to start with some really basic individual courses. Line up, wait until the mom ahead of you is halfway along before you enter the course, and most of all, support each other!"

The moms all *woo*'d. Adrienne contemplated if there was a way to cover her ears for the rest of the summit. Then she thought of Lisa's words—that her pride would keep her in the dark. Pride needed to take a back seat for the weekend. She let out what she hoped was a believable, if slightly less passionate, *woo* of her own.

Tamarind turned to the PA system, and soon every speaker disguised as a rock was pumping out the synth beat and chopped-vocal opening of Beyoncé's "Run the World (Girls)."

The ropes course started off easy: two logs on a slight incline. Adrienne could do that, no problem, easily toggling her weight back and forth while keeping her balance centered.

The next section was a single, skinny log with a loose rope suspended overhead for her to hold on to. Adrienne grabbed the rope and slowly made her way. Despite herself, Adrienne cracked her first smile. Who could resist the joy of playing outside while Beyoncé commands girls to run the world? No one. Not even a woman on a mission.

Adrienne got stuck midway on the suspended tire bridge. She flailed and struggled.

A couple of the moms nearby started yelling encouragements:

"You got this, Mom!"

"Go, Mama! Go!"

"Yes, yes! Imagine your baby is on the other side—use that power!"

A very athletic mom who clearly knew her way around a ropes course came and stood just underneath Adrienne. She spoke calmly. "I'm here. You won't fall. Trust yourself."

"Trust yourself!" another mom echoed. And then suddenly, they were all chanting at Adrienne, "Trust! Trust! Trust!"

If this exact scenario had been described to Adrienne before this moment, she would have eaten a hive of bees to get out of it. But somehow it wasn't a horrid display of #Friendship. It felt really good to hear a group of smiling faces boost her confidence.

The athletic mom was still beneath her. "You have the strength in your grip. Now, just take one leg off and swing it. Get some momentum."

Adrienne looked in her eyes and was startled to see nothing but complete confidence reflected back to her. How long had it been since anyone had looked at Adrienne with anything besides annoyance, suspicion, or pity? At least a year? Maybe eighteen months? She felt an unexpected rush of energy as she followed the woman's instructions to regain her movement.

By the power of the group belief in her ("Trust! Trust! Trust!") and Beyoncé's vocals, Adrienne stretched through that last bit and crossed the finish line, where she was met by a group of moms all cheering and giving her high-fives. It felt so damn good.

Thea was back on the platform. "All right, we knew you could complete the solo events. I mean, what *can't* moms do, amiright? But it's time to rely on each other. Let's move on to what it's all about: teamwork. Or should we say, MOMwork! That's the coMOMunity that makes our days bright!"

The moms *woo*'d, but Adrienne didn't cover her ears this time. She even let loose a little shoulder shimmy. *I'm blending in,* she told herself. *That's all.* She was sure it would take more than Beyoncé to make her lose sight of her purpose this weekend . . . right?

Ashleigh came forward. "Okay, let's divide up by birthday. Winter Babies here with Opal; Fall Babies, meet Tamarind there; Spring Babies are with McKenna; and Summer Babies, follow me."

A minute later, with the rest of the Summer Babies, Adrienne was standing on one side of an eight-foot web made of metal cables suspended between two trees.

Ashleigh stood to the side, shouting instructions, "Every mom must make it through the web to the other side! But don't let any part of your bodies touch the cables; otherwise, you start over."

At first, the event was going well, and three women contorted themselves to the other side. One woman, Maddie, who was so skinny Adrienne could only assume she hadn't eaten a full meal since the aughts, was slowly navigating her lower half through a hole while other women supported her upper body.

A mom in head-to-toe lululemon was coaching her. "Keep going, Maddie. You can do this."

But Maddie was getting frantic. "My leg is starting to cramp!"

Lululemon Mom's stress started rising. *"Focus, Maddie!"*

Ashleigh sighed with semi-mock impatience. "Other groups have already finished. Just saying."

A mom who was trying to guide Maddie's torso on the other side of the web yelled, "My hands are slipping! They're slipping!"

Adrienne was sweating. She looked around; turned out, everyone was sweating. This was hard.

Ashleigh looked at her watch. "Wow, I am glad this isn't a timed event."

Adrienne was confused. She felt the coMOMunity with the other moms, but Ashleigh was being a real bitch right now. Did she think that was motivating? Did she not care?

And in a span of seconds, one hand slipped, setting off a chain reaction until the entire group collapsed.

Ashleigh was visibly bored. "Well, at least that's over."

The women disbanded immediately, frustrated, leaving Maddie awkwardly trapped in the web.

Maddie was trying to keep her cool. "Guys? Guys. Are my extensions stuck in the cable? I feel like my hair extensions got stuck."

An air horn sounded, signaling for the groups to switch events. The Summer Babies moved on with Ashleigh in the lead, leaving Maddie behind, as she was still trying to get her hair extensions out of the cables. Adrienne felt torn. To blend in with the group meant leaving Maddie, but that didn't feel right to her. She had seen a pair of scissors in the first aid kit, and got them for Maddie.

Maddie awkwardly tried to make eye contact but couldn't turn her head that way. "Thanks so much."

"Don't mention it," Adrienne said. "How do you want me to do this? It's really caught."

"Oh, I don't care. I got my photo with Ashleigh already. Just cut it so we don't get left behind."

Adrienne heard the frantic tone in that last bit. "Left behind? They're right there." She pointed to their Summer Babies group, which had merely moved on to the next course a few feet away.

"They're starting the next event! They're starting!" Maddie fretted. "Wait for me!" she yelled at the top of her lungs. She snatched the scissors from Adrienne's hand and cut the extensions at nearly the root of her hair. Once free, she ran to catch up without giving Adrienne a second look.

Adrienne had spent a lot of time with tweakers, and as such, she thought she knew how to anticipate the most unpredictable people. Yet no moment of this was going how she'd expected, including a woman choosing to give herself a bald spot.

As the groups switched locations, Adrienne decided this shuffle was the perfect opportunity to find out who'd been here at the last summit and therefore could have any information about Chiara.

She couldn't admit to herself how flimsy this method was, randomly asking two hundred women if they'd seen Chiara last year while also trying not to share anything about herself. Her hope was, if she could get any usable information, Bautista would have to interview them, maybe find a witness or at least a lead.

Adrienne started her #CasualNotCasual questioning with a sweet southern mom who had strayed from the mommy pack when she stopped to tie the laces on her neon-floral HOKAs.

"Hey, great work back there," Adrienne said, doing her best bestie impression.

"Thank you. I get up at four thirty a.m. every day to exercise. It's my happy place!" Southern Mom said in a tone that Adrienne had last experienced with people who were desperately trying to convince themselves they weren't having a bad acid trip and, in fact, loved that plaid vampires were chewing on their pant leg.

"Gotta love a happy place! Speaking of which, this summit . . . So happy, right? Like, the happiest! Happiest place on earth!"

Southern Mom's tone was dead serious. "No. That's Disneyland."

Adrienne nodded effusively. "Yes. Obviously. Mickey, what a guy—er, mouse. So, back to this summit. You seem to really know what's what. Did you come last year?"

Her eyes narrowed slightly. "Why?"

Adrienne really pushed herself to be breezy. "Oh, just trying to see how this year stacks up compared to last year." She paused and held it, desperately willing the woman to fill the awkward silence. Southern Mom made no sign of budging, so Adrienne started jabbering. "Is this year better? The same? This all seems so supportive. Was last year supportive? Like this? Or were the vibes off? Were there different moms?"

"Why does it matter?" Southern Mom replied, her eyes narrowing just a tiny bit more.

Adrienne sputtered for an answer that was clear but also open-ended. "I guess I'm curious if the summit is consistently this . . . fun."

"Fun?"

"Yeah. Fun. I love fun." Inside, Adrienne was screaming, *Fun?!*

Southern Mom's face spread into a giant grin that was as toothy as it was joyless. "I see your desire to know more. I imagine it's frustrating to feel that way. But unfortunately, I can't help you."

And with that, she sailed away on a sea of medium-teased hair and clinking David Yurman jewelry, rejoining the rest of the Summer Babies.

Adrienne quickly convinced herself that she had just chosen the wrong person to ask. She needed to find the opposite of that mom, and she spotted her immediately: a yoga mom with visible gray hair who wore stretch linen overalls that Adrienne felt certain were purchased at Whole Foods. Sure, she was wearing those flowy overalls over a sports bra that pushed her boobs up so high they were touching her chin, but she was still a million miles from Southern Mom. Adrienne knew this exchange would go down differently.

Yogini Mom was doing an elaborate backbend, using a tree to steady herself. Adrienne tried to do the same bend but only made it about 10 percent of the way down. If the yogini was in the shape of a lowercase *n*, Adrienne was a mild parenthesis. "Wow, great stretch," she wheezed out.

Yogini Mom took a deep breath and somehow went even deeper into the bend. "Yes. Really opens the chakras."

"Mm-hmm," Adrienne said, standing up before all her blood rushed to her head. "Hey, I was curious—did they do a ropes course last year?"

"You want to know about last year?" the yogini asked, incredulous.

"Yeah, the summit last year? Were you here? I'm just trying to get context on one year versus another."

"That's a unique framework for this experience. That said, I never look back. It's not part of my mindfulness practice," Yogini Mom said with a tiny bow as she backed away, linen flowing, chin resting on boobs.

Adrienne rubbed her eyes furiously. As she did so, she felt something smoosh against her cornea—fake hair. *Maddie!* She would ask Maddie. Surely their scissor snafu could break through the niceties and into the truth.

Adrienne caught up to her as the Summer Babies were getting their harnesses checked for the next event. "Maddie, wait up!"

Maddie was smiling until she saw who it was. "Oh, hey."

"Just wanted to make sure you're feeling okay after the whole hair thing."

Maddie was all business, looking over Adrienne's shoulder and waving at someone in another group. "Yeah. Totally."

Adrienne nodded. "Hey, I'm curious: Did you come last year?"

Maddie's eyes snapped into focus, "I come every year. Haven't missed one. Twenty-six, total. That includes all of the style summits, and every official quarterly meetup. You know how many moms can say that?"

"Cool. Yeah, you seem like you have everything dialed in. One hundred percent in the know. So, considering that, do you remember a woman last year—her name was Chiara?"

Maddie waved to someone else. "Hi! OMG, let's catch up at dinner!" Then her attention went back to Adrienne. "I don't know. Maybe. How many followers does she have?"

Adrienne was startled at the question but tried to hide it. "Um, I don't know. Like one hundred, maybe?"

"One hundred *thousand*?" Maddie was interested now.

"No. Like one hundred, period."

"Oh, then no. I don't know her. I only talk to Elite Moms, or moms with follower counts higher than me."

Adrienne couldn't help her snark. "Then why are you talking to me?"

Maddie was very clear. "Oh, because it would look bad to other moms if I ignored you."

Adrienne bit her tongue, literally and metaphorically. "Right, of course. So, you don't remember a woman last year named Chiara?"

Adrienne had barely even finished asking the question when Maddie cut in. "I hear that you want information about last year. However, I am focused on completing the summit's current goals on the ropes course. I hope you find what you are looking for."

With that, Adrienne saw the pattern in all three of their answers. They'd identified her want, validated her desire, and then set a hard boundary of *No*. Even in their apparent variations as people, their uniform responses felt like canned buzzwords from social media therapists.

Emotional regulation by fridge magnets.

Adrienne talked to a few other moms at the water bottle refilling station and at the coMOMunity organic-sunscreen pump, but got absolutely nowhere. Either people hadn't been there last year, or they pegged her as no one they needed to know and wriggled out of the conversation as fast as they could.

Adrienne had to stomp away for a minute to blow off some steam.

"Stupid healthy attachment-style gentle parenting," she huffed as she threw some rocks at a tree, a coping mechanism she hadn't used since sixth grade.

When she ran out of rocks, Adrienne thought about Chiara in her college cap and gown. The flush of pride on her face. A world of possibilities in her eyes.

"You did it!" Adrienne had yelled, pulling Chi into a big hug.

"*We* did it. How many times did you keep me from dropping out?"

"Mmm, eleven times?"

"Thank you for never giving up on me," Chiara had said.

"Of course! I'll never give up on you," Adrienne had replied.

She had kept that promise all the way to this ranch in the middle of nowhere, and no snooty moms were going to make her give up.

When she rejoined the group, the whole summit was together now, but the birthday groups were still divided. There were two rows of logs thirty feet apart, with everyone gathered on one side. Between the logs were perpendicular lengths of rope that created four lanes from one log side to the other. Adrienne was reminded of a high school track, but these running lanes were much wider. And instead of hurdles, the lanes were evenly littered with flat 4x4 squares of wood. Adrienne thought it answered the question *What would a Cro-Magnon 100-yard dash look like?* Not that anyone had ever asked it.

Thea was back on her platform. "I want you to imagine that where you are standing now is a riverbank. This open space here"—she pointed to the lanes—"is your river of motherhood. You need to work together to cross from this side of the river to the other." Thea pointed to the row of logs opposite them, where Tamarind and McKenna stood, waving. "But your feet cannot touch the dirt. You will get across the river by stepping on the 'stepping stones.' If anyone's foot touches the dirt, you are out. And that's a big deal because as you move forward, you need to pick up the stepping stones and carry them with you to the other side." She pointed to the small wooden squares. "These are all the things you keep track of every day, moms."

Looking closer, Adrienne saw that each wooden square had something written on it: *laundry*, *birthday parties*, *pediatrician appointments*, *field trip forms*, etc.

Thea gave them a second to read and then continued. "All that invisible emotional labor. That mental load that you handle like a boss. This is about seeing how much you do, how well you can prioritize, and how much we need to rely on each other. But it can't be *that* easy—right, moms?"

Easy? Adrienne felt like she had already forgotten half the rules!

"When I blow the whistle, if a stepping stone doesn't have a foot on it? We take it away. Because sometimes we can't do it all. Sometimes stuff falls through the cracks. So what will you choose to let fall to the wayside? What important things will you miss? Now, not all stepping stones are created equal, just like not everything we do for our families is equal." Thea held up an example square to reveal a number written on the back. "These are the point values for each square. When the last mom reaches the far bank, the group that has not just carried the most stones across but also the stones worth the most *points* wins something pretty great. I wish I was down there with you so I could win it."

A hyped-up mom in the crowd yelled, "What is it?"

Thea played coy. "You want to know? You don't want it to be a surprise?"

The crowd frenzied at the bait:

"Tell us!"

"We want to know!"

"What is it?"

Thea allowed herself to be persuaded. "Okay. The winning team will meet with my Mom Squad for a quiz evaluation and a one-on-one consultation!"

At this, the crowd actually went berserk. On a scale from one to ten, the enthusiasm jumped to an eleven with a side of full-blown rabies. But there was something else, something just below the surface. Adrienne saw the mothers sneering at the other teams, sizing each other up, cracking their necks, and rubbing dirt into their hands.

On a dime, the game had changed.

But it had changed for Adrienne, too. While Thea was clearly too removed to access, Adrienne saw this as an opportunity to get closer to the Squad, and she needed that closeness if she were to have any hope of getting a clue about Chiara. The women in the Squad were the only ones she knew for sure had been here last year, and could tell her who else had been, too.

Thea blew a whistle, and the teams started to make their way across the "river."

Within seconds, Thea blew her whistle again. Everyone looked up.

Thea pointed. "Winter Babies, I see three stones without a foot. Fall Babies, I see one stone without a foot. Spring Babies, you're good. Summer, you're good."

Tamarind and Opal walked over and took the unattended wooden squares.

Thea almost blew the whistle to restart the game but then stopped herself. "Tamarind, can you read out the things that the Winter Babies missed out on?"

Tamarind read out what was written on the front and then the back of the wooden squares she had just collected from the Winter Baby–river lane. "End-of-year teacher gifts." There was a collective groan from the summit. "That was worth two points. Dentist appointment was missed; that's three points." Another groan. "And . . . oh no . . . wow, you guys didn't get organized for a family Halloween costume. Four points."

This was met with audible gasps.

Thea grimaced. "Wow. Winter Babies, you are already down nine points. I hope you can catch up."

Thea blew her whistle, and shit got very real.

As everyone moved forward, Thea reminded them, "Laundry can wait, but that birthday party . . . If you have to leave one stone behind, which is more important? Priorities, mamas!"

The event moved quickly, and as Thea blew her whistle again and again, more stones were removed. As the moms carried more stones, their balance worsened, and several participants from each team touched dirt and were escorted to the side. The women were getting frustrated with each other and eyeing the other teams with shrewd calculus. At one point, a Spring Baby lost her balance, and Adrienne could have sworn that she tried to reach across the lane line to take a Fall Baby down with her, narrowly missing.

Adrienne noticed that the stones most often left without a foot, and therefore picked up by the Squad, were the ones left behind when the group moved forward. She had no idea how this point-priority system worked; to her, missing a dentist appointment, for example, was way worse than a missed family Halloween costume. She needed to figure out how to get the maximum points writ large instead of trying to glean which random woodblock would be worth the most.

At the next sweep, when everyone was still, Adrienne whispered to a mom on her team, "Hey, do you have pockets?"

"What?"

It wasn't a complicated question. Adrienne pointed to her own pocketless lululemon pants and then to the other woman's. "Do you have pockets to put the stones in when we move past them?"

Her teammate got it. "No, but . . ." She reached into her fanny pack, which was stylishly slung around her shoulder, and pulled out a reusable shopping bag in an Americana pattern that was just shy of jingoism. "It's from Ashleigh's fall line. I was hoping she'd sign it."

Adrienne snatched it. "Give it."

The woman tugged on the bag. "No! Get your own!"

As they both pulled on either side, they teetered close, almost losing their footing.

Adrienne dug deep for a calm voice. "We don't know how much each block is worth until they turn it over. We have a better chance of winning if we don't lose any stones at all. Bring them all with us." And then, with emphasis: "In the bag."

Adrienne slid her foot off one stone and then picked it up, placing it in the bag. Her teammate's eyes went wide as she saw the easy plan in action. She whispered to the moms on their team to pass the stones over to them when they moved forward.

The other teams were moving faster than Adrienne's, with more moms already past the finish line. Adrienne could see the women in the front of her team were feeling stressed about being last, but she kept her focus. Being first wasn't how to win. The bag was heavy, and her balance was almost gone by the time her team crossed the finish line. Fourth place of four. But that was when Adrienne proudly handed her bag to McKenna to be counted.

Thea checked out the bag and smiled. "We have a winner: Summer Babies!"

The summer team coalesced around Adrienne, and she was swept up in the moment. Hugs, high fives, smiles for days.

However, beyond her cheering team, she saw the faces of the other mothers. Flashes of anger, fear, and panic.

She may have won face time with the Mom Squad, but she realized she'd also just put a target on her back.

Chapter 7

Your Self, Your Brand

The Summer Babies arrived at the main event tent positively buzzing with anticipation. The jovial vibe from earlier had returned, and each of them were clutching their *What Kind of Mama Are You?* quizzes. There were clear instructions to deposit their quizzes into Ashleigh's basket so they could be "evaluated" by the Squad.

As they waited, Maddie, with the bald spot, ran up to Adrienne and squeezed her. "I am so excited. This kind of one-on-one is worth thousands!"

It took Adrienne a second to realize she meant thousands of not just *followers* but also *dollars*. She felt a blast of clarity: *This isn't what type of mom you are; it's what type of brand you are.*

Adrienne hated this in every facet of life, but particularly here. Since when did everyone become brands? Since when did this word apply to regular people? Accountants and dentists and teachers? It was as if when the Supreme Court decided "corporations are people," humans collectively decided "people should be corporations." Suddenly, every person on the planet was supposed to have cohesive strategies for their personalities and a unifying colorway for their aesthetic, all with an accessible price point. Or not, if *that's* your brand.

Adrienne remembered a video a friend took of her after they'd done too many edibles. (As if there was any amount to do other than "too many.") Adrienne was lying in the back of a Honda, eating a hot dog from the 7-Eleven roller grill and railing, "Is everyone waiting for the great Coca-Cola God in the sky and a trademarked Holy Spirit in their heart to tap them on the shoulder and say, 'It's time for you to sell yourself to the masses'? Mattel Hot Wheels Jesus isn't coming, and yet you're all waiting for him to tell you to slap a price tag on your Instagram bio. Because once you do that—once you sell your personality like it's an estate sale—what are you left with? You don't own yourself anymore. You have exported your inner world for a QR code and ten percent off your first order."

It was one of those marijuana-induced moments of certainty, and Adrienne stuck to her position even when her friends tried to tease her about her soapbox tendencies.

But this was no place for Adrienne to release one of her (unfortunately) signature stoned tirades. She just had to clutch herself like the rest of the hopefuls, nodding emphatically when every person thought they were the first one to cleverly say "golden ticket."

After forty-five minutes Opal came out from behind a curtain, holding the reviewed quizzes. "Wow. What an incredible and diverse group of women," she said.

Adrienne looked around. Nearly every woman was white, between a size 0 and a size 6, had long hair, was visibly wealthy (engagement rings, subtle nose jobs, recently facial'd skin), and was positively chattering with anticipation. The only thing less diverse than this group was a eugenics pamphlet.

"Now, I know the goal in life is to be the best at everything—crafts, traditional values, style, health, wealth—but we wanted to see in these quizzes where each of you really felt your strongest. Where did *you* see *you*."

In bizzarro horoscope vernacular, Opal told the moms to get ready to learn their *Mom Sign*. Apparently, even the zodiac calendar was too scientific for this world and needed to be zhuzhed further.

"All right, starting with the A's . . . ," Opal said dramatically.

Adrienne knew the chances she could be first were high, unless there was an *Abby* in the group. She wasn't excited to be the guinea pig. She wanted a tired Squad with their guard down—not fresh-faced first-candidate attention.

Opal looked over the quiz on top of the large stack. "First up is . . . Adrienne!" The other moms politely clapped like this was an accomplishment. "Adrienne, you have a . . . Tamarind sign with a McKenna rising!"

Everyone clapped more as Adrienne took her quiz back and was directed to a side area where Tamarind and McKenna were seated on the ubiquitous Adirondack chairs. It was like a job interview, but the only qualifications were "How cute are you?"

It was just the three of them, and Adrienne had to steady her nerves as she took her seat. Who knew if she would get a chance like this again by the end of the weekend. She needed to play this perfectly.

McKenna started the consultation. "So, we looked over your quiz. It was . . ." She drifted off and looked to Tamarind for help.

Tamarind finally came up with, "Different." Tamarind looked to McKenna, passing the buck right on back.

Despite clearly hoping for more from her partner, McKenna soldiered on. "You didn't seem to really fit with any of the Mom Squad types."

They both had strained smiles, and it was apparent to Adrienne that they were also unhappy her quiz was first.

Tamarind added on, a little too enthusiastically, "And we love that. We love a unique mom."

This was obviously bullshit, but Adrienne found her biggest smile yet. "Yeah, I guess I just move to the beat of my own drum."

Tamarind cozied up like they were BFFs. "So, what drives you to be the best mom you can be?"

Adrienne hadn't expected to be questioned and had nothing prepared. "Um . . . my kids."

McKenna nodded. "Right. Of course. But like what do you see as your mom brand? Are you a Craft Mom? Or a Fitness Mom?"

Adrienne thought of her own mother, who was exhausted every second of every day for her entire life. "I think I'm just a Barely Making It to Bedtime Mom, ya know?" She tried a self-deprecating laugh that went over like a lead balloon.

There was an awkward silence, and Adrienne started to panic a bit. If this was her only face-to-face, she was blowing it. She fought the urge to bite her nails—good mommies don't bite their nails.

Tamarind grabbed her iPad from a leather magazine caddy that was draped on the side of the Adirondack. "Here, we are connected to Thea's private Wi-Fi. Let's pull up your Instagram. Maybe we can help you."

Adrienne was truly scrambling now. Two months ago, when she had realized she would need an Online Mommy presence to pass, she had deleted her "Best Lesbian Bars in San Diego" blog post, pasted in stock photos of babies, and had ChatGPT fill in the captions. All nicely backdated. But she didn't have the confidence to create a new Instagram; that was *their* home turf. A paltry grid felt like an easy way to be found out.

Adrienne nervously blurted out, "I don't have an Instagram."

Tamarind and McKenna shared a worried look. This was probably like saying she didn't believe in matching family pajamas on Christmas morning.

McKenna, suddenly getting it, said, "Ah, you're kind of an Offline Earth Mom. I get that. So, more of an Ashleigh. No computers. Homeschool."

Adrienne scoffed so hard she almost choked. "Homeschool? Are you nuts? Who can afford that?"

Another shocked silence.

Adrienne needed to course-correct right now. "I mean, I worry about mothers who don't have means. Lots of moms need to work full-time. Lots of moms *like* to work full-time."

It was Tamarind's turn to think she understood. "So you're an Opal? A girl boss always looking to save a penny?"

Adrienne realized she needed to lead this a bit more, because she honestly couldn't keep any of these women and their precious brands straight. "I guess I want to focus on, um, building community with other mothers who, um . . . uh, don't look like me." Adrienne grimaced internally. The Miracle on the Hudson had been a smoother landing than that, but she'd have to take it.

McKenna leaned in. "So you're kind of a *me*? Always reaching out?"

Tamarind let out a snort, and McKenna shot her a look of spite. Tamarind dodged the conflict by turning the attention back to the real problem in the room: Adrienne. "Seems like you are an individual mom who likes to trail-blaze. We love that here."

"Sure." Adrienne could fake "trailblazer" for the next five minutes. At least, she could fake it better than crafts.

The relief from Tamarind and McKenna was swift—these women did not like mystery. Tamarind focused in. "We encourage you to make that the cornerstone of your brand. Seems like that's how you like to operate: alone."

This was actually annoyingly accurate to Adrienne's real life, especially recently, and she didn't like that. She pushed back. "I have friends."

Tamarind tried to hide the note of surprise. "You do?"

Adrienne, a little offended, shot back, "Yes. My sister is my best friend."

McKenna leaned in even farther; she was practically folded in half at this point. "Does she have kids?"

"Yes."

McKenna needed more. "So do you pool childcare?"

Tamarind added, "Alternate school pickups?"

Before Adrienne could respond, it was rapid-fire:

"Meal plan?"

"Community garden?"

"Holiday vacays?"

"Group Halloween costumes?"

"Share extracurriculars?"

"Soccer moms?"

"Room parents?"

"PTA?"

"Girls' trips?"

"Booty Bootcamp?"

"Zooga?"

"Mommy and Me Music?"

"Mommy and Me Sign Language?"

"Mommy and Me Pottery?"

Adrienne's head was spinning. "No. No, we don't do any of that."

Tamarind was confused again, and not happy about it. "But you said she's your best friend."

Adrienne was fully on the defensive now. "She is."

A cloud of confusion dulled McKenna's big smile. "But you don't see her daily and you don't spend time with her kids?"

"There are other ways to be close," Adrienne responded, crossing her arms. Then immediately uncrossed them to look less defensive.

Tamarind shook her head vigorously. "Not for mothers."

McKenna's interest had moved on, as she was already leafing through the pile of other quizzes. "We need to meet with our next mom. But it has been a pleasure spending this quality time with you, Adrienne. We wish you luck with your Lone-Wolf Mommy brand."

Tamarind's eyes lit up. "Ooh, that's good. You should write that down."

Adrienne was trying to reengage, trying to get control of this, but was completely spun out. "I don't think *lone wolf* is accurate."

Shoulder to shoulder, McKenna and Tamarind escorted Adrienne from the consult area.

McKenna gave her a sad little smile. "Don't try to change. It never works."

Tamarind agreed. "A forced brand is never authentic."

"Byeeeeeeeee!" they said in the same nauseating singsong.

McKenna and Tamarind gently ushered Adrienne out as another eager mom entered.

Adrienne returned to her cabin, completely dejected.

She picked up her phone. Still no service. She looked through her photos and pulled up her favorite album: the one of her and Chiara. To be fair, it was really short, and didn't show anything that actually made them *them*.

Adrienne wondered if maybe this was part of her all-consuming resentment. So much of her life with Chiara had been their interior worlds coming together. Their shared memories. Their inside jokes. There were no videos from their childhood. There wasn't a photo of them when they got matching tattoos. There wasn't a single picture from that one trip they took to Mexico in the middle of the night, and woke up in time for sunrise on the beach.

At the time, Chiara had lamented, "We should have taken a picture!"

And Adrienne had responded, "We don't need a picture. We were there."

Instead, Chiara had bought them both postcards in town with a photo of the beach and drew two little stick figures on top of the sand.

Adrienne took one look and couldn't stop laughing. Finally, she composed herself long enough to show Chiara. "This isn't the beach we were on!"

Chiara took a closer look and collapsed into hysterics. "Holy shit, it's not the right beach!"

They laughed for so long and so loudly that the *policia* had come to make sure they weren't drunk or insane. This only made them laugh harder; who else but them would almost get arrested over a postcard?

Adrienne loved that stupid postcard of the wrong beach with the bad stick figures. She loved that no one would know what it meant but them.

Their bond was stronger than anything on this planet, yet it was dismissed entirely by the wider world because it wasn't obsessively cataloged for others to consume. They hadn't reduced their life to photo shoots and merch. But now that Chiara was gone, Adrienne felt like she had to scream out to convince people that she was dying inside, her anguish undercut and outweighed by the lack of a significant digital footprint.

So Adrienne clung to the few photos she did have. Old photos of them partying. Being young. Being messy. Being fun. Images scanned from disposable cameras. Then, as the photos progressed through time, Chiara cleaned up. And the photos got further between. There was only one of them together while Chiara was pregnant. A handful of the babies. And then . . . nothing.

When Adrienne made the Missing flyers, she had to copy a recent photo from Chiara's Instagram because she didn't have one herself.

Adrienne went to look at the bathroom wall. She had *Suspects* underlined, but nothing written. She had *Motive* underlined, but nothing written.

This was going poorly.

She was embarrassed at how little she had thought this out. She had no plan, no leads, no idea what she was doing. She tried to think back to the certainty she'd felt the day she bought this stupidly expensive ticket. She had been sure that day that the key to finding Chiara was somewhere on this ranch. But the reality of being here was so much looser.

Her only saving grace was that she hadn't told anyone else she was coming.

If she wanted to, she could slink home and never speak of this weekend again. No one would know how hard she had failed.

She looked at Chiara's photo, though. And that swept the thought from her mind. She at least had to get some intel on what the last summit had been like. All she needed was one solid lead for Bautista to go on.

With her new goal clear, she readied herself for the next event. Nothing could be worse than the ropes course, she assured herself.

She was wrong.

Chapter 8

Theories Abound

Gabrielle Bautista woke up to the smell of melting plastic and the microwave beeping.

After pulling an overnight shift, she had come home, pulled out a mystery Tupperware from the freezer to reheat, and promptly fallen asleep on the couch in all her clothes. She wiped her face and felt a little trail of drool.

Bautista got up from the couch slowly, feeling her back creak, and inspected her meal. Just the edges of the container had melted, and the contents (oxtails from her mom—yum) were safe. She poured the kare-kare into a large bowl and let it cool while she put on pajamas and a fluffy bathrobe in a red chili pepper pattern.

Once situated on the couch, she breathed in the peanut-based broth, catching the smallest notes of fish sauce and shallot. It smelled like home. Bautista's mom came up from LA every six months to ostensibly cook like crazy and stock her daughter's freezer. The ulterior motive was a three-day guilt trip for Gabrielle to move home. Gabrielle took the trade-off because the food sustained her physically and emotionally for months. And kare-kare was her absolute favorite. She couldn't believe she had forgotten this in the back of the freezer, and was grateful to have it now. She didn't even mind the eggplant her mom had put in against her wishes.

Bautista's home was a small one-bedroom bungalow that had been built as a guesthouse in the 1940s. Later, when Hayward was rezoned, the guesthouse was deemed its own domicile, and as such, it was tucked away in the center of a residential block at the end of a long, easy-to-miss driveway, behind all the other homes, not a street in sight. Bautista loved it. It felt like her little cocoon. A hidey-hole for only her and no one else.

Last year she had bought fifteen self-watering plants off an Instagram ad. After a lifetime of killing cacti, her home was now a lush wonderland. She didn't mind getting marketed to. All day at work, she searched for suspects who did not want to be found, pulling information from witnesses like molars. Because of that, in her off-hours, she loved the feeling of being sought. Even if it was just a plant company that had bought her data. With her plants in place, Bautista had painted her home in cheerful colors and had every shade of green in her furnishings. Soft-yellow walls in the living room with a jade couch. A peach kitchen framing sage cabinets. Jewel tones of mauve off-setting emerald tiles in the bathroom. She had humidifiers in every room and loved to light sandalwood-scented candles. Last visit, her mother had said it felt like a terrarium. Bautista said she felt like it was her own little forest. Except the only monsters here were the ones she invited in.

It had been a long shift of nothing. Paperwork, following up on a domestic dispute, more paperwork, prepping for a hearing coming up next week. Bautista didn't mind the paperwork so much. She loved order, and finishing a file felt like putting a nice bow on a messy situation. But for that reason, the cases that never sat right with her made her absolutely nuts. They were like a mental hangnail she couldn't stop tugging at. And when this happened, she broke one of the cardinal rules: never take your work home with you.

Bautista was ready to go to bed now for a few more hours before her next night shift started. Fed, face washed, pajamas on. She was filling up her bedside humidifier when there was a knock at her door.

She hooked the window curtain next to the door aside and saw her partner standing there. Bautista grimaced, tugged her fluffy bathrobe tightly around her, and opened the door.

Jarvis cheerfully greeted her, "Gabby!"

Gabrielle shook her head.

Jarvis tried again. "Gabrielle?"

Gabrielle shook her head once more.

Jarvis admitted defeat. "Bautista."

"What are you doing here, Jarvis?"

Jarvis was freshly promoted, and she gleamed with an enthusiasm Bautista had lost five years prior. "I just thought you needed to see this."

Jarvis handed an envelope to Bautista, and when her attention was diverted down, Jarvis entered the house in one swift motion.

Bautista was startled and not interested in company. "Jarvis, it's not really a good time."

Jarvis hadn't heard, though—or, more likely, pretended not to hear—and was already in the living room. "Cool place! Hard to find."

"Not hard enough, apparently," Bautista grumbled, shutting the front door. But as she closed it, she was pleasantly surprised to see that Jarvis had taken off her shoes and lined them up neatly with Bautista's own. How had she done that so quickly?

"Damn, Bautista, what the hell is this?" Jarvis called out.

Bautista gasped and hustled into the dining area, already well aware what Jarvis was talking about. The dining room wall was a giant map of Mendocino County. Thea's ranch was clearly marked, and every road out of the area highlighted. There was also a long list of names, with dark lines drawn through each of them. A timeline of the June weekend was written out hour by hour on a large calendar with things like *arrival* and *last text* time-stamped. At the top of it all was a photo of Chiara.

Jarvis's mouth was agape. "The Shaw case? I thought you told the sister to give up."

"I did."

Jarvis pointed to the map. "But clearly you didn't."

Bautista knew when her options were down to one, so she came clean. "The junkie sister is annoying, I agree. And her efforts to help have really bugged the hell out of me. I mean, my God, you should hear these voicemails she leaves me. 5150 material. But this case has never felt right to me, either."

Jarvis nodded. "Yeah, no one likes this case. That's why we got stuck with it."

It was true. The case had been passed around several departments like a cursed amulet, and Bautista didn't have anyone under her to pin it on.

"I just needed to follow up on those last leads. For me."

Jarvis's face was the definition of skepticism. "Uh-huh. Are these *leads* or are they *theories*?"

"I hear your tone, and I don't like it." Bautista tightened her bathrobe again and went to her list. "Firstly, I double-checked all of the husband's reported whereabouts."

"You suspect him of being involved? That guy? The wimp?"

"Well, his mom was his alibi," Bautista said through an eye roll. "That might have been enough for the captain, but it was not enough for me. And not to sound like the crazy sister, but why did it take him two days to call us after she didn't come home? What was that? Felt off. So I tracked his movements."

"And?"

"It all checks out. Restaurants he said he went to had his credit card on file. The toddler art class on Saturday is in a mini mall with CCTV, and he was on that. I even checked the toll booth on the Richmond Bridge—never crossed it. He was definitely in the East Bay, and not in Mendocino, all weekend."

"Could he have gone north through Vallejo?"

Bautista shook her head. "Nope, I checked those bridges, too."

Jarvis was on the hook, even as she tried to poke holes. "Wow, you have been busy. Okay, could he have hired someone to do it?"

Bautista shook her head again. "I asked for twelve months of bank statements. No big cash withdrawals. No regular small cash withdrawals leading up to, but not after, the weekend in question. No new credit cards taken out. Nothing that would suggest a contract."

Bautista could tell Jarvis was turning the Rubik's Cube now, her brow furrowed as she paced in front of the wall collage. "So maybe he waits for her to come home, kills her when she gets back. Says he never saw her."

"I thought of that, too. I got Richmond Bridge footage going east—her minivan never crossed back. Also, for the husband, motive wasn't there. No big savings account. No life insurance policy. No girlfriend waiting in the wings. He gains nothing from his wife's death."

Jarvis wasn't impressed yet. "A lot of legwork for nothing."

Bautista said gruffly, "I like certainty. I got certainty."

"Fair enough."

"The next lead Adrienne wouldn't let go of was all of Chiara's ex-boyfriends. She helpfully gave me a list. She unhelpfully included everyone going back to when Chiara was in high school." Bautista pointed to the very long handwritten list of names pinned to the wall.

"Uff," Jarvis said. "That would take forever to check."

"Thirteen months and six days, to be exact. Everyone accounted for—I got the last confirmation two days ago. One ex was a good possible perp: rap sheet, had a history of threatening voicemails to the vic, the sister had to beat him off with a bat once."

"But?"

"But he was in jail in Colorado."

Jarvis addressed the elephant in the room. "So what's with the map?"

Bautista stared at the map like it was her nemesis. "People don't disappear. We know where she was. The question is, where did she go?"

Jarvis smiled. "Well, that explains the thick envelope. Your Canada-border checkpoints came back. When they called your desk, I thought they had the wrong number."

Bautista had forgotten she was even holding an envelope and ripped it open, but Jarvis gave her the highlights: "No record of Chiara, her passport, California ID, or minivan plates crossing into Canada between Washington, Idaho, or Montana."

Bautista looked through the report. "Damn. I was hoping she had snuck up north."

"Asking the Canada Border Services Agency was definitely a reach. Our people weren't enough? Had to go to CBSA?"

"Like I said, I like certainty." Bautista felt sick. She hadn't realized just how much hope she had pinned on this last theory, that Chiara had cracked and absconded to start over. Jarvis was frowning, too, and Bautista knew this meant she had an idea. "What are you thinking, Jarvis?"

"One time my mom and I went to an A's game . . ."

"Here we go," Bautista sighed. They had only been partners for eight months, but she had already heard enough of Jarvis's rambling stories for a lifetime.

"Shut up, I'm going somewhere with this. Okay. So we go to an A's game. Great time. I had a malt and almost caught a foul ball—"

Bautista cleared her throat with the message *Get to the point.*

Jarvis nodded. "Game is a nail-biter, so no one is leaving in the seventh inning to beat traffic. A's cinch it in the ninth. Beautiful double for the winning run. So, game ends and we kind of get swept up with the crowd, got totally turned around. We leave the stadium; we have no idea where we parked. Like, no idea. We walk in the direction we think our car is in—it's not there. Nothing looks familiar. It's a disaster. We walked for two hours."

"Two hours?"

"Two hours and nada—still can't find the car and are even more turned around than when we started."

"What did you do?"

"The only thing we could. We found a security guard in a golf cart and waited until everyone—and I mean *everyone*—capable of driving left. Then we did a full lap around the parking lot. Still took an hour in the golf cart, but we found it. Spent more time looking for our car than we did watching the game."

"How is this relevant?"

"What if she got swept up in the crowd leaving, got turned around, and got lost?"

"We already chased that theory down. Checked every road."

"Every road headed *south*." Jarvis points to the map and the roads Bautista had marked as canvassed.

Bautista was picking up what Jarvis was putting down. "Not every road going north."

"Exactly."

"GPS up there is a mess, so little reception."

"It's dark as hell, so few street signs."

"It is the husband's preferred theory."

Jarvis was smiling big, thrilled to have contributed something. "You checked with local PD up there, yeah?"

"Of course. The sister was sure they were covering for their local celebrity," Bautista said with exasperation.

"Maybe not covering, but maybe not really looking, either."

"True. But look at that map. I don't have enough sick days to cover that many back roads."

"But you know who might? Highway Patrol."

Bautista liked this idea. "Where are they based up there?"

Jarvis pointed at the map. "Ukiah."

Bautista felt a flicker of hope now. "Do you know anyone in that office?"

"Only my most obnoxious cousin. I'll call him, see if he can pass the car ID around, have fresh eyes out there looking as they drive in circles."

Bautista was really feeling good now. "Yes, yes. And they won't have the ties local PD does. Might actually put in a little effort. This is great. We could really find something!"

Jarvis shook her head. "I don't get you. Out on patrol, you are stone cold. You tell the sister to move on, pass the husband to Victim Services, close the case at work—"

"I never closed this case at work," Bautista cut in with a little annoyance.

Jarvis rolled her eyes. "God, you're such a stickler. You know what I mean. You moved it to *Inactive*. Refocused, blah, blah. But now I come here, and you've secretly gone full conspiracy theory in your off time. What gives?"

Bautista bit her lip. "I hate to say it, but that damn junkie sister wouldn't let it go—so neither could I."

Chapter 9

What Doesn't Serve You

Adrienne entered the Gorgeous Gourds tent to find twenty tables set up with every squash ever dreamed of and several ring lights.

Ashleigh stood in the center of the worktables. She was in yet another flowing cotton prairie dress (#DÔEN) and yet another $800 Stetson. Her stupid basket with the ribbons was there, too. Everyone chatted quietly until Ashleigh raised her hand—her middle and ring finger pressed to her thumb, her pinkie and index finger sticking straight up.

Ashleigh spoke in a high-pitched yet dreamy voice barely above a whisper. "Quiet Coyote. Quiet Coyote."

Adrienne realized her hand was supposed to be the coyote and wanted to balk, until the room of adult women fell silent at the sight of a finger dog.

Ashleigh smiled. "Thank you. Welcome to Gorgeous Gourds. Table-scaping is crucial for any successful holiday meal, or *photo* of a holiday meal. Now, if you have been paying attention to my Stories recently, you know we need three elements . . ."

The entire tent chimed in: "Thrillers, fillers, and spillers!"

Adrienne practically jumped when they spoke.

She was visibly pleased. "Good. So good. I'm so proud of you. Once you get your gourds set and your spillers—love these tendrils of pampas—we need to add lighting. I love to use these vintage jars." She pulled out a series of Ball jars with special lids that had a wick inserted. "The kerosene inside is flammable, but I know your babies know about fire safety. Right, moms?"

Everyone nodded. Their babies did know; their babies were perfect. *Perfect* perfect. Ashleigh lit the wicks and Adrienne had to admit, the light did actually give out a stunning glow over the centerpiece.

Ashleigh's eyes stayed on the flame for a second too long for Adrienne's comfort. "This will give a natural—and dare I say, timeless—light for all your holiday-dinner photos. But I also recommend three ring lights and a soft-bounce flash." Every mother there took notes. "Okay, let's get started."

Adrienne arranged some gourds on her table, but she couldn't get any of them to balance. She leaned over to the mother on her right. "Have you done this before?"

The mother looked down at her own absolutely spectacular arrangement as if to say *Bitch, what do you think?* She looked at Adrienne's table and snorted. "Your sugar squash is dull."

So that mom was not here to be a friend. Fine. Who *did* seem like a possible friend? Adrienne looked around the tent and was struck by how controlled every single one of these women were. There was no joy, only white-hot intensity as they balanced their tableaux.

Adrienne leaned over to the mom on her left, who was furiously buffing a kabocha. "Did you come to the last summit?"

Kabocha Mom whipped her head around, furious to have been disturbed and even more furious when she saw who exactly was talking to her. "That trick you pulled on the ropes course? With the bag? That was cheating."

Adrienne had been in some scrapes, but few things had been as instant as this mother's seething. "W-what?" she stammered.

"I needed that consultation. And you stole it from me."

Adrienne tried to respond, but before she could, Ashleigh gently tapped her on the shoulder and whispered, "If you're talking to your neighbor, you won't be able to hear the gourds speaking to you."

Adrienne tried to point Ashleigh's attention to the hissing kabocha psycho, but that woman was now calm, smiling, serene, matching Ashleigh's energy exactly.

"Ashleigh, can I move workstations? I just don't feel the right flow here," Kabocha Mom cooed.

Ashleigh smiled. "Of course." She turned back to Adrienne and looked at the sad little pile of squash around her jar. "Remember, it's not about the posting—it's about the present."

Adrienne smiled through her teeth, but underneath the table, she ripped a pile of fall foliage to shreds. This was like if the Stepford Wives had Stepford'd themselves.

As Kabocha Mom moved stations, she yanked hard on Adrienne's tablecloth, causing her entire failed tableau to tumble to the ground. The kerosene jar smashed as it fell, and eight moms bum-rushed it to be the Best Safety Mom. They shoved each other as they gathered the doused pampas; another mom brought over a bucket of sand from the fire-safety station.

"Ashleigh, don't worry, I got it! Stand back, everyone!" she yelled as she expertly covered the wet spot in sand, with unnecessary flourishes that seemed purposefully directed at the other moms' eyes.

Ashleigh watched this madness without a flicker of concern. In fact, Adrienne felt like she looked entertained to see these women compete for her attention.

Then there was a loud pressurized hiss as another mom sprayed not just the kerosene puddle, but also 100 percent deliberately sprayed every mom in the scrum with a tiny pink fire extinguisher. The moms sputtered and coughed, choking on the chemical foam in their mouths. They gasped and desperately tried to clean their eyes. But still the mom sprayed and sprayed.

As she drenched her peers, Fire Extinguisher Mom turned to Ashleigh and said with a smile, "I brought this from home. Safety first."

Ashleigh's face oozed into a smile that was closer to a leer, "Well done, Mini Mom. I am so proud of you." She linked arms with Fire Extinguisher Mom as the other women desperately tried to wipe the fire retardant from their clothes and regain a shred of dignity that was long gone.

No one else spoke. No one else moved.

Ashleigh guided her new chosen favorite back to the dais and said, "Quiet Coyote wants to say thank you. Who will join me?"

She raised her coyote finger puppet in the air and howled. And every woman howled back. Including the moms who were still soaked from the chemical foam, their humiliation complete.

Then it was over. The chatter started up again, and everyone moved on. Except Adrienne, who once again felt so outside this culture she couldn't believe they didn't smell her lies.

After what felt like seven years (but was really only an hour), Adrienne was back in her cabin. She went into her bathroom/command center and wrote *Kabocha Mom? Fire Extinguisher Mom?* on her list of suspects. Even she didn't believe that was a real lead, but the blank space was too depressing.

As Adrienne got ready for dinner, she was dismayed at her lack of any new information. Day one was almost over, and the clock was quite literally ticking. She had observed enough. No one was going to voluntarily confess to hurting Chiara as Adrienne happened to be ear hustling nearby. Never a joiner, Adrienne needed to go against type and truly infiltrate.

It's time to stop pussyfooting around the groups, she told herself in the nice combination of pep talk and self-criticism that was her specialty.

She thought back to the week she'd spent in juvie after breaking into a house (misdemeanor, dismissed). Santa Rita Juvenile Correctional wasn't her idea of a good time, but she'd had her wits about her then. She arrived first at mealtime and stuck to the wall so she could watch the rest of the girls arrive and understand the social structure of the world she had just been dropped into. Who came together. Who avoided each other. Which groups were loud, loving being the center of attention. Which groups were the human equivalent of circled wagons, just trying to get to their release date in one piece. By the end of that one breakfast, she knew who to mess with, who to hang with, and most importantly, who to avoid at all costs.

Adrienne needed to do the same thing tonight at dinner. The good news was, Adrienne knew Chiara was shy in new situations, and Adrienne felt she could suss out who she would have seen as a possible friend pretty quickly. Especially since Chiara's own text from dinner last year had said that she wasn't enjoying herself.

When Adrienne entered the barn, she was met with an incredible layout of food on long buffet tables. The decor was #Aspirational, and every inch of the place was on theme. Every pumpkin had been painted some combination of cream, bronze, or a marbled effect of both, to match the crisp cotton table settings. Silk witch hats seemingly floated through the air, as they had been expertly hung on the thinnest fishing line, invisible to the diners below. There was even an eight-strand braid of corn-husk leaves as a table runner, like a desiccated challah from Gluten-Free Hell.

The menu was #HealthyHarvest: whole grains, a variety of squash, and gently seasoned (i.e., bland) lean meats. While the moms *ooh*ed and *ahh*ed at each and every hot station, tucking the hand-printed recipe cards into their pockets, Adrienne recognized this menu for what it really was: what you feed a dog who had explosive diarrhea.

However, she was grateful for the taste-free, spice-free, allergen-free dinner, as she could eat it without looking at her plate, allowing her eyes to be glued to the door as every mom group made their entrance.

First came the Caitlin, Kate, Katie, Chrissy, and Katherine (never Kathy) faction. They were outside before the dinner started, waiting in an organized line. Chiara was a time optimist, a.k.a. always ten minutes late. These women (if they had been here last year) would have been seated and mid-meal before Chiara had even gotten out of the shower. It was entirely possible she would have missed them altogether, and even if they'd overlapped, the Chiara Adrienne knew wouldn't sit down with an established group.

Next to arrive was the Jennifer/Jessica/Jacqueline/Janelle group. Adrienne immediately ruled them out. These were the women who genuinely enjoyed CrossFit, and who'd continued playing on the ropes course long after the event was over today. Chiara was the least coordinated person on the planet. She'd once managed to get her own hair caught in the back end of her blow-dryer, causing a small fire that torched their apartment carpet. Even though Adrienne recognized a few of them as her cheerleaders from the earlier tire-bridge debacle and felt a rush of genuine affection for them, these were not Chiara's people.

The next wave—the moms who were mostly named some variation of Emily, Emma, Eleanor, Ellie, Courtney, or Claire—was the self-styled posh geniuses. Adrienne had lingered by their table long enough to hear them prefacing every conversation with "While I was at Bryn Mawr . . ." and "Well, at Brown . . ." and "See, the thing about Vassar is . . ." Their desperation to distinguish themselves as "women who were once on the fast-track" was as subtle as chum. It didn't matter that their daily lives looked identical to everyone else's. Once upon a time, they were supposed to be more than this, and had *chosen* to opt out. Or at least, they wanted to *project* that they had chosen. And they definitely wanted to give the impression that they could opt back in at any moment—the world was waiting for them. Chiara, on the other hand, had felt lucky to transfer to Cal State East Bay after spending way too long aimlessly bouncing around Laney Junior College. Chiara's rough edges wouldn't have meshed well with them. And besides, after listening to eight women faux-complain about "going to Paris too much" and "the cost of new ski instructors," Adrienne knew they wouldn't have liked Chiara, either.

The Nikki, Becca, Stephanie, and Amanda group was next. They were what Adrienne would classify as the gentle bimbos. At no point had these women been in anything other than full hair and makeup. Their femininity wasn't an issue. Adrienne's repulsion (which she was sure Chiara would share) was due to the fact that every single one of them, after every single bite of food, would cover their mouths while chewing. A hooked finger over the lips. A flattened palm cupping their cheeks. A napkin daintily blocking watching eyes from the unspeakable act of eating. Chiara had always found joy in sharing meals with people. She wouldn't have spent time with women who saw consuming the calories necessary for living as a social liability.

Finally, one group did arrive that seemed promising. They were the hippie-adjacent self-described "Relaxed Moms." Moms whose energy was *I don't care, it's all good.* Granted, it was only chill and all good after copious amounts of planning. Nevertheless, when they went to the bar first and asked to just take a bottle of wine to their table instead of refilling one glass at a time, Adrienne felt certain that this was who Chiara would have gravitated toward. As a bonus, they even reminded Adrienne of Chiara's only known friends from last year—Andie and Michelle. Adrienne felt sure they were her best bet. As they lined up at the buffet, she fell in with them, adopting a meek energy.

"Hi. Can I sit with you guys?"

A chorus of yeses was followed by their names: Hannah, Maya, Naomi, Anya.

To make sure this wouldn't be a waste of a meal, Adrienne asked the most crucial question first: "Did you guys come to the summit last year?"

Maya nodded a little too vigorously. "Oh, yes. It was so fun."

As a clear callback to the previous year, Hannah started singing that Katy Perry song about being a firework.

The other friends joined in, all hitting the high notes about letting their colors burst.

They dissolved into laughter.

Naomi said, "Sorry. Inside joke from the last summit."

Adrienne smiled. Perhaps she was finally onto something.

They sent the wine bottle around, and Adrienne passed it along without filling her own glass. Her mouth twitched. She wanted a drink so badly, and being around other drunk people made her cravings spike. She could tell by their generous pours that this meal was going to be especially excruciating. It didn't matter that these women were actually pretty nice. Her sobriety sometimes manifested as a loneliness that felt like a creeping flu, making her skin cold and her head swim.

During a slight pause in the conversation, Adrienne decided it was time to shoot for the moon. "I heard a woman went missing last year."

This was met with pure shock. Maya asked, "Are you serious?"

Adrienne nodded. "Yeah. She came here and no one saw her again."

Hannah's eyes were closed in the effort to remember. "Oh, wait. I do remember hearing that."

Adrienne tried to play it cool. "Do you remember her?"

Hannah wasn't really listening, though. "You guys remember. She came here, and then like a month later she was reported missing—"

"It wasn't a month," Adrienne corrected, cutting in too quickly. The curious looks from everyone made her pull back a little. "At least, I thought it wasn't a month."

Maya looked genuinely sad. "That's terrible. Did she ever come back home?"

Adrienne shook her head. "I don't think so. Did you guys meet her last year?"

There was quick shared look between the foursome. It was so fast that Adrienne couldn't even be sure it really happened.

Naomi shrugged a little. "No. We actually joked that none of us spoke to anyone but each other last summit. Which is kind of embarrassing to say out loud."

Anya frowned. "Made us feel cliquey. We aren't like that."

Adrienne smiled. "Yeah. I can tell."

By the time the organic gluten-free Stevia-only dessert came out, Adrienne decided she had to call it a night. These four women were perfectly lovely, but they weren't saying anything interesting, and the risk of Adrienne taking a drink was rising by the second. She worried if she stayed, she wouldn't be able to resist the bar much longer, and she knew if she had one drink, she would have eight. And that would mean she'd lose half of tomorrow to a hangover.

Making the choice to leave early gave Adrienne a strange mix of pride and regret. Any minute she wasn't with other women was time lost to find information. However, she was also seeing her own limitations, and that was growth! Still, Adrienne wished she had been able to grow without her entire world being ripped apart. The small accomplishment felt undercut by its high price.

Adrienne wiped her mouth and started to gather up her plate to leave.

Hannah, who was the loudest of the four but not in an obnoxious way, said, "You're not leaving are you? No!"

The other moms mock-pouted.

Anya tugged on Adrienne's sleeve. "Stay!"

Adrienne thanked them but assured them she needed to go to bed.

Maya looked to her friends, conspiracy in her voice. "Should we tell her?"

Adrienne's ears tingled. "Tell me what?"

Naomi shook her head. "You can't tell her. We will sound insane."

Adrienne had to put her fork down, worried that it would rattle on her stacked plate and cup as the adrenaline hit her system.

"Naomi is right," Hannah agreed. "We can't tell her."

Adrienne's heart sank. Her mind was buzzing—how could she get these women to open up? But before she could even start to try, Hannah got very serious. "We can't tell her because we should show her. But first"—she turned her eyes to Adrienne—"are you cool?"

Maya whispered, "Can you keep a secret?"

Anya, however, didn't seem to be on board with this. "Guys, she wasn't here last year."

Naomi was on the fence, too. "She will tell everyone. No offense, Adrienne."

Adrienne was desperate to know more. "I won't. I won't tell a soul. I promise."

Hannah nodded. "I believe her. Let's go."

In unison, the foursome stood up, and Adrienne trotted after them, out of the barn, and into the dark.

They stopped at the edge of the cabins.

Hannah turned to Adrienne. "Do you have anything from your past in your cabin?"

Adrienne didn't understand, and she definitely didn't want them being "helpful" by investigating her cabin for her. "Um, can you be more specific?"

Hannah responded elliptically, "We can't have you come and not participate. Do you have anything from your past in your cabin? A journal? A piece of clothing from an old boyfriend? A photo?"

Adrienne was so confused, but she went along. Thinking of her photo of Chiara in the bathroom, she said, "I have a picture of an . . . old friend."

Hannah looked to the other women in a silent conferring. "That'll work."

Maya looked around. "Meet back here in five minutes?"

Everyone nodded and dispersed.

Adrienne ran to her cabin. As she pulled Chiara's photo off the shower wall, she thought this might just be perfect. She could see if any of them recognized her from last year.

Adrienne rejoined the group. Each of them had a bag or a backpack now. Adrienne was about to show them her photo when Naomi stopped her.

Naomi looked around. "I don't want to do it here."

Maya agreed, "It's too exposed. Someone will see us."

Adrienne wanted to yell *What? What? What will they see?* but instead stayed quiet.

The night had turned chilly since dinner started, and a heavy wetness was collecting on the ground. Adrienne wished she had a jacket, but she was scared to leave the group again.

Anya thought for a minute. "Maybe the ropes course? Then we won't have to sit in the wet grass."

Hannah piped up, "I know where we should go."

Maya's nerves seemed to be piquing. "Let's just get going before everyone else leaves dinner."

The group agreed and moved quickly into the oak grove.

Hannah led the way. "It's over here."

As they walked, the women wordlessly gathered small sticks and branches. Adrienne followed suit. All the while, her mind was racing. One thousand guesses of what "it" was Rolodexed in her eyes, and she had to really work hard to not telegraph disappointment when Hannah found what she was looking for: a bougie firepit.

Instead of the dirt hole with cinder blocks that Adrienne had spent her teenage years drinking 40s around, this was a large copper bowl with industrial legs and a gentle pebbled finish. This was a firepit for people who imported olive oil and felt strongly about car interiors.

Anya was still looking around nervously. "Can we just start already?"

Naomi lit kindling in the firepit and then deftly layered the sticks in ascending size until she had made a perfect little cone of branches. As it all seemed to effortlessly catch fire, she propped two of the larger logs on top, which also started to burn at the loose edges of bark.

Naomi was pleased and did a little salute. "Once a Girl Scout, always a Girl Scout."

Adrienne wanted to press for information, but she knew she had to play it cool. She couldn't spook them.

The women pulled out their small parcels.

Maya looked into each of their eyes. "Are we ready?"

They all nodded.

Adrienne gingerly asked, "What are we doing?"

Anya replied, "We have all held on to parts of ourselves that are holding us back."

Naomi added, "Becoming a mother was really hard, and I realized it was because I was fighting it too much."

Anya stared into the flames. "We all were."

"What was the word she used?" Hannah asked.

Maya knew. "*Surrender*. She told us to surrender."

Adrienne's skin was tingling. "Who told you to surrender?"

There was a long pause, until Hannah finally whispered, "Opal."

This didn't track for Adrienne at all. Nothing about Opal's vibe was *surrender*. Her vibe was somewhere between *doing your taxes* and *Stalingrad*.

Hannah kept going. "Opal has been helping us reach the next level."

Adrienne was confused. "Next level of what?"

Hannah smiled. "Ourselves."

Naomi took Hannah's hand. "We have been waiting for this moment for a year. Everyone ready?"

The other three women clutched their parcels and nodded.

Maya was the first one to step toward the fire. She held out a little envelope. "These are all the letters from my ex-boyfriend. Thinking about him has kept me from fully investing in my marriage and my children."

She tossed the envelope into the fire and, for good measure, pushed it down into the hottest flames.

After a minute of silence, she looked around at the group. "I feel good. Opal was right."

It was Naomi's turn. "These are all my badges from my various jobs over the years."

Adrienne could see the ID cards on long lanyards, several eras of Naomi's face beaming with *first day at a new job* energy.

"I haven't deeply engaged with my children because I thought I would go back to work. But that idea was holding me back from my true purpose." She threw the badges into the flames, and Adrienne watched as the ten little Naomi faces warped and melted.

Anya was hesitant. "Do I have to do the whole thing?"

Naomi pushed her closer to the firepit. "You got Opal's last message. We have to commit."

Anya was resigned. She pulled out a stack of photographs. "These are pictures from my annual girls' trip with my friends from college. They all stayed in the city and are still living it up while I live in the burbs now. I haven't made it on the trip for the last four years because I was either pregnant or postpartum."

Maya was gentle but firm. "That's not true, Anya. Opal said we have to be honest if this is going to work."

Anya's eyes welled with tears. "Yeah. I guess I could have gone on one, but they wouldn't move the date for me. Even though they hadn't booked anything yet. They just really didn't care if I made it or not." Two big tears streaked down Anya's cheeks. "That hurt. Confirmation that I am on the outside."

Anya passed the photos around so everyone could look at them one last time. There was nothing particularly salacious, just drunk women being stupid in foreign countries and possibly (definitely) wearing the local traditional garb like it was a costume. None of these women were going to be able to run for Senate if these insensitive images got out.

Anya gathered the pictures back up. "So I am just going to tell them to plan the trips without me from now on."

Naomi put her hand on Anya's shoulder. "You outgrew them."

Anya smiled. "I don't totally believe that, but I'm grateful for a version where I'm not the loser who got kicked out of the friend group."

Last up was Hannah. She was very emotional. Her breath was coming in big heaving sobs. Everyone was quiet and endlessly patient. They had nowhere to go.

Finally, Hannah pulled out her stack of journals. "These are my journals from the years when my dad was in prison. Well, he's still in prison. But this was when we were still in contact. I pasted some of his letters in here. And I wrote a lot about how hard it was to have him away. But I have to let him go."

Very slowly, Hannah fed her journals into the base of the flames. The covers slowly charred; then the pages were alight, and at last they were perfect cubes of ash.

"This is what no longer serves us and our higher selves," Hannah said.

Adrienne had to ask. "What are your higher selves?"

"Being the best mothers we can be," Maya said, in a tone that asked *Isn't it obvious?*

Naomi added, "Being the mothers we wished we had."

Adrienne felt a twitch of recognition in this, and then knew that Chiara would have twitched the same. Their mom had been the difficult boulder they'd built their emotional lives around. Not in a good way; not in a bedrock way. She had been unpredictable. Suffocating one minute, utterly devoid of emotion the next. Their childhood was a roller coaster Adrienne couldn't wait to get off of, and once she did, she'd never looked back. When their mom died, the scaffolding of their personalities was suddenly comical, so intricate but with a big void in the middle where she used to be. Adrienne had filled her void with drugs, parties, and self-sabotage. Chiara had filled hers with a husband, two children, and a beige couch. It didn't matter that they'd shared a past when their coping now drove them to opposite ends of the spectrum.

However, the women at this firepit were going beyond just trying to undo old family patterns. They were singular now, the new all-encompassing Mommy Identity. To Adrienne, these women honestly seemed like cheaters. They were bailing on everything, past and present, that couldn't fit in a sippy cup. They were lopping off every part of themselves that clashed with the family portrait in the pumpkin patch. Sure, who hasn't pretended they'd never gotten an STD or dreamed of telling a shitty boss to go to hell. But where did it end? How could they know these were the only parts of themselves that would be deemed inconvenient?

The foursome looked to Adrienne. "Your turn," Hannah said.

Adrienne replied, "I am one hundred percent on board. I think I just need to understand more about what we are achieving here."

This was met with more intense shared looks.

Hannah said, "We have been talking with Opal and Tamarind about coming on as a new wave of the Squad."

"Oh, wow." Adrienne was genuinely surprised that there was even a whiff of open enrollment from people who clearly cherished the exclusivity of their current position.

Naomi nodded. "Yeah. A big deal. But they needed to know what was holding us back."

Maya added, "If there were things in our past that we couldn't let go of or that wouldn't let *us* go."

Adrienne didn't understand that last bit. "Wouldn't let *you* go?"

Maya sighed. "Well, that ex-boyfriend. We had been back in touch. Nothing happened. But there were texts, so many texts. And long emails. I sent some to Tamarind, and she told me that if those came out, it could look bad. So I needed to really cut him out once and for all."

Adrienne was putting it together but didn't want to assume. "Was some version of that true for each of you?"

They all nodded.

Naomi pointed to one of her melted ID badges. "At my last job, my boss got caught embezzling a ton of money. He named me in the deposition. It's public record. But Opal said if I didn't go back into the corporate world and I took my husband's name, she would help me leave it behind. Scrub my public profile of the connection."

Anya frowned. "My girls trips were just stupid. So many Facebook photos and idiotic outfits. But there was one trip where one of my friends trashed a hotel room when she was drunk. Security came. There is a video of her screaming some pretty messed-up stuff at the staff, and I'm in the background. The local news picked it up."

Hannah made a face. "Dad in jail. Not a good look for a mommy brand."

"So, if you wanted to be put up for the Squad, Opal and Tamarind needed to know your pasts were clean?"

They all nodded.

"And you proved that by"—she was reaching here but needed confirmation—"bringing this stuff at their instruction. They told you to bring it here and burn it."

They all nodded again.

Adrienne thought that sounded like blackmail material they had just hand-delivered to Tamarind and Opal. These moms were very nice but not exceptional. If they were willing to give Tamarind their darkest secrets in a DM and follow elaborate instructions from Opal to prove their dedication, they probably weren't the only ones. Also, blackmail works both ways. These compromising tidbits could be used to keep all these moms (and any other mom who shared secrets) out of the running for Squad consideration.

"So are you going to find out this weekend if you are part of the new Squad?" Adrienne asked.

Hannah shook her head. "We need to get through this summit without . . ." She searched for the word. "Incident."

"Incident?"

Naomi looked ashamed. "Last year's summit was . . . different."

The women shared uncomfortable looks, guilty looks.

Adrienne felt her pulse quicken. "How was last year different?"

Hannah looked down. "It almost broke us."

Anya whispered, "Our loyalty to the coMOMunity was put to the ultimate test."

Adrienne squeezed her hands into fists, pressing her nails into her palms as a release for the tension.

Anya went on. "We came together in Naomi's car. But before the first welcome dinner, we were screwing around, drinking, having fun."

Naomi said sadly, "And then I ruined it."

Hannah put her arm around Naomi. "No. *We* ruined it."

Naomi shook her head. "I was being stupid. I climbed onto the bar, trying to sneak an extra bottle of wine, and jumped off like an idiot. I broke my ankle."

Hannah nudged her. "First off, stealing the wine was my idea. And then what happened? You needed to go to the hospital—but instead of being supportive friends, we were awful."

Anya winced. "We had this big blowup because we didn't want to leave. Caused a huge scene."

Maya added, "We were so happy to be away from our kids. We weren't ready to go back. But we were all yelling at each other, and then Opal asked us to leave."

"We didn't even make it to the first dinner," Hannah said.

Adrienne thought back to the last selfie Chiara had sent her from the welcome dinner. These women had been long gone.

Adrienne was, in a word, furious. This was the big secret? This was their traumatic bond? Being assholes to each other when one of them ruined a vacation? Moreover, from what she could tell, all this higher-self garbage was maybe necessary, since the secrets they had burned were directly related to their behavior last year—theft, being tangential to schemes, not wanting to be with their families, being a crappy friend. And now she had wasted an entire evening with them.

She pulled out the photo of Chiara. "This is what I have to burn." She looked at each of their faces, knowing already that she had run into a dead end.

They genuinely did not recognize Chiara.

"Who is she?" Hannah said after taking a closer look at the picture.

"A friend."

Anya asked, "How is she holding you back?"

Adrienne paused for a moment, looking for a banal way to describe the emotional Chernobyl at the center of her life. "We grew apart."

"Do you think you could be close again?" Naomi asked.

"I really have no idea."

"Is she a good mother?"

Adrienne smiled. "She's a very good mother."

Hannah pressed the photo back into Adrienne's hands and away from the fire. "Then maybe see if you can repair things. Maybe she will make you better."

Adrienne nodded. "That's the hope."

Chapter 10

Day Two

Since Chiara disappeared, Adrienne hadn't cried once. Crying felt like mourning, and mourning felt like an acceptance that her sister was gone. Adrienne assumed she would cry eventually, and really cultivated a cavalier attitude about it when anyone asked her. The reality was, Adrienne was terrified that if/when she started to cry, she would never, ever stop. Logically, she knew that she would stop at some point—it was physically impossible to cry to death—but it felt akin to blowing up a dam. Sure, the flood would *eventually* recede, but only *after* everything in its path was utterly destroyed and submerged in a watery grave for all time. Adrienne didn't know how that destruction would manifest in her life, and so she held the tears at bay.

Except at night.

When Adrienne slept, she would almost always dream of Chiara.

So much of her late-night drinking had been an effort to slosh her mind to bits, praying for a nonsensical, run-of-the-mill nightmare that would fade as soon as she opened her eyes. The two shots before she brushed her teeth? The mug of wine by the bed in case she woke up? A vape pen under her pillow? These were just her nocturnal emotional anesthetics.

Since she had gotten sober, she had no such protection, and her dreams had taken a weird turn. The beginnings were always mildly surreal—for example, a real walk they had taken down the Embarcadero on New Year's Eve, except in the dream they were eight feet tall. Then at some point, the dream would coalesce into a faithful rehash of a real day, no detail too small, every color and object a lesson in accuracy.

This night was no different.

The dream started with Adrienne and Chiara waiting for a BART train at the 16th Street Mission Station, but instead of the regular silver rapid-rail fuselage, an open-air vintage cable car rumbled down the tracks. It was one of those frantic dreams where they were definitely late but could never tell what time it was despite constantly looking at their blank watches and the glitching wall clocks. In their haste, they got on the cable car and were trying to figure out how they would hold their breath as they descended beneath the choppy Bay water between the Embarcadero station and West Oakland. Instead of a BART map, on the wall of the cable car was a life-size drawing of a human lined with lights like a blue thermometer. As the cable car hurdled through the dark with the sharp careening familiar to every Bay Area resident, lights lit up the human to indicate the water levels rising up to Chiara's and Adrienne's faces. This was the countdown so they could get ready to take their last breath at the last-possible second and hopefully make it to the other side. *Beep beep beep* the lights went as the water level rose.

Beep beep beep.

Beep beep beep.

Then, as was the pattern, the dream shifted from surreal scenario to very real memory.

The *beep beep beep* from the cable car became the soft *beep beep beep* of a heart monitor. Chiara was sitting up in a hospital bed, Adrienne beside her.

A distracted doctor was running through the post-op care, "All right, twenty-six-year-old female, recovering from a laparoscopic appendectomy. Procedure went well. You will need to take it easy for a couple of weeks—no heavy lifting, maybe wait a week to drive."

Adrienne made a loud noise of disgust. "So I guess I'm your taxi for a while? Typical! Typical, typical, *typical.* My bird can't feed himself, you know."

The doctor didn't know how to read this deadpan delivery. That only made it funnier.

Chiara was trying to keep her composure. "How should I care for the stitches?"

"Glue," the doctor corrected her. "I used glue."

"Okay, how should I care for the glue?"

"Don't touch it—"

"Is this going to scar?" Adrienne cut in.

The doctor clearly did not enjoy Adrienne's vibe. "Yes."

"Goddamnit!" Adrienne yelled. "We have a very elaborate crime planned that requires us to be *identical.*"

The doctor looked back and forth between their two distinct faces, baffled. "But you aren't identical."

"Well, yeah. Not *now.* Not with her scars. How about this: I slip you a fifty and you give me a couple scratches to match. What do you say?"

Adrienne lifted her shirt, exposing some of her stomach and pointing to where she would like her own faux incisions.

The doctor grew flustered. "What? No!"

"Fine. A hundred dollars."

The doctor gathered up his things and basically ran to the door as Adrienne yelled larger and larger dollar amounts at him.

At this, Chiara dissolved into fits of giggles. "Don't make me laugh! Ow! Laughing hurts!"

"That guy was a dork. Come on, let's have some fun."

Adrienne practically carried a sore Chiara into the tattoo shop that sat on the fringes of the Tenderloin neighborhood.

Chiara looked around, nervously chewing her nails. "I think I've been poked with enough things today."

Adrienne waved this away. "That's exactly why it's the best time to do it! You won't even notice!"

"How do I let you talk me into this stuff?" Chiara smiled as she leafed through a binder of tattoo ideas.

"Because you love me! How's this for compromise: you and I both get tattoos today and you get to choose."

"For both of us?"

"Yup."

"Deal."

It took some time to find the right image. Chiara was spontaneous enough to get a tattoo on the fly, but she still wanted to choose something actually meaningful. After what felt like a dog's age, Chiara's eyes lit up.

"Do you trust me, Ade?"

"Absolutely."

Chiara turned to the artist and showed only him the image. "We'll get this."

A few hours later, Adrienne was finally allowed to see what Chiara had chosen for them.

On the back of both their upper arms, just above the elbow, was a tiny lighthouse with tiny pointillist details, right down to the scalloped pattern of the lenses. The lighthouses were identical except for the daymarks; the spiral lines down the towers mirrored each other so that when they lined their arms up (Chiara's left, Adrienne's right), the diagonal lines created an inverted V shape pointing up, up, up.

As they looked at their fresh ink in the mirror, their skin shiny and irritated from the needle, Chiara asked Adrienne, "Do you remember?"

Adrienne nodded. Of course she did. Ostensibly, she'd explained it to the tattoo artist, but really she wanted to cement the meaning by saying it aloud. "When we were kids we learned about a pair of lighthouses on adjacent bluffs that were built so that if sailors lined them up, they knew they were facing truth north."

Chiara's eyes were brimming with emotion. "Twin lighthouses."

Adrienne said it back, "Twin lighthouses."

Adrienne woke up aching with sadness. The hyperrealistic dreams took longer to wear off, and there were always a few seconds in which she was so disoriented that she wondered where she was. *When* she was. But she was not in the tattoo shop, watching the fog roll in. She was in her little Style Summit cabin, all alone. Adrienne willed herself to go back to sleep, to hold on to that day a little longer. Instead, her lighthouse tattoo itched something awful, in a psychosomatic expression as subtle as a chain saw on an Amish farm. She let herself wallow for a few minutes, then succumbed to reality. It was the last full day of the summit for her ticket level, and she didn't have time to let that dream annihilate her. Annihilation was for later.

Adrienne dragged herself out of bed; she was physically and emotionally worn out. The crushing of last night's high expectations had really hit her already low confidence. She still wanted to judge those women, burning their own identities, but she was the one who had followed them like a damn dog and hung on their every word.

As Adrienne hustled to catch the end of breakfast—which ended unnecessarily early, by her standards: 9:00 a.m.?!—she didn't even notice that she had joined the coffee line behind Hannah and Anya.

"Hi, Adrienne," Hannah said sweetly.

"Did you sleep well?" Anya asked.

Adrienne felt a little sheepish, like she was running into a one-night stand the morning after. "Yeah. Pretty good."

As Hannah and Anya chatted idly about which events they were going to attend that day, Adrienne was struck by their very happy, casual attitude. Even though Adrienne hadn't burned her photo, they didn't seem to have any judgment toward her. She had assumed there would be an emotional hangover between them, or that they would at least freeze her out for not going all the way. Instead, it was all kindness for everyone. Maya had even saved a seat for Adrienne at their table! Naomi refilled her coffee! This trust and vulnerability was intoxicating. Adrienne wanted to spend the day in this little friendly glow, but she couldn't. They weren't suspects, and they didn't know anything. So instead, she had to pass on the massages they had booked for after breakfast and opt for every afternoon activity they were declining so she could remain a free agent. Saying goodbye to them and returning to her cabin alone hurt more than she'd expected.

Even though Adrienne cringed every time someone said *coMOMunity* aloud, was it possible that the bonds made here were not totally phony? Sure, the crafts were insane and the forced seasonal ✨ childhood magic ✨ machine was just a money grab dressed in the trend of the moment. But Adrienne was finally seeing what Chiara had seen: a place to meet mom friends. Just that term alone only yesterday would have seemed like bullshit. Today it sounded like a promise.

Once, Chiara had asked her mom, Heidi, "Mommy, why don't you have friends?"

Their mom had replied, not unkindly, "Mommy has no time to make friends."

How different could life have been if Heidi had had a coMOMunity, or whatever the equivalent was in the eighties? The other waitresses at the diner where Heidi had worked fell into two categories: Half were ancient, so old their skin rustled—corn-husk dolls with an apron and a name tag. The other half were college kids who never stayed longer than a semester. Neither group were in the trenches of young motherhood. So Heidi went on alone, making ends meet, marking the time.

Adrienne realized that Chiara had been on the same track of social isolation. Was it really so shocking that Chiara had apparently been feeling as low as their mom? Battling dark emotions? Chiara had been asking for connection, and Adrienne had turned her back.

Just like I did to Mom, she thought, the parallel feeling like a thousand paper cuts on her heart.

So of course Chiara had been looking anywhere for friends. Even here.

But if Chiara had been hurt here, it wasn't by a friend. Or was it? What did *friend* mean in this world? Adrienne felt friendships happening around her, but were they real? Or were friends just a means to an end? A stepping stone with unknown point values used to get to the next marker of success?

Back in her cabin, Adrienne tried to regain the shrewd mind that had helped her decipher dinner the previous night.

She imagined Bautista had walked in the door and asked for the most salient facts she had gathered so far. Adrienne knew the answer: she had learned just how far women were willing to go to impress the Mom Squad—the shoving, the sabotage, the blackmail material. The math was clear: the closer her proximity to the Mom Squad, the more the knives came out. Letting that direct her next steps, Adrienne decided she needed to get close to them, too, and, unlike the brand consultation, do so in a way that kept the focus on them and off her. She looked at the day's itinerary, hoping to see something promising. Instead, she saw that the first activity to kick off day two was capture the flag.

What adults chose to play capture the flag on a vacation? Why did they hate themselves? Why were they dragging Adrienne down with them? Where were these steam facials and vagina eggs that had been plastered on her social media targeted ads? That was what she'd been sold, not this extended P.E. class.

Adrienne huffed as she pulled out some more of her new clothes—namely lululemon leggings, which she had shoplifted because she couldn't stomach paying $100 to Saran Wrap her own ass in nylon. Ahem, not nylon—*luon*, their fake-science proprietary fabric. Adrienne wore long sleeves to hide her tattoos, especially the twin lighthouse, just in case. She covered the hole in her pants left by the sensor she'd cut off and put her hair in the highest ponytail she could manage before her arms gave out from all the back-combing.

She thought maybe this was good. Her sadness had given way to anger, and that gave Adrienne a boost of energy.

It was surprisingly hot that day, with no clouds to provide any filter from the sun. Within seconds of arriving at the corn maze, Adrienne was sweating from every crevice on her body, had dirt in her eye, and was scratching a mosquito-bite mosaic on her leg. What a great time. Totally worth maxing out a credit card for this.

The smells of #Fall were all around her—some real, some synthetic, all stomach churning. If pressed to describe it, Adrienne would have gone with cinnamon-vanilla-bean candy-coated Spirit Halloween Store.

Tamarind—with her size 0 ass, bone-thin upper arms, and perfect bouncy ponytail—stood on an observation deck in the maze's center clearing. She was looking down at the group of moms below. Two moms, clearly thrilled to relive their childhood roles as teacher's pet, passed out belts with little flags Velcro'd to the side to divide everyone into two teams.

Tamarind, too loud and too happy, yelled, "Welcome to day two! You made it!"

Everyone screamed with joy.

Tamarind pinched her nonexistent stomach fat. "We've all had those few extra pounds after baby that we wish we could lose—right, mama? But who has time for the gym? As if! Please! Remember, playing with your kids is cardio!"

"Woo!"

Adrienne winced. So many *woo*s. *Woo*s that could cause permanent hearing loss.

But she was the only one bothered. Everyone else loved the pump-it-up vibes, and Tamarind was their living, breathing *Jock Jams* CD.

"So let's play—and remember," Tamarind prompted, "it can be fun . . ."

"To keep it tight!" the group called back.

The way they said it made it clear this was a signature catchphrase. These group activities all seemed to have well-established scripts and slogans that Adrienne found herself mouthing along to or trying to cough so people wouldn't see that she wasn't in the know.

Tamarind pointed to the screen behind her where the corn maze was laid out. The maze was a large rectangle, with two smaller cleared circles inside it and the large center clearing where they currently stood.

Little Miss *Jock Jams* pointed. "Fall Feathers, your flag is in this circle. Autumnal Equinox, your flag is in this circle. If your flags get pulled, you come to jail right here. Let's go!"

After the whistle was blown, Adrienne walked through the corn maze alone, putting about 25 percent effort into the game. But she had to admit, being away from Tamarind was a vague improvement.

Suddenly, a scream ripped through the corn.

Adrienne jumped.

She spun around, looking for the person in trouble. But then the scream turned to innocent laughter as two women led a third to "jail."

How were their screams of fun so close to the sound of being murdered?

Had Chiara screamed like that here? In joy? In pain? Had anyone heard her? Had anyone recognized her voice? Would Adrienne ever hear her voice again?

As the laughing trio passed, Adrienne tucked behind some cornstalks so they couldn't see her. Once they were gone, Adrienne tried to find a dead end she could hide in until it was over. She was exhausted in every respect. Keeping up this charade had been grueling, and it wasn't as if she was coming into this weekend in peak physical or emotional shape. Add in a bad night's sleep peppered with stress dreams and she was feeling rough.

Forget real hangovers—emotional hangovers were just as bad. There was no Gatorade for shame!

As Adrienne got farther away from the group, the maze got eerily quiet. For a second she enjoyed the birdsong and the trilling of crickets.

Then.

The dry cornstalks rustled.

Here.

There.

Then back again.

Was it just the stalks, or was there someone in there with her?

Rustle, rustle.

Then silence.

A trio of birds suddenly took flight, disturbed from their perch. But disturbed by what? Perhaps just an unexpected breeze.

Or maybe a person.

Adrienne tried to look deeply into the corn, but couldn't see anything beyond three stalks' depth.

"Hello?" she called.

Nothing. Then . . .

Rustle, rustle.

Each and every time the sound perked her ears, Adrienne panicked a little.

She kept turning, trying to find the source of the noise, but it always seemed to be right behind her.

Rustle, rustle.

Rustle, rustle.

In a matter of seconds, before she even knew what she was doing, she was chasing the sound.

But then, suddenly, the positions reversed, and the sound was chasing her.

Then they reversed again.

She didn't know which was worse.

Adrienne couldn't take it anymore. Panic, fear, anxiety were all rising in her throat. She needed to get out of here.

Except, after all the turning around and dead sprints, she had no idea where she was in the maze. She had completely lost her bearings.

And then the sound came for her again.

Rustle, rustle.

Rustle, rustle.

Adrienne was sweating now. She ran a few paces and then hit a dead end.

She turned around and found herself in another corner.

All the while, the rustling was intensifying, then whizzing past her, like a sonic shark brushing past her leg in the ocean.

She thought she heard steps.

She felt herself being watched.

Adrienne was sure she saw the end of a ponytail whip around a corner, and she ran after it, only to see no one there.

She called out, "Chi!" and her voice caught in her throat. She knew it was insane. Chiara hadn't spent a year in a corn maze, for God's sake. But Adrienne ran after the shadow, faster and faster, until she realized her sweat was augmented by bitter tears. "Come back! It's me!" she croaked out.

Then, out of absolutely nowhere, Tamarind aggressively pounced on Adrienne, knocking her down, seizing both her wrists and pinning her to the ground. Adrienne struggled, the breath knocked out of her and unable to move more than an inch in any direction.

Tamarind leaned her face really close to Adrienne's, their noses nearly touching.

"Boo," Tamarind whispered. "You're dead."

Tamarind pulled Adrienne's wrists together over Adrienne's head so she could hold them both tightly in her left hand. Then Tamarind moved her right hand behind her back. Adrienne tried to see what she was reaching for. A weapon? A gun? Adrienne struggled, but it was no use against Tamarind's shockingly strong grip.

In a flash, Tamarind stood up, her right hand not holding anything, but instead ripping Adrienne's flags off her belt before she bounced away.

Adrienne was left in the dirt, wondering what had just happened.

Back in the center of the maze, she took a seat in the capture the flag jail by the tractor, trying to find a sliver of shade. The dirt had mixed with her sweat and sunscreen to make a disgusting paste that had gotten into her mouth. That said, she noted that this was her fifth time going to jail but her first time being happy about it.

The woman next to her leaned over. "I'm Bernice. Cabin 5."

"Adrienne, Cabin 4."

"Neighbors! I thought I saw you earlier."

Adrienne gave her a half-hearted thumbs-up.

"I live in south Utah. Mom of three."

"Cool." Adrienne really wasn't feeling the small talk right now.

Bernice was short, a little awkward, and clearly trying hard for acceptance. And failing. As evidenced by her perfectly lovely but not at all aspirational sportswear.

Bernice was undeterred. "Can I tell you a secret?"

Even though Adrienne knew this was exactly what she'd come here for, nothing about Bernice said *in the know*, so Adrienne felt confident in brushing her off.

But Bernice would not be brushed. She made sure the coast was clear and then leaned even closer to Adrienne. "I pulled off my own flags so I could come sit down."

Tamarind popped out of some corn, scaring the shit out of them.

"Jesus!" (Adrienne.)

"Mother of pearl!" (Bernice.)

Tamarind didn't notice them at all.

The shared scare softened Adrienne to her new neighbor. "Pulled off your own flags, huh? You're smart. I got tackled by the Cardio Bratz Doll."

Tamarind got on the PA system. "The Fall Feathers are winning. Autumnal Equinox, you ladies better pick it up!" Tamarind hustled past the tractor and back into the maze, not a drop of sweat in sight.

Up close for the first time, Adrienne looked at the giant metal spikes mounted to the front of the tractor. "That doesn't seem safe."

Bernice nodded. "Oh, it's not. You should never leave a grappler attachment on heavy machinery while unattended." Bernice caught Adrienne's shock and quickly added, "One of my sons loves trucks, tractors, all that stuff. I can spot a front loader a mile away now." She ran her finger along the sharp farm blade. "Leaving the grappler on, though . . . Guess it's cuter this way?"

Adrienne's eyebrows went up. "Cuter?"

"Cuter is everything." Bernice had a little knowing smile. "This your first style summit?"

"Is it that obvious?" Adrienne asked.

"It's my first time, too."

Adrienne relaxed at this. If Bernice wasn't here last year, then Adrienne didn't have to pump her for information. "I'm exhausted. I feel like they are speaking a different language."

"Oh, are you not big on Instagram?"

Adrienne shook her head. "No. I have a mommy blog."

Bernice seemed genuinely impressed that Adrienne wasn't on Instagram. "A blog! Wow. Must be so fun to have all that freedom."

"Yeah, I guess," Adrienne replied, clocking the word *freedom*.

"You'll pick up the Insta stuff in a second—it's all pretty straightforward. You just gotta know the signs. Okay, like here . . ." Bernice pointed to a woman with a long braid, prairie dress, and a blank serene stare. "That's a #TradWife, a.k.a. Traditional Wife."

Once decoded, Adrienne could totally see the Type. "Whoa. Very high-end department store meets 'waiting in a bunker for the Rapture.'"

Bernice nodded. "Probably."

Adrienne pointed to the screen behind the podium, which had been playing a loop of mom memes the entire weekend. "What does *Please the Algo* mean?"

"It means, game the algorithm to put you at the top of the Explore page."

"Why?" Adrienne asked.

"If you get to the top, you can get sponsorships, paid ads, all kinds of free stuff. One brand partnership and your baby's college fund is set."

Adrienne couldn't quite make the math add up. "So in order to care for human babies, you have to trick a nonhuman computer program?"

"Pretty much."

"But that makes it sound like you work for Instagram instead of Instagram working for you."

"Oh, you don't know the half of it. You gotta post multiple times per day, every day. You have to build engagement with hashtags, trends, polls, and now Reels. If you don't do Reels, you are dead in the water. The algo only notices Reels and constant positive attention on your page."

"What is 'positive attention'?" Adrienne asked. She would have felt bad asking so many questions, but she was getting the sense that Bernice didn't get to feel like the smartest person in the room very often. Adrienne knew the type—the permanently and unfairly underestimated woman who'd worn her role like a scarlet letter for so long she eventually believed it herself. Adrienne was happy to give Bernice a long-deserved spotlight on her knowledge.

Bernice ticked off the topics on her fingers. "Keep it all organic to your life, no pop-culture stuff, and definitely no politics."

"So, like, don't mention vaccines?"

"OMG. Not on your life!" Bernice let out a snort that was not cute, and therefore adorable.

Tamarind was at the top of the platform again, blowing her whistle with zeal and announcing the winners. But all Adrienne heard was that it was finally lunch.

Adrienne and Bernice walked over to the buffet line. Adrienne was thrilled because now she not only had everyone in one place, but she also had her Rosetta Stone: Bernice.

"So, Bernice, what's the deal with Thea? I've barely even seen her. Isn't this her thing? I only see all these other moms in charge of stuff."

Bernice nodded. "Okay, obviously, Thea is at the center—her brand is top notch—but even she can't do it all alone. So there are four women who never leave her side: McKenna, Ashleigh, Tamarind, and Opal. They call themselves the Mom Squad."

True to form, the four women sat at the head table. Adrienne took them in. They all looked so happy, so perfect, so motherly.

Bernice pointed to McKenna. "McKenna is the Multiples Mom from the south. Two sets of twins, naturally. She's the craft wizard. Anything she makes, Pottery Barn rips off next season. McKenna is the one who made llamas trend."

Adrienne could totally see that. Chiara had decorated the boys' room with llamas, and in a muted desert palate that felt closer to Palm Springs Spa than Preschool Spawn.

Bernice continued, "McKenna's a double big deal because her husband is a dad influencer now, and they do these marriage-bootcamp weekends."

Adrienne smelled bullshit. "What the hell is a marriage bootcamp?"

Bernice shrugged. "I think that just means they tell you all the ways your marriage stinks? I don't know. Every morning they live-stream themselves in bed, giving each other affirmations. It's cringe, but they seem really happy, so maybe it works."

"Do you and your husband affirm each other first thing every morning?"

Bernice let out one of her snorts, and Adrienne loved her for it.

Bernice pointed discreetly with her fork. "Ashleigh is the ultimate TradWife, all about breastfeeding, homesteading, homeschooling. You get it. Big *back to the land* vibes."

"That's kind of cool, I guess," Adrienne said.

Ashleigh's whole energy was serene. Her long, (naturally?) platinum-blond hair was a mix of soft Dutch braids across her head and flowing waves down her back. She wore no makeup and glowed. Her eyes were so blue they were unsettling.

"Yeah, but does homesteading count if her husband is loaded? Like *family owns a professional basketball team and dabbles in private jets* loaded?"

Adrienne was genuinely surprised. "Damn, that's serious wealth."

"Oh yeah."

It was Adrienne's turn to point discreetly, this time at Tamarind. "Cardio Bratz, I know."

Bernice nodded along. "Yeah, Tamarind is Mommy Fitness, the former Peloton instructor who shows you how to keep it tight by doing squats during diaper changes. Not a stitch of plastic surgery after five kids."

Cough, cough, bullshit, cough. Adrienne remembered Chiara doing this shit and then crying when she was still not fitting in her jeans.

Adrienne's tone was harsh. "Let me guess: she is all about snapback bodies."

Bernice nodded. "Oh yeah. Then there was a big dustup when she also tried to do some body-positivity posts. People called her a hypocrite. It got so bad she had to *turn off comments for a month.*"

From Bernice's scandalized tone, Adrienne could tell turning off comments was the biggest deal in the world.

Bernice whispered the next part: "There was even a rumor going around that Thea was going to drop her from the Squad. Eventually, it all evened out. But it was dicey for a minute. She missed two birthday parties in a row for the other Mom Squad kids."

Bernice pointed to the last woman on the dais, who sat directly next to Thea. "Last but definitely not least is Opal—the former corporate shark who left it all behind for motherhood. She's all about super couponing, gaming Costco to pay you to shop, DIY home improvements that can scale into flipping if you're serious. These summits were her idea. She's a big part of why Thea's reach goes way beyond just social media now."

Adrienne was begrudgingly impressed. "And she really doesn't work anymore?"

"You mean, work outside the home?" Bernice corrected her.

Adrienne needed to watch that kind of stuff. "Right. That's what I meant."

"After she left her corporate job but before she got on Instagram, she had a mail-order business. It was supposed to be like a company where you would get educational toys shipped to you, and then when your kid aged out of them, you would mail the toys back to trade with other people in the company. So basically, you would buy the first toy and then that would actually turn into five years of toys for free. She pitched it as ethical toys without the consumption or the price tag."

Again, Adrienne was impressed. "That doesn't sound bad."

Bernice winced. "Yeah, but it didn't work. They rejected toys for trade that had any wear at all. Which is insane because, *hello*, kids play with them. They're gonna get messed up. But also, the toys were super cheap, so they broke really easily, and sometimes even broke during shipping. When toys were rejected for re-trade, you were charged to replace what you broke and re-charged for the next toy level up, and without notice. So you ended up buying like five times more toys than you would have otherwise, automatic charges to people's cards in the thousands. That kind of stuff."

"Um, that sounds like a scam."

"I don't know. *Scam* is harsh, but it was definitely a mess. Opal apologized. Did a whole live stream telling people how sorry she was. She shut the company down for not living up to its promise."

Adrienne could see the corporate experience in that savvy damage control. No wonder Opal was the one handing out NDAs. She knew how to build, and then protect, a brand.

Adrienne made a note to look more closely at Tamarind and Opal. When Tamarind's precarious Squad status was viewed in conjunction with her gathering blackmail material on moms, perhaps Tamarind was ready to go further than anyone thought to protect her spot next to Thea. And Opal was no saint. She was pressuring moms to essentially perform loyalty tests, and had had her own brush with cancellation. Adrienne thought back to Chiara's viral post and how the paid-sponsorship offers had rolled in. Could she have been in the running for a Mom Squad spot? Could Tamarind or Opal have been threatened to the point of harming someone? The walk from blackmail to assault didn't seem long from where Adrienne was sitting.

She thought back to her hours of research. She had spent days scrolling through these women's posts.

McKenna's two sets of multiples doing RISD-level crafts. Her kids all in car seats while they held pinwheels they had made themselves. The caption: Easy Breezy. #MultiplesMom #LinkInBio.

Ashleigh's jars of peaches (#FromTheOrchard, #BackToNature), handmade seasonal wreaths of wheat.

Tamarind's tiny sets of butt lifts, bench presses using her smiling baby, stroller squats for days. All while her kids crawled around her feet.

Opal finding Halloween costumes that could be repurposed year after year, courting sponsorships, perfect lighting tips under ten dollars to make your home beautiful.

Adrienne also remembered what she had initially thought of as duplicates—reposts of each other's Stories, reposts of reposts, an M.C. Escher–level of posts within a post within a post—but now she saw them as proof of their overlapping real-life coMOMunity. Proof they really were together, really were friends. Parties together with rainbow charcuterie boards on perfect bamboo dining sets. Cute kid sleepovers in MIT engineering–level pillow forts. Movie nights in the backyard with s'mores and themed decor.

Adrienne was embarrassed that she hadn't seen their obvious brands at first; she was too blinded by her own prejudice, jealousy, anger. She'd only taken in what had appeared to be effortless motherhood. In fact, several times, what started as focused research became hours of mindless scrolling. It all went down so easy, so quickly. Too quickly. When she finally managed to put her phone down, Adrienne was always left with the same sick feeling in her stomach.

Something about it brought back memories of when she and Chiara, for a school assignment, had made a castle out of the sugar cubes her mom had pilfered from her diner job. The girls had each snuck an entire sugar cube into their mouths. Adrienne could still taste the sweetness on her tongue and feel the rough corners softening in her cheek. The school project stood tall and solid, with a tiny toothpick flag at the top turret. However, later that night, a pipe burst in their rundown apartment, drowning the castle. In a matter of seconds, what had once sparkled was reduced to a tiny puddle of goo.

That was these posts. Once flattened into brands, the images ceased to be 3D and became nothing but saccharine waste.

Even with that sick feeling in her stomach, though, Thea felt different.

"Tell me about Thea," Adrienne said.

Bernice let out a sincere sigh of admiration. "Thea is amazing. See, Thea doesn't have one thing; she is *every* brand. She does everything these moms specialize in. Authentically. None of it is perfect—well, her design stuff is, because that's her background. But the rest of it was just her trying. She's so open. You really get to know the real her. And so many of us have been following her for years, well over a decade. Maybe two?"

Adrienne was taken aback. "Two decades?"

Bernice nodded. "Oh yeah. Some moms followed her before Instagram even existed—when she just had a blog! I started following her . . . sixteen years ago, I think? I remember when she met her husband. I remember her engagement. I remember her announcing her pregnancies. I was the first one of my friends to have kids and just didn't have a single person to talk to about how I felt. Thea was that person for me. By the time the words *Mom* and *Influencer* were put together? Thea was already so much more than that to us. She was my sister, my friend, my sleep-training consultant, my mom."

Adrienne could hear the genuine emotion in Bernice's voice, and under it, a current of true devotion. "Does anyone feel this way about the moms on the Squad?" she asked, although she was sure she already knew the answer.

Bernice considered the question for a minute, then answered. "I don't think so. Thea already had her followers, but she wanted to build a bigger community to help more moms feel supported. After a few years she said it was a lot of pressure to be all things. She worried she was failing the coMOMunity, which we all totally understood. We all feel like we are failing our kids, and Thea was feeling that exact same thing, just on such a large scale. So these were the first moms she brought into her brand."

Adrienne found herself less impressed than ever with the Squad and more intrigued than ever with Thea. Every gut instinct she had had about these women hadn't been right. She felt destabilized in her own judgment, and that made her worry—if danger was lurking somewhere here, there was a big chance she wasn't going to see it until it was too late.

Chapter 11

Halloween Past and Present

Adrienne wanted to go back to her cabin for a few hours, digest everything Bernice had told her, review her research, and try to get her bearings in this subculture she couldn't quite get a handle on. But time was running out, so she went off to a pumpkin-carving tutorial with McKenna, Bernice chattering along as they went.

Much to her surprise, Adrienne found Bernice's patter soothing. She prattled on about funny things she'd seen on the internet, recipes she had spectacularly failed to emulate, and the ways her body had changed into an unknown entity over her pregnancies. ("Pregnancy is basically puberty again, but twice, and sped up. And no one tells you until you are covered in weird hair and your boobs are so heavy you tip over.") Bernice wasn't self-deprecating so much as she was just refreshingly without guile.

Bernice was mid-story when they found the Pumpkin Carving tent. "So I am making these cupcakes. I have everything in my KitchenAid. Do you have a KitchenAid? I only have one because a rich aunt got it for me for my wedding. She doesn't have kids. It's yellow! Makes me so happy! Anyway, I put it all in the mixer, but then one of my boys comes out holding scissors. And I'm like *Oh, beans, what did he cut?* Because he definitely cut something! Turns out he cut his own hair—and whatever.

Who cares. As long as it wasn't curtains like last time. So anyway, I get back to the stand mixer, and the batter looks weird, but I figure it's fine. Oh man. So not fine. My husband ate one and said it was the worst *cupcake* ever but the best giant cupcake-shaped marshmallow. I had beat it so long I had made meringue! It was so funny."

This little tale wasn't going to make it on NPR's *The Moth* anytime soon, but every part of it charmed Adrienne. Each tiny detail more darling than the last, like a little Beatrix Potter book.

Bernice ended the scissors anecdote with the same closer as all her other domestic anecdotes: "When you meet my boys . . ." or "You'll see when you come over . . .", etc., etc. These invitations weren't conditional. Bernice had clearly decided they were real friends and was planning for all the great ways they would stay close after the summit.

Most shocking of all was Adrienne hearing her own voice say, "Oh yes, I can't wait to meet them!" And realizing she really truly meant it. She really did want to meet these little rascals, and the adoring husband who felt very passionately about getting a physical paper delivered and happily ate every disastrous new recipe Bernice tried. She wanted to laugh at the burn mark on the dining room table from the left-behind magnifying glass, and the painting done in Wite-Out that had destroyed the wallpaper, and the "vase" her sons had worked so hard on that they wanted prominently displayed on the mantel even though it looked, in Bernice's words, "exactly like a pile of wet cow poop."

Except these sweet future hangouts were all utterly impossible. Because Bernice wasn't just inviting Adrienne. She was inviting Adrienne, and Adrienne's fake husband, and Adrienne's nonexistent children. Bernice was friends with a lie—and Adrienne was a lot of shitty things, but she wasn't a liar. The push-pull of enjoying this easy camaraderie while also knowing that it would eventually dissolve when Bernice learned the truth made Adrienne feel like she was on a slingshot between realities.

But what choice did she have? She had to do this.

Moreover—or perhaps, specifically—Adrienne knew part of the allure of Bernice's invitations was that they echoed all Chiara's invitations. Hundreds of hours of closeness offered that Adrienne had almost uniformly declined. She had refused to spend time with Chiara with the babies, or with DH, and looking back now Adrienne had acted like a jealous lover. Unable to share Chiara's attention for even a dinner.

Instead, she had opted for nothing over an afternoon of split focus from her other half. Her regret was so strong—tasting like a mouth full of battery acid—that she had to push the thought away before it flattened her and instead live in the fantasy of accepting these new invitations from Bernice while they were still extended.

In the tent, McKenna stood at the dais, her perfect messy bun just so, as per usual. She had on a cute skeleton apron with leather accents (available for purchase) and was putting the finishing touches on a child's portrait carved into a pumpkin.

McKenna talked without ever breaking her megawatt smile. "Okay, y'all. Almost done. My little baby girl needs her signature wisps that frame her face—and done. Oh my God, y'all! My pumpkin is a pumpkin!"

McKenna turned her pumpkin around, and holy shit it was amazing. Police sketches wished they were this accurate.

The whole tent let out a uniform *"Awwwww!"*

McKenna lifted the pumpkin. "So, now we take our pumpkin portrait and put it onto our scarecrow form."

Next to her was a full-size scarecrow, a perfect replica of her child. It was equally impressive and terrifying. She placed the pumpkin head on the scarecrow body, which was dressed as a tiny witch. All the moms gasped and clapped.

McKenna turned and gave a little bow. "The great thing about this project is its versatility. In October, it's a fun life-size family portrait."

It was true—she had her entire family represented up there: her husband, Tod (one D); her twin boys, Cyan and Navy; and her twin girls, Indigo and Azure.

Bernice whispered, "Aren't her themed names cute? Their rooms and belongings are all decorated in their signature color."

Adrienne whispered back, "But they're all . . . blue? So it's all just shades of blue?"

Bernice, missing the point, said, "McKenna says it helps her keep her home organized!"

McKenna wiped her brow. "Wow, call Tamarind because I worked up a bit of a sweat, y'all!" She took a slug from her personalized Stanley tumbler, and Adrienne swore she saw the small shudder of someone who'd just done a shot cross McKenna's face.

McKenna stood behind the scarecrows representing her family. "But once Halloween is over, you can remove the clothes." She undressed her "husband" to reveal a chicken wire form underneath, with straw woven in the visible parts; then she pointed a remote at the screen behind her and clicked, projecting a photo of the chicken wire form dressed for Halloween. As she talked, new decor appeared and disappeared on the form like in Cher Horowitz's *Clueless* closet. "As we turn to November, this can be made into a traditional scarecrow for a harvest tableau. Then, come December first, you can redress again and make it . . ." She clicked the cue forward. "Santa, Mrs. Claus, and elves!"

The tent was clapping, clapping, clapping. The moms around Adrienne were enraptured.

"Ingenious!"

"So versatile!"

"Love the multipurpose!"

"These forms can get heavy, so make sure you put this on your Honey-Do List. And if your husbands grumble, you can always—"

She gave her husband scarecrow a swift shove off the stage. It careened into the dirt, the pumpkin smashing into pieces, McKenna's husband's face split into a slick pile of mess.

Even though it was only a bizarre dummy, Adrienne was taken aback at this pumpkin murder. The humor of the shove was the sugar sheen on a callous act. But what came next disturbed her more: the tidal wave of laughter. McKenna started to laugh first. Then the other women laughed. Louder. Harder.

McKenna catcalled over the edge of the stage. "Whoops! Sorry, honey!"

Laugh, laugh, laugh. The mamas were lapping it up. Had anything ever been so funny to them? No.

McKenna clearly liked having an audience to egg on and kept it going. "You got a little something on your face, sweetie. Did you cut yourself shaving?" she sneered. (More laughing.) "Honestly, so nice of Tod to be quiet for once!"

The peals of laughter increased, tipping closely to an angry crowd jeering.

And just before it became truly unsettling, McKenna pulled out of the skid and wrapped it up. "Okay, time for you to work on your pumpkin!"

Adrienne hoped Bernice wasn't feeling this, but she was laughing right along. If Adrienne's mom almost went insane with one set of twins, had McKenna's second set really pushed her into a permanent postpartum psychosis? This presentation seemed to say yes.

But by that math, where was Chiara's mental state last year? Adrienne barely knew. And then a smaller thought that wasn't new at all came forward: What if partying hadn't been the big problem between them? What if the big problem was that Adrienne had rejected the person most precious to her for doing an extremely normal thing—having children? Adrienne tried to lock the thought away, back into the vault of shame, but it wouldn't go. Chiara had needed Adrienne, and Adrienne had refused to go to her. The drugs were just a means to an end. The red herring that had allowed Adrienne to totally avoid her responsibility. If Chiara had been as low as Bautista said—recurrent uncontrollable thoughts of death, refusing medication—maybe she really did leave her family, drive away, and never looked back. Adrienne struggled to believe that, but at the same time, what did she know? She couldn't even return Chiara's texts by the end.

Amid a chicken wire "family," Adrienne started hacking away at her pumpkin. She had seeds in her hair and pumpkin guts on her face. It was not great. Suddenly, she longed for the cleanliness of gourd table-scaping, even if it meant dodging a social climber with a fire extinguisher. She used the electric eggbeater to clean the inside of her pumpkin like the other moms. However, her gooey hands were too slick, and the pumpkin spun away, crashing to the ground, eggbeaters spinning in the air, spraying even more mess onto her already sullied apron.

Everyone was looking. This was not blending in.

A woman walked through with Thea/McKenna-branded pumpkin-carving utensils. She gave one to Adrienne but not to Bernice (again with that bitchy *Sorry, not sorry* smile).

Adrienne called after her, "Hey, you missed Bernice."

Bernice held up her blue wristband and shrugged. "Festive Friend Level doesn't get merch perks."

Adrienne reacted with perhaps outsize indignation. "What? Ew. Here, you can have my carving set. I'm clearly not gifted at this."

Bernice refused to take it. "It's okay. It's not the only thing I won't get this weekend. You neither."

"What's off-limits?" Adrienne asked, striving for casual, devil may care. She knew forcing her way into an event would draw unwanted attention, but she still needed to understand what was happening behind those closed doors. Those smaller rooms of inner-circle moms seemed like prime territory for answers.

Bernice pointed to a couple of moms with the coveted gold wristbands, "There's a whole upper tier only for Elite Level Mini Moms. Obviously, the third day is only for Elite, but even before that, they keep the lower levels separate. Especially anywhere Thea is—that is definitely only for Elite."

Adrienne scoffed; a lifetime of sneaking into clubs and out of drug dens had given her a few skills. "Come on, how hard can it be to walk into a tent?"

Bernice shook her head. "No tents. Those all happen at Thea's house."

She pointed to the two-story whitewashed farmhouse set back on the property, well away from the tents and cabins. It had a wide wraparound porch with swings and hanging baskets of marigolds. A matte-black tin roof, dormers with cute witch hats suspended on fishing line poking out in pairs. It was not welcoming, but it was impressive, like *American Gothic* by way of HGTV.

Adrienne had somehow not even really noticed the house, but now knowing that it was off-limits immediately got under her skin and made her teeth itch. She tried to keep her voice from coming out as a hiss. "That's messed up."

Used to the quiet caste system of this world, Bernice shrugged it off. "I guess. But I get it. We can't all have time with Thea. I'm just happy to be near her. My husband got me the cheapest ticket here as a gift." The volume of her voice dropped down several notches. "It was the only one we could afford."

This hit Adrienne in her own soft spot. "I get it. We didn't grow up with any money, either."

Adrienne thought back to the small apartment she'd grown up in, her and her sister sleeping in the living room with bedsheets hanging from the ceiling as makeshift walls. Adrienne's mom making dinner for the three of them from an empty fridge, stretching ramen packages and thinly slicing mealy apples. Her mom's pained expressions and the girls pumping up their happiness to try to cheer her, terrified that any darkened mood that had taken hold would last for days or weeks, as it had done so many times in the past.

These memories were still so painful that Adrienne physically winced. They flew to the front of her mind without warning or invitation, leaving her depleted. These were wounds she had been trying to outrun, outdrink, outsex for years. Now she was left with all the old pain of her mom, the new pain of Chiara missing, and no coping mechanisms. The intergenerational connections felt so obvious now. How had she not seen that Chiara was struggling exactly like their mom had? How had she been so spiteful that she couldn't see her own twin was drowning? How had Adrienne grown so little in so many years that she repeated the pattern of turning away from someone who needed her help? Or at the very least, her love.

Bernice was clearly in her own mental swirl. "I mean, I didn't grow up rich. But it seems harder now. Life is so expensive. It barely made sense for me to go back to work after my son was born. Once I had the twins? Forget it."

Bernice's voice stayed the same, but her frustration grew as she talked, and Adrienne remembered she wasn't the only one with a complicated past. Then she felt ashamed that she had to remember that at all. For all her cynicism, she still bought the social media highlight reel people presented of their lives and was always shocked to see behind the curtain.

Bernice continued, "We did the math. Me going back to work would actually cost us thirty thousand dollars. So yes, this weekend was a gift from my husband, and my first break from the kids in years—but I'm hoping this weekend is an investment. Maybe if I make the right connections here, I could make us a little extra pocket money with some social media something. I don't know."

Adrienne felt for Bernice. And then, in a common pattern, she decided to attack what made her feel bad. Her voice was quiet and salty as hell. "But, Bernice, this isn't the real world. This isn't the only way to be a mom."

Bernice seemed startled by this. "What do you mean?"

"Well, like, where are the moms who actually don't have money for crafts and shit? Where are the moms who have to work or are on food stamps? Hell, where are the moms who aren't white? Where are the moms who aren't cis? Where are the queer moms? All I see here is this white-lady fantasy where your brain ends at your uterus. These expectations of perfect motherhood that torture you are created by these exact women. They made the problems they are selling you solutions for. What if you just stopped following them?"

Bernice was flummoxed. "But then who would I follow?"

Adrienne's voice rose. "No one! Yourself! Your own mind!"

She wanted to push this conversation further, but McKenna was suddenly at her shoulder, inspecting their pumpkins. Her presence felt like supervision, as if she knew that Adrienne was questioning their dogma. Instead of Big Brother it was Big Mommy. Adrienne plastered a smile on as fast as she could.

McKenna leaned in. "Wow. I love the detail on your pumpkin portrait, Bernice. So cute!" She pulled out her phone and snapped a selfie with Bernice, who was thrilled. "I'll post this when the weekend is over . . ." Hitting the catchphrase with Bernice chiming in: "It's about the present!"

Then McKenna turned to Adrienne's pumpkin, which was less *charming family* and more *inadvertent homage to Leatherface*. "And that's . . . fun, too. In a kind of informal way."

McKenna pulled Bernice to the front of the group so they could admire her work.

Left alone at the table, the insult still stinging, Adrienne's memory kicked in, back to another Halloween.

It was 1996. Adrienne and Chiara were seven years old, and their mom was putting the finishing touches on their homemade costumes. Both of the girls were Wonder Woman. They had on bathing suits over sweats and little crowns of tinfoil. They were all having so much fun.

Heidi was clearly loving this as much as her girls. "Look at me, my little Wonder Women!"

She took their photo as the little girls struck a powerful pose. The Polaroid slipped out of the front of the camera, and they all crowded around while it developed, eventually revealing a truly adorable picture, the light from the flash glinting off the foil, making it look like diamonds.

Heidi looked at the Polaroid. "Perfect! I am going to keep this photo with me always." She slipped the photo into her shirt pocket and gave it a little pat.

Chiara was breathless. "Always?"

Heidi reached out her pinkies to her girls for a pinkie promise. "Always. So we are never apart."

That was why Chiara had the precious photo of her boys on her car visor; that was where she'd gotten it from.

Heidi smiled and said, "One more pose, now! Show me the Invisible Plane! Show me the Lasso of Truth!"

All three of them were laughing, giggling, hugging. A puddle of affection. It was one of those rare moments in life where they all knew this was special and so they soaked in every iota of feeling, cataloging the now for a lifetime of joy.

Later that day, the girls and Heidi went to the school for the Halloween parade. They were all brimming with pride.

But within seconds of joining their class, the girls heard a laugh.

No. More than one. A whole chorus of laughs.

A freckled kid with an expensive haircut yelled, "Oh my God, did you make that?"

Another kid yelled, "What are you even supposed to be?"

Adrienne tried to project strength, anger, a *don't you dare* attitude she would perfect later in life. "We—we are Wonder Woman," she yelled back, hands on her tiny hips, chest puffed out.

A girl behind her chirped, "Me too. But my costume is from a store." Her costume was clearly sanctioned merchandise, every detail perfect, right down to the lasso. Nothing about it was smooshed tinfoil.

The other moms were there in borderline sexy costumes. They made no effort to correct their kids. Instead, they hid their own faces and shot each other looks of secondhand embarrassment.

Finally, one mom spoke up. "Cute costume, Heidi."

Another mom in a leotard and a witch hat stepped forward. "Oh, honey, that's not her costume. It's her uniform at the diner. Late for your shift?"

Heidi shrank in shame and tried to smooth out her apron. Adrienne, Chiara, and their mom were all crushed. Every good feeling, every giggle from that morning, was gone. Evaporated like it had been in the path of a bitchy hydrogen bomb.

Later that night Chiara and Adrienne wanted to go trick-or-treating, but their mom wouldn't get out of bed.

Chiara pled their case, pulling on Heidi's arm. "Mommy, please. Please come with us. We want you to come!"

Heidi yanked her arm back. "Go by yourself. I'm tired."

Adrienne's child-size fury burned white hot at everyone and everything. "Let's go, Chiara. It's just like last year."

Though Adrienne itched to storm off, Chiara held her back, hoping against hope that their mom would rally.

At the last second, Heidi did roll over, but only to say, "And turn out the porch light when you leave. I don't want anyone knocking."

Adrienne grabbed Chiara and marched her out the door. "Told you."

They both had enough experience with their mom's depression to know that this mood wasn't going to pass soon. They would be living under the cloud of this day until Thanksgiving, at least. Maybe even Christmas.

It didn't matter that decades had passed—Adrienne's head roiled as she relived that day yet again. Time hadn't lessened it at all. If anything, the laughter had become louder. The other moms seemed more loathsome. And her mother's shame was even more heartbreaking. The morning of putting together the costumes with Chiara and her mom was Adrienne's most cherished memory. One of the few moments of unbridled happiness from her childhood. But her mind always had to play the tape to the end, and it was excruciating to remember the rest of the day. The two memories being next to each other in her mind felt like a hideous trap. In order to revisit the joy, she also had to prepare herself to be slapped with misery. No matter the warmth in her heart at the start, the sting on her cheek always lasted longer.

And now, that memory was even worse. Her mother had died, and Chiara was missing. Adrienne felt so responsible for their entire lives. She was the only keeper of their shared history. The small, beautiful glimpses of love and the aching disappointments. It was too much to hold alone, and yet here she was, up to her elbows in pumpkin guts, matching McKenna's fake smile, which was the same as those moms in the schoolyard.

Something between vomit and tears rose in her throat; she had to get out of here. She couldn't stand being in the tent a second longer.

She walked as fast as she could across the property without drawing attention to herself, her legs taking long strides and her arms swinging with tight fists. Every smiling, laughing face she saw triggered a wave of fury. She knew these weren't those same moms from her childhood, but they hit the same chord regardless.

Adrienne got back to her cabin, slamming the door so hard that the entire post-and-beam frame rattled. She grabbed the bottle of wine from the welcome basket. It didn't matter that it was the disgusting trifecta of cheap plus warm plus chardonnay—the cork was out in seconds, the mouth millimeters from her own.

Bautista had laid out the theories so many times: car accident, self-harm, or the long shot of being a victim of a crime. Adrienne had never entertained the first two, and now she knew that was because those were the ones that implicated her and her emotional neglect. She couldn't take it. The regret felt like a live animal trapped under her skin, ripping at her emotional sinew, and only the alcohol would let it out.

Just as the bottle was about to hit her lips, she stopped.

Adrienne couldn't check out. Something had happened to Chiara, and Adrienne couldn't lay down and hide like her mom did all those years ago. Like DH had for the last year. Even though that was all she wanted. She could anticipate the loose warmth that slugging half of that wine would give her. She craved that release. The need for it set her teeth on edge and made the back of her tongue plump with thirst.

For a second she thought maybe she could have just a glass.

No, just a sip. One sip.

But Chiara . . . Wherever Chiara was, she needed Adrienne.

Painfully, Adrienne poured all the wine down the bathroom sink.

Then Adrienne heard a soft knock at her door.

She opened the door to find Bernice.

Bernice's eyes were soft, her voice kind. "Hey. I just wanted to check in on you. You kind of stormed out of the tent."

Adrienne's voice came out harsh, harder than she intended. "Yeah, I'm fine."

Bernice waited a beat, then gently, genuinely asked, "Are you?"

Adrienne was ready to protest again, ready to push Bernice away just like she did to everyone else. What did this Utah Mommy Nitwit know about her? About Chiara? Nothing. Zero. Less than zero. She was a distraction.

As if she could sense the rejection coming, Bernice said, "You don't have to tell me. I don't want to pry. I'm just here for you."

It was when Bernice turned to go that Adrienne finally saw how taxing the isolation of her mission was. Yes, telling Bernice the truth was a major risk, but Adrienne was too exhausted to lie anymore. She needed a friend more than she needed perfect control.

"Come in," Adrienne said.

She led Bernice to the bathroom and showed her Chiara's photo.

Bernice took in the collage and let out a breathless "Holy guacamole."

Adrienne pointed. "This is my sister Chiara. She came to the Fourth of July Style Summit last year. And she hasn't been seen since."

Bernice's face was the definition of legitimate shock. "Oh no. That's terrible."

"The police think she snapped, bailed on her kids, and ran off to Canada. Her postpartum was really bad—not that I noticed. Her stupid husband seems to be hoping she just got lost in the mountains on the way home, drove off the road in the dark."

"It happens more than you think." Bernice took in Adrienne's face and read the situation exactly. "But you think something different?"

Adrienne nodded. "I think *something* happened to her."

Bernice was connecting the dots now. "And you think it happened at the style summit?"

"Yes."

"And that someone in the coMOMunity is responsible?"

"Yes."

"Why?"

This was the question that had gotten Adrienne's back up every day since Chiara had disappeared. It always felt like a rebuke when Bautista said it, when DH said it, when her idiot friends said it because they complained Adrienne was "always killing the vibe now." But Bernice wasn't challenging Adrienne; she just wanted to know more.

"I don't know. I just do. I'm the only one. So I came here to infiltrate, I guess."

"You don't really have kids?"

Adrienne shook her head.

"Husband?"

"Nope."

"And the blog?"

"Fake. I know I sound unhinged, but you have to believe me. These mommies are not her people. Chiara was independent. She was out there living to the extreme, every day."

Bernice nodded solemnly. "Okay."

Adrienne was confused. "Okay what?"

Bernice answered in the most matter-of-fact tone, "Okay, I believe you."

Adrienne's knees almost gave out from relief. She didn't realize how much she'd needed that. How much she'd needed just *one* ally after the last fifteen months of railing against everyone and everything that had swept Chiara away like a piece of inconvenient trash.

Bernice was all business now. "So, who is your main suspect?"

Adrienne shook her head. "I don't have one."

Bernice nodded. "Okay, what about motive?"

Adrienne shrugged.

"Timeline?" Bernice asked.

"What's that?"

"I don't know. They just always say that on cop shows."

Adrienne leveled with Bernice. "I know I seem nuts. And I have basically nothing to go on. I don't even have a coherent theory. The one lead I thought I had was a complete bust. But I can't shake the feeling that someone here knows what happened. I just can't get these psychos to talk to me."

Bernice laughed. "Oh, that's easy." Bernice went to the summit schedule taped to the bathroom wall and pointed to the next event. "#WineTime."

Chapter 12

Wine Time

The wine-tasting event was all set up, the tent flaps securely tied together until the appointed hour. Yet another chalkboard-pen-calligraphy sign saying Keep Out. Adrienne had started to think calligraphy was the default *Sorry, not sorry* font. While the rest of the summit guests were at dinner, Adrienne and Bernice went around the long way and approached the tent from behind. Adrienne shifted a few of the sandbags that held the vinyl to the ground, then lifted a section open for Bernice to climb through. Adrienne followed her into the tent, tucking the sandbags back into place as best she could. Neat rows of endless wineglasses were already filled a quarter of the way up, along with platters of fruit, cheese, and crackers.

Adrienne asked, "Who set this stuff up?"

"The Elite Level moms."

Adrienne let out a guffaw. "Are you serious?"

Bernice didn't see the problem. "Elite Moms set up these big group events for the lower-level moms, and that's when they get to do their exclusive meet and greets with the Mom Squad. It's how they keep it feeling equal. We all get something special."

"Uh-huh. What I hear is they pay more and then have to work the event."

Bernice scrunched her face. "Wow, I never thought of it like that. Opal presented it as more one-on-one time, seeing behind the curtain."

Adrienne snarked, "What's 'behind the curtain' is, they don't have to pay any staff this weekend and get to keep all the money."

Opal may have done the perfect corporate two-step of apology/accountability when her last scam ran aground, but she clearly hadn't given up on making a buck off an easy mark.

Bernice and Adrienne worked in silence. First, they topped off every wineglass to the brim—no delicate-tasting pours here. Then they removed the water jugs, the cheese and crackers, and the spittoons. Chances of some mommies getting wasted had just gone up by 200 percent, and hopefully so had the likelihood of their guard going down.

As moms started to file in from dinner, Adrienne headed toward them, ready to grill some sloshed women, but Bernice stopped her.

"Hey, maybe I should ask around," she said gently.

Adrienne disagreed, her chest puffing out. "But Chiara is my sister."

Bernice leveled with her. "I know, but you aren't very popular after winning the ropes course."

Adrienne rolled her eyes. "No shit."

"So maybe let a beta mom try."

Adrienne recognized immediately that Bernice had a better read on how to work the room. "Okay, you run point. What should I do?"

"How good are you at getting people drunk?"

"Bernice, it's one of my top skills."

"I had a feeling."

As Bernice mingled, chatting up the other moms, Adrienne filled glasses surreptitiously. At first, the women weren't drinking enough, and she wondered if perhaps the process of going to the bar was slowing them down, or at least keeping them keenly aware of how much they (and others) were drinking. Adrienne removed the hurdle by placing open bottles of red, white, and rosé at every table and next to each Adirondack circle. Then she had a stroke of brilliance. She tucked under the podium and found the control center for the speaker system. She clicked through the connected iPod. Scrolling, scrolling, scrolling—and then her eyes lit up.

"Oh yes."

She pressed play.

A few ears turned when the piano chords started . . . Then the breathless contralto of Adele's "Hello" came forth.

Every woman in that tent loosened three notches immediately as Adele crooned about being younger and free in California. Because, really, who didn't want to drink six glasses of wine away from their kids and sing along to Adele?

By the time Adele belted out from the other side, the women were getting absolutely sloshed and Adrienne was enjoying her backstage role. However, she couldn't help but try to stand close to the groups, desperate to hear a whisper of Chiara's name, followed by furtive glances and a quick exit. Part of this was due to the fact that her weekend was nearly over; the vast majority of the attendees would leave first thing tomorrow morning. But the quiet part of her mind also whispered that it was because she wanted to be the hero.

She wanted to be the One Who Saved Chiara. It was hard for her to admit that, to admit that her own ego was still so hungry for recognition, to be the center of Chiara's life and now possibly her death. She could hear her sponsor chiding her, telling her to give up her pride.

A good sister wouldn't care where the information came from.

Maybe I'm not a good sister after all.

Adrienne's head was starting to hurt. This train of thought had been zinging around the edges of her mind since she'd gotten sober thirty days ago. She remembered getting out of the ocean once, her skin numb, and how her hot shower had felt like knives before her body recognized it was warming up. That was what sobriety felt like so far. Knives. Forgotten parts of her pain coming back alive to burn anew in order to heal.

Adrienne had to take a step outside the tent to steady herself and hope her headache would subside. The air was cooler out here by a not-insignificant margin. It was her favorite time of day—when the grass was cool but the air was warm, and the twilight sky was a wash of yellows into lavenders. It only lasted a few minutes, and she watched as the darkness from one horizon spread forward, pushing the sun below the hills.

From this vantage point, Adrienne could take in the moms as a group, and she was struck by how relaxed and happy they all seemed right then. And it was more than the wine. Adrienne tallied up the weekend so far and found a startling trend. When the Mom Squad wasn't around, the mothers were open, breezy. Just regular women worn out from life, desperately trying to recuperate and connect. Alternatively, every moment when the Squad was leading events, every woman projected severity and a willingness to fight for the slightest advantage. The mere presence of the branded foursome and whatever they were offering in that moment—attention, sponsorships, advice—got everyone's hackles up.

She remembered watching aerial footage of a sheep dog herding a flock of sheep in Ireland. The border collie had navigated and instigated perfect swirls, exerting total control. When the Squad was there, they controlled the vibe, and these moms were their emotional sheep. The air crackled with frenzy, desperation, and competition. Scarcity mindset in *Life, Laugh, Love* format.

But Adrienne didn't know if that was directly the Mom Squad's fault. They were definitely the cause, but perhaps unintentionally so. Was the Squad a frantic pack of collies at cross purposes, inadvertently rattling their charges? Or were they predators rustling the group to find the strays and, more importantly, any threats.

She didn't know.

Nevertheless, there had to be a predator here somewhere.

By the time it was dark, her headache was gone, and Adrienne saw Bernice frantically waving her back into the tent.

Bernice linked arms with her. "There you are. I've been looking everywhere. I think I found something." She dragged her to a corner far from the speakers.

Bernice presented Adrienne to a little group of women heaped into CB2 lounge chairs that were all painted a garish retro orange. "Everyone, this is Adrienne. Adrienne, this is Lauren, Lauren, Lauren, and . . ."

"Laurel," the last mom replied with a not-insignificant amount of attitude.

Bernice laid on the apology. "Right. Of course. So sorry. Adrienne, they remember some drama last summit." Bernice raised her eyebrows in a very not-slick *We have a lead*–type vibe.

Adrienne showed them her photo of Chiara. "Do you recognize this woman?"

Lauren 1: "Oh yeah, I remember her."

Lauren 2: "Her most popular post? It was about . . ." She dropped her voice to a whisper that was somehow louder than her speaking voice. "Drug use."

Lauren 3 was clearly still scandalized, even though she wouldn't be able to pass an eye exam, she was so hammered. "Our local Mini-Mom group emailed to see if she was coming back."

Bernice was clearly thrilled that she had found a clue. "And?"

Lauren 3: "Our local group didn't know. So they checked with the official Mom Squad."

Lauren 1 was slurring. "And they assured us she was not."

Adrienne's breath caught. "Who was 'they'?"

Lauren 1 was confused. "Who was who?"

Adrienne took a deep breath. "You said *they* assured you she was not coming. Meaning the Mom Squad. Who was 'they' in the Squad? Who did you email?"

Lauren 1 shrugged. "I didn't write the email. It was another mom in my group. She told us."

"So you don't know who exactly from the Squad wrote you back?"

"Nope."

"Could it have been Tamarind?"

"I don't know."

Adrienne looked around. "Is that mom who wrote the email here? Can I talk to her?"

Lauren 2 shook her head. "Nope. All her kids got impetigo and her husband freeeeeeeeaked out. So she had to stay home."

That was not the answer Adrienne wanted, but she needed to get any drop of information from these women before they blacked out. Adrienne tried another approach: "When was this?"

Lauren 2 looked at her weird. "The impetigo?"

"No. Not the impetigo. The email. When did your local Mini-Mom group email the Squad?"

Lauren 1 thought hard—too hard. "Must have been mmmm . . ."

Lauren 2 tried to help but was also way out of it. "Mmmmm . . . March?"

"Yes! It was *March!*" Lauren 3 agreed.

Laurel nodded along. "Yes, definitely March. I remember because that was when my husband slept with the nanny."

Lauren 3 was shocked. "No!"

Laurel brushed it aside. "Look, I was happy for a night off."

The Laurens and Laurel dissolved into hysterics, and the women cheers'd sloppily, wine splashing everywhere.

Lauren 3 piped up, her right hand raised like she was in court, "I swear to God, I will choose my nanny over my husband."

Lauren 2 nodded, raising her left hand. "One hundred percent." Then she realized her mistake and raised her right hand. "One hundred percent."

Adrienne wanted to keep them on track. She snapped her fingers. "But how did they know that already?"

Lauren 1 was confused, seeming to have forgotten everyone and everything that had happened in the last thirty seconds. "Know what?"

Adrienne tried to swallow her frustration. This was like attempting to get a witness statement from a school of goldfish. "How did they know back in March that this woman wasn't coming back?"

Lauren 2 breezed past Adrienne's question, if she'd even heard it in the first place. "So important to keep the mom quality as high as possible," she said through hiccups.

Adrienne was about to snap her fingers again, but Bernice knew how to get info and it was not with Adrienne's laser focus. She slid in, faking it. "Totally. Can't agree more."

Lauren 2 squinted her eyes. "I mean, first it's drugs, and next it's"—cue the loud whisper—"lesbians."

Lauren 1 nodded. "My neighbor is a lesbian. She's very nice, very handy, but I always feel like she's, ya know, watching me."

Adrienne's frustration was obvious now. "Did they say why that mom wasn't coming back? Did they say how they already knew?"

Lauren 3 ignored Adrienne completely. "But here's the thing: I think *I'm* a lesbian."

Adrienne was ready to go five more rounds of questioning with the Chardonnay Quartet, but Bernice appeared to recognize that this was going absolutely nowhere and not even an act of God could get it back on track. She led Adrienne away.

They went to Bernice's cabin and closed the door behind them.

Bernice was breathless. "Cheese and rice, that was so exciting!"

Adrienne was flush with renewed energy, and talking a mile a minute. "I knew it! I knew it. I knew these bitches didn't get Chiara. How did the Mom Squad know in March Chiara wasn't coming to this year's summit? Unless they *knew* she wasn't coming. In March, I was still holding press conferences and hoping her credit cards would ping. Bautista was still checking hospitals on the way to Canada to see if she had been admitted. But these women—who she met exactly once, who claimed to the cops to not even know her—knew where Chiara would not be seven months later? No. That's fishy as hell."

Bernice couldn't quite follow. "Huh?"

Adrienne was all business now. "I think this is enough to get renewed interest in Chiara's case. It has to be. I need to call the police."

"Yes! They will totally listen to you," Bernice agreed.

Adrienne winced. "Actually, our last conversation didn't go so great. But I do have someone who will care. Wait . . . No phones."

Bernice nodded knowingly. "Oh, there's a phone."

"Where?"

Bernice pointed out the window to Thea's house. "We should go soon, while most of the coMOMunity are in the wine tent."

Adrienne smiled. "Great point, Bernice. Thank you so much. I couldn't have done this without you."

Bernice smiled back. "Of course." She winked. "This is what coMOMunity is all about."

Adrienne was pleasantly surprised. "Did you just make a little joke at the expense of the coMOMunity?"

"You're a bad influence on me."

"Not the first time I've heard that."

Bernice looked a little sheepish. "Don't tell anyone, though, okay? I still really want a partnership with Melissa & Doug."

Adrienne was confused. "Who are they? Are they here?"

Bernice laughed. "Wow, you really don't have kids. Come on, let's go break into Thea's house."

Chapter 13

Never Zebras

Bautista tried to get five minutes of sleep in her cruiser in the parking lot. These stupid night shifts were killing her. She felt like, while she was technically sleeping enough hours on paper, none of it tracked with her body. She had just drifted off when she heard a gentle *tap tap* on the window.

Bautista didn't even have to open her eyes. "Yes, Jarvis?"

Jarvis's voice was uncharacteristically low. "We got something."

Bautista opened one eye and saw Jarvis's hangdog face. "You don't sound happy."

Jarvis shrugged like a sulky preteen. "See for yourself."

Bautista followed Jarvis inside and up to the second floor of their office building. The detective's bullpen was a linoleum box from the seventies, with harsh fluorescent lights that gave Bautista a migraine every time she worked a double.

Jarvis turned her computer so Bautista could see the screen. "My cousin at CHP came through. He's going to be insufferable at Christmas."

Bautista saw a zip file of photos—a minivan wrapped around a tree at the base of a ravine. The airbags had deployed. Everything inside was tossed from hell to breakfast. Bautista squinted closer at the driver's seat. "Blood?"

Jarvis replied, "We don't know for sure yet, but my cousin thinks yes. That dark stain there, too." Jarvis pointed to a smear on the airbag. "CHP also took photos of the inside driver's door; check out the handle. They think that dark stain is blood from the vic exiting the vehicle."

"Where is this?"

"Twenty miles north of the ranch," Jarvis said.

"So your theory was correct: she got turned around when she left the event, got lost, and then had an accident. Good job, Jarvis." But there was no enthusiasm in her voice. Then, almost to herself, Bautista asked, "Why did it take them so long to find this damn car?"

"Car is at the base of a service road that no one thought to check. The guardrail was taken down for repair but never replaced." Jarvis clicked open a photo showing the posts where a guardrail should be. "Three other cars have gotten lost and stranded that way. Seems like when she tried to turn around, she slid down the ravine or maybe, in the dark, lost control altogether."

"Any sign of a body?" But Bautista didn't know why she'd asked. She knew the answer. No body . . . yet.

Jarvis clicked another window and a map of Mendocino came to the front of the screen with a whoosh. "Car was found here, so they are setting a ten-mile search radius here. They think they will find her in the next couple of days."

Bautista thought back to her map on her dining room wall. She had spent a year staring at the little highlighted squiggles that created a spiderweb with the ranch at the center. This road wasn't on there, she was pretty sure. But then she also laughed at herself, imagining she had committed the entire county to memory.

Jarvis stood there for a minute, not moving.

Finally, Bautista asked, "What's wrong?"

Jarvis thought for a second. "I don't know, actually. I guess after all this legwork, I thought the truth would be . . . more."

"Me too. But it's true: When you hear hooves, think horses, not zebras."

"Do you want CHP to call the family?" Jarvis asked.

Bautista rubbed her temples. "No, I'll do it."

Without thinking, Bautista picked up her phone and called Adrienne, not the husband. This was against protocol. The husband was next of kin. But Bautista didn't hang up to correct the error. She just listened to the ringing.

The phone connected, and Adrienne's terse voice said, "I'm out." Then an automated voice said, "The voicemail box you are trying to reach is full. Please call back later. Goodbye." The line went dead.

Bautista growled. Of course even the smallest task with that woman would be a pain. She tried again and got the same message. Bautista pulled out her cell phone and texted Adrienne. *This is Detective Bautista. Call me when you get this message.*

Now it was time to call the husband.

He picked up on the third ring and barely said a word as Bautista filled him in.

"I'll call the sitter. See you in twenty minutes," he said, and he hung up before Bautista could respond.

Twenty minutes later on the dot, Bautista led Chiara's husband from the elevator to her desk. She was gentle both in vocal tone and physical presence. "There really was no rush. You could have come later."

Chiara's husband mumbled so quietly Bautista had to lean in to catch it. "I have waited long enough. The sitter can spend the night, so I'm here as long as you need."

"'Spend the night'?" Bautista echoed. She realized he was expecting a big process, a major wrap-up, something time consuming to reflect the enormity of the loss. Except this was going to be nothing of the sort. This was the worst part of the job—bad answers with no conclusions.

Bautista sighed. There was no stopping this train, so she was resigned to see it through. "They found Chiara's car, driven off a ravine twenty miles from the Instagram-mommy event. Like I said, the road should have been blocked off, and your wife wasn't the first person to take it by accident. What probably happened was she crashed her car and then went looking for help. People have head injuries. They get lost."

Chiara's husband was dazed, unable to take in any more information. "Right. Makes sense."

Bautista handed him a manila envelope. "I have photos here for insurance. I can also email you copies. Sometimes life insurance needs this to process claims."

"Uh-huh," he responded as he mindlessly opened the manila envelope and looked through the photos.

Bautista winced. The car was in bad shape, and she hadn't really intended for him to open the envelope here. "There's not much you need to see in there. Maybe ask a friend to help you."

Bautista gently took the photos from his hands and tucked them back in the envelope. He didn't even react, and she was struck by how placid he was, like a giant drugged baby just being moved along the assembly line of time without effort or intention. The feeling was so strong she had to stop herself from helping him zip up his coat as he slowly walked to the door, his shoes making a soft shuffling sound on the linoleum.

After he left, Bautista sat at her desk for a long time without moving or speaking. She didn't even take a sip of water. She just stared into the middle distance at nothing. She felt like a rookie, oddly devastated by the completely mundane end point of this investigation.

This was the obvious outcome. The most likely. The one with the fewest questions.

So why did she feel so empty about it all?

On her first day as a cop, her training officer had said, "Prepare yourself, kid. This job will make you see the worst of humanity."

But that had not been Bautista's experience. Quite the opposite. This job had shown her the complete dumb luck of it all. Someone in Ukiah three years ago had forgotten to file a work order to replace a guardrail and now a family was destroyed. That was all it took. The sheer randomness of the universe was scarier than any perp Bautista had seen.

A mere slip of the wind was the only difference between life and death.

Chapter 14

The Farmhouse

Adrienne and Bernice snuck up to Thea's house, tucking themselves into the nearby trees until their direct path in the open was as short as possible. They agreed before they made their casual sprint to the porch that the front door was too exposed to the rest of the coMOMunity event, so they decided to make a break for a set of heavy cedar benches on the back porch. There, they could hide behind the benches to get their bearings.

At the edge of the trees Adrienne whispered, "One, two, three . . ."

She crouched low and moved as quickly as possible. She caught a glimpse of Bernice running just behind her. Bernice had hinged at her waist and scurried with her arms wide. She looked like a child pretending to be plane.

Adrienne whispered as she ran, "What are you doing?"

Bernice held her position firm. "For balance."

Once crouched behind the benches and leaning out as far as they dared, they found a Dutch door at the back of the house. They crawled down until they were sitting with their backs on the door. Adrienne popped her head up and looked through the window. She didn't see anyone directly inside.

Adrienne whispered, "I think this is our best bet. Seems like a utility closet or something."

Bernice peeked in. "Oh, this is her laundry room slash doggy-bathing station."

Adrienne was confused. "What the hell is a doggy-bathing station?"

Bernice pointed at the waist-high walk-in shower with a detachable showerhead.

Adrienne admired the pearlescent tile mosaic. "Jesus. That's for her dog? That's nicer than my apartment."

Bernice looked Adrienne up and down. "Okay, what size is your butt?"

"What?"

Bernice pointed to the small doggy door behind Adrienne, and then her face crumbled into shame. "I fell off Atkins, so my butt will not fit."

Adrienne shook her head. "Everyone falls off Atkins! It's impossible!"

Bernice looked so relieved. "Really?"

Adrienne tried the lower knob. "It's locked."

"Corn nuts!" Bernice huffed.

Adrienne took a breath. "Bernice, I really appreciate your help, but if you don't start swearing like a normal person . . ."

Adrienne reached in through the doggy door and felt the locked doorknob. "The knob needs a key to unlock. But . . ." She pushed her shoulder as far as she could into the doggy door, reaching, reaching . . . There was the *click* of a lock, and the top half of the Dutch door swung open.

Bernice was impressed. "How did you know to do that?"

"A mild drug problem for most of my life means I have some dubious but helpful skills," Adrienne replied, enjoying Bernice's slightly scandalized reaction.

Bernice nudged Adrienne. "I'll say."

Bernice gave Adrienne a boost up and over the Dutch door. It was not graceful, but it got the job done.

Adrienne popped her head up Whack-A-Mole style, and so did Bernice. A pair of grown women kneeling at a half door like some kind of demented two-way puppet theater.

Bernice urgently whispered, "When I've seen Thea's office in photos, it looks like it's on the ground floor, facing the back of the house. Great golden-hour light there at sunset."

Adrienne whispered back, "It's super creepy that you know that, but thank you."

Bernice bit her lip. "What should I do?"

Adrienne shrugged. "Be a lookout?"

Bernice looked around. "Look out for what?"

Adrienne shrugged. "I don't know. Use your motherly instincts."

Bernice looked worried. "But I'm more of a craft mom."

"Then I don't know, craft me an excuse for why I'm in the house."

With that, Adrienne closed the top of the Dutch door. She stood up slowly and listened for any sounds on the other side of the interior door, pressing herself up against a wall of perfectly folded towels. She took a deep breath to steady her nerves. Then she sniffed. She sniffed again. She buried her face in the towels.

Adrienne couldn't help but let out a little sigh. "Oooh, sage lavender."

Snapping back to focus, Adrienne snuck out of the doggy-bathing station room, which led directly into the kitchen. It was absolutely giant, with brass pots hanging from a ceiling rack, charming arrays of fruits in adorable baskets of every size, and two kitchen islands topped with the finest marble.

Adrienne was impressed. "Damn, *two* islands?"

She was about to turn the corner into the foyer when, in a ludicrously large oval mirror hanging on a rustic leather strap, she saw the reflection of a figure coming toward her. She ducked back into the kitchen and tucked herself under the country-style breakfast nook. It was a shitty hiding spot, but it was all she could find in the split second before McKenna hustled in.

McKenna wasn't as bouncy as normal, and was looking around a bit too much, her forced casual air betraying her.

McKenna beelined to the fridge (Sub-Zero, hidden cabinet door) and selected a bottle of rosé from the back of the shelf. She uncorked it quickly, dumped half of the contents into her Stanley tumbler on the counter, and exited out of the side door. The entire errand took merely seconds, and Adrienne recognized another addict's dexterity. No one's hands were steadier than someone getting their fix.

Alone again, Adrienne crept out from under the nook, found the office off the foyer right where Bernice said it would be, and gently closed the door behind her. She grabbed the landline on the desk and dialed. It was a legitimate corded office phone, with multiple extensions and a button for quick video conferencing—reminding Adrienne yet again that as folksy as this whole weekend presented, it was, in fact, a multimillion-dollar enterprise. She was surprised that she didn't have to dial nine to get an outside line.

Adrienne's nerves were high as she listened to the ringing. "Come on, come on. Come on."

Finally, the call connected.

"Hey, it's Adrienne."

On the other end of the line was Chiara's husband. Before he could get a word out, she started talking. "Look, I don't have a lot of time."

"Adrienne, did you get my message?"

She was confused for a moment. "What? No. There's no phones here."

And now it was DH's turn to sound confused. "Where are you? And what number is this?"

Adrienne winced; she knew this wasn't going to go over well. "I'm at the CoMOMunity Style Summit." She couldn't see him grimace, but she could feel it happening through the phone and was immediately on offense. "I'm telling you, something happened to her here!"

She expected DH to yell. To fight. But instead, what he did next was so much worse: he pleaded.

"Adrienne, please, I can't."

"No, seriously! Listen to me. They knew Chiara wasn't coming back in March! How did they know that in March?"

"Adrienne, we have been over this—"

"These women are weird, okay? Like Stepford–*American Psycho* weird! No one likes their kids this much!"

"Jesus Christ, Adrienne. Will you just stop?" he snapped.

And there it was. Adrienne wouldn't back down, though. She had come too far, and his anger just fueled hers. "No! I won't! She was my sister!"

"And she was my wife. The mother of my children."

"I have to find out what happened to her."

"That's why I have been trying to get in touch with you. The CHP found her car crashed off a steep hill."

This stopped Adrienne in her tracks. "What?"

DH was barely holding it together now. "I just left Bautista's office. CHP found her car off a service road or something. She went the wrong way, got turned around. The guardrail had been taken down, and a couple people had already gotten lost that way."

Adrienne wasn't convinced. "Did they find a body?"

"Jesus Christ, what is wrong with you!" DH never swore, and the fact that he was now told Adrienne how callous he found her question. "No, not yet. But now they have a search area, and it won't be long. Looks like it's exactly what they said: she had an accident, then got lost looking for help."

Adrienne was furious that he was giving up. "It's not true!"

"It is! They literally found her car wrapped around a tree at the base of a dark road!"

"Don't you think it's a little convenient that their blameless theory of events just happens to be exactly what happened?"

"No! I think my wife dying is the opposite of convenient, actually!" he yelled.

He was really angry now, and Adrienne hated how much she loved it. It felt so good to push against someone who was as furious as her instead of the wet noodle he had been since Chiara had disappeared.

"You know what I meant," she shot back.

"Yes. I know that instead of a very basic accident, you think the more likely scenario is a group of mommies who love beading and shit murdered a woman they had never met before."

"I'm going to get proof. You watch!"

"Proof of what? We have the car!"

"But no body! And why did it take so long for them to find the car? Why did no one check that road if people had already gotten lost on it? Maybe they did check the road last year and the car wasn't there yet? Maybe someone put it there just now because they know I'm getting close!"

"Who is 'they'? You're close to what?"

"The truth!"

"This *is* the truth! Adrienne, not everything is a conspiracy theory. Sometimes bad shit just happens." His anger had burned white hot, and now it had burned out. "I know you loved her. But holding a grudge? Never letting anything go? That's not the only way to love someone."

This hit Adrienne harder and closer than she'd expected. She tried to retort back, to keep the volley going, but he wasn't going to comply.

DH said, "Call me when you get home. It's time to plan a funeral."

He hung up.

Adrienne stood with the receiver at her ear, listening to the dial tone.

Against her own will, Adrienne's mind flew back a few years to a diner, where Chiara and Adrienne sat at a booth. Chiara was clean, put together, but a little nervous. Adrienne was still grungy, and definitely coming down off of something.

Chiara's voice was delicate. "Is that a black eye?"

Adrienne let out a little chuckle. "Ha, barely. You're so soft now."

"What happened?"

Adrienne was matter-of-fact: "This new dealer tried to short me." Chiara started to ask more questions, but Adrienne waved her away. "It's fine. I'm fine. He didn't know we took a self-defense class in juvie."

Adrienne did a few shadowboxing moves. Chiara smiled despite herself.

"So, what's up? I got up early for this," Adrienne said as she dumped five spoons of sugar into her coffee.

"It's two p.m.," Chiara said with an arched eyebrow.

"Like I said."

Chiara took a deep breath. "I have to tell you something. I know you never understood our relationship, but we—"

Adrienne cut in with a wave of relief. "You're getting divorced? Thank God, that guy is such a drip. You are not that suburban wife he wants. Dear Husband has got to go. And you? You need to get back out there. People miss you, Chi. Our friends miss you. I was at a party last night—well, this morning, really—and everyone was saying, 'Where's Chi! Where's Chi!' Oh man. When I told them you were living in Walnut Creek? In a gated community? No one believed me. Time to get you out! Back to real life! I can borrow Carlos's truck and get your shit today."

"We're not getting divorced. We're having a baby. Twins, actually."

Adrienne couldn't hide her absolute shock, followed by a flush of anger. Her mood darkened on a dime, like only an addict's could. "Are you serious? With that guy?"

"Yes. He's not who you think."

Adrienne dismissed this. "He's exactly who I think."

Uncharacteristically, Chiara pushed back. "You never gave him a second of a chance."

But before Chiara could launch any kind of argument, Adrienne was mentally gone. She tried to flag the waitress, barking, "Check, please!" but was ignored.

Adrienne reached into her pocket and pulled out a crumpled twenty bucks. "Here you go. Call it a baby shower gift."

And at that, Adrienne had left.

Except, she hadn't really.

She'd stood outside the diner in the shaded end of the parking lot. From behind a large delivery truck, she watched as Chiara sat alone in the booth for a long time. Adrienne was crying a bit, and she wanted to see Chiara cry, too, to know that this was just as painful for her. But Chiara didn't cry. She quietly finished her coffee and politely declined the waitress's offer of a refill. No big drama. No hysterics or coming after Adrienne. After a while, Chiara calmly got up, went to her car, and drove home.

To this day Adrienne couldn't move beyond Chiara's face: a mix of resignation and a complete lack of surprise. She had expected to see fear on Chiara's face, fear that this was the end of their bond, a mirror to Adrienne's own fear. Instead, she saw Chiara's sorrow that her sister wasn't happy for her to become a mother, which had always been Chiara's most earnest and guarded wish.

Adrienne wanted to blame Chiara for leaving her behind, but she knew that was only half of it. Maybe not even half. She had pushed Chiara away as hard as she could, even when Chiara came back again and again.

In truth, the spat in the coffee shop was just the newest version of an argument they had been having for years. And when Adrienne was really honest with herself, she felt like she had been having the same arguments over and over again with everyone. Fighting with DH. Fighting with friends. Hell, fights she had with herself in her own head. She was stuck in her own loop, and the record of her thoughts couldn't pop out of the scratch and into a new groove.

She had been jealous. She had watched her sister slowly build a perfect family life, and Adrienne was angry that she wasn't the center of Chiara's world anymore. That was the horrid truth. Her own ego had pushed Chiara away and into this mega-mommy world.

As the din of the diner memory faded back into the dial tone, she heard something else: stressed voices. Instead of worried, Adrienne was relieved to have something external to focus her attention on.

Adrienne followed the voices to a beautiful living room off the entryway. Six large four-pane windows with gauzy white curtains lined one wall, creating a perfect view of the rest of the property. Overstuffed couches in dark-caramel leather faced a tall brick fireplace that was stacked with unlit cedar. Either side of the fireplace was framed with built-in shelving in a luxurious navy blue, picture lamps highlighting perfectly chosen items—a Nambé vase, a sepia portrait of someone's great-grandmother, a tiny oil painting of the landscape outside. Corners of the room that would have been left to collect dust in other homes had been transformed into cozy reading nooks with special loungers and lamps, or perfect spots for board games on inlaid custom-wood tables. Family photographs—some posed, some candid—lined the creamy-colored walls above the country-style wainscoting. This wasn't a showroom. This was truly a room to live in and feel like part of a family.

According to the little banner over the french doors, this was Opal's seminar on WHAT'S NEXT, MAMA! TREND FORECASTING FOR NEXT YEAR. It was an Elite Level event, so the group was extremely small. Twenty women only. These were the hard-core followers who'd shelled out the $10,000 to be in this room.

However, they didn't sound like die-hard fans. They sounded like restless troops who wouldn't be bought off with a shitty gift in the main tent.

Adrienne snuck into the room, hiding behind a tight cluster of frantic moms. Within seconds, she saw a major crack in the Mom Squad armor that had only been visible at the edges of the larger group events.

Opal was digging deep for her best rabble-rousing tone. "We all know the mom-influencer world is changing—"

A panicked mom cut her off. "Yeah, no kidding. We have banked our lives—our children's futures—on this income. If one more brand drops me? Could mean the end of private school! And what the hell is a Reel?"

Another mom, who was vibrating from stress, jumped in. "I have literal nightmares about the algo now. It murders me in my sleep. Ones and zeros smothering me until I choke!"

Opal was still hoping to regain control. "I have heard your very valid concerns. I have read your DMs and your comments. That's why we are here. If *we* pick the trends together, the algorithm will choose *us*."

Another voice from the back called out, "But how can you know? How can you predict?"

Opal pivoted to Capital S *Strategy*, all her corporate Fortune 500 skills coming out. "It's all about finding the most authentic version of yourself and your family. What speaks to you is what will work."

But this did not land. The panicked mom was at her wit's end. "None of that means anything! We paid to be here so we can know what to do. No more buzzword bullshit. What do we *do*?"

Opal's voice was soothing, calm, strong, but her shaky hands betrayed her anxiousness, and there was a sheen of sweat across her forehead. "You can build a local community outside of social media. Try asking nearby restaurants to sponsor you. That's what Ashleigh did."

Another woman, who was clearly on the edge of a nervous breakdown, shrieked, "*Her husband owns a professional basketball team! Those restaurants are in the arena!* What about those of us who are just moms and not secretly also rich?"

The room was unruly, and people started yelling out their fears.

A mom with too-thick bangs shouted from the back, "My kids are teens now. They don't want to be in my posts anymore. What do I do? They are *my brand*."

Another mom practically bawled, "If I renovate my house again, my husband said he's taking the kids. But shiplap is *so out*."

Another mom was on the verge of tears. "Everyone said TikTok is the new Instagram—I cannot go on TikTok! Gen Z made fun of my side part! But I don't have the bone structure for a middle part!" At this, she fully broke down into the arms of the woman next to her.

Opal said, "Yes, engagement is down. But that's okay. People were just getting back into school. Once the holidays start up—"

She couldn't even finish her sentence before a midwestern mom yelled, "I did a whole back-to-school series, and nothing! Why isn't this working anymore?"

Opal was grasping now: "Maybe it's time to branch out?"

An angry voice cut in from the side, "Oh, are you starting your pyramid scheme again?"

A quiet hush came over the room. This was like yelling the emperor had no clothes, but instead of just yelling it, they'd also put it on a blimp to fly over the emperor's house on his birthday for twelve hours and drop water balloons. Opal was silent, unable to mount any response.

It struck Adrienne that what the Mom Squad was really selling—beneath the art projects and the holiday magic—was something altogether more nebulous, and therefore more pernicious. They were modeling how to grift. The product wasn't what they were "Linking In Bio"; the product was the moms in this room, the moms in their follower count who dedicated their lives and their dollars to emulating the perfect Instagrammable moment. The Squad was selling these moms to the corporations and keeping every penny for themselves. These regular moms not being able to make a dime wasn't a bug—it was a feature of their own unwitting self-exploitation. They couldn't hear the subtext of *Find your own scam, this one is all ours*. The mothers' failure to understand that, and their failure to build a brand, only exalted and proved the unique worthiness of the few who could. Namely, the Mom Squad.

Finally, Thea stood and took the reins. "Whoa, whoa, whoa, Mini Moms. Money should never motivate you. This is about coMOMunity. And our coMOMunity can handle anything! We have hand-sewn costumes. We have made head lice fun. We navigated Racially Sensitive Thanksgiving. We will get through this. Together. No matter what."

Adrienne couldn't tell if this was the ultimate spin or if Thea really believed that this wasn't about money. Because if Thea really believed that, then she had surrounded her mommy utopia with opportunists. She was promising deliverance, and instead was delivering marks to the schemers. Worst of all, she didn't even see it.

Thea took the hands of a couple of moms in the front row. "I hear your stress. It makes sense that you are feeling this way, and I am so sorry that I cannot solve that for you. I don't want anyone to feel like they are being left behind. What I think we all need is more emotional support from each other." This was met with sincere gratitude from the group. "Let's break into smaller groups and talk about our fears. Let's be there for each other. Maybe we will find solutions to the social media machine. Maybe we won't. But if you leave here feeling loved, and seen? That is what I want more than anything."

Thea's words were like a balm. It was if the air in the room changed. The energy went from frantic to comfortable in seconds. Unlike Opal, she wasn't offering shaky promises or half-baked media speak. She was tangibly committing to caring about them and their children. The emotional connection was the only reward that mattered.

Adrienne knew she couldn't hide in the small-group format, so as the rest of the Elite Moms coalesced, she used the movement to back away toward the foyer. As she did, Adrienne saw something on the flat-screen behind Thea: a photo from the last summit. A row of women, all wearing the same perfect Fourth of July palette.

And there, in the middle, was Chiara. Smiling, happy, alive.

And just as quickly, the photo swiped away, the slideshow moved on and jolted Adrienne back into herself. She needed that photo to figure out who'd talked to Chiara last year, and to find out if they were here this year. Instead of leaving Thea's house as she had planned, Adrienne quietly backed into the front hall and looked for somewhere to hide until Opal's event ended. She ducked into a hall closet and left the door cracked so she could see when the living room emptied. She took a deep breath to settle herself and was once again hit with a beautiful scent.

Was that cedar? And maybe some juniper? Whatever it was, it smelled good as hell, and Adrienne leaned into the fragrance, which seemed to waft from every corner of the dim closet.

The stark difference between the easy-breezy wine tent with no Mom Squad and the searing intensity of Opal's event churned in Adrienne's mind. Just being near the Mom Squad seemed to make every woman here unhinged, even when the Squad was doing their best to be helpful or supportive. Actually, *especially* when they were trying to be helpful and supportive.

But Thea was the opposite. She so easily soothed their frayed nerves.

Was Thea just a sheep, too? That seemed impossible, considering all that she had accomplished. Perhaps, instead, she was the ultimate shepherd of the coMOMunity, above even the border collies of her Squad. And if that was the case, then maybe, if the right moment came, Thea could be Adrienne's ultimate ally in finding out what happened to Chiara.

Twenty minutes later the event wrapped up. Adrienne didn't hear any resolutions, but the women seemed calmer now as they exited out the front door (black, brass fixtures, modernist pendant light above).

A little Halloween tableau was set in the doorframe, and as every woman passed by, a tiny motion-sensor-activated witch yelled, *"Have a spook-tacular day! Have a spook-tacular day! Have a spook-tacular day!"* over and over.

Adrienne gave it a few more minutes until she felt sure the living room was empty of any stragglers hoping for more guidance. She heard nothing, only her own muted breathing. The coast was clear.

Adrienne gently pushed open the closet door and it let out a heavy, reverberating creak. She grimaced but thought it was okay, until she heard another door in the hallway open.

What the hell? She had been sure the house was empty. Or was that the front door? Had someone been just out of sight on the porch?

Then her fear spiked as she heard steps coming down the entryway, followed by "*Have a spook-tacular day! Have a spook-tacular day! Have a spook-tac—*"

Adrienne heard the cord get ripped out of the wall, cutting the witch off midsentence. She stopped moving and stopped breathing.

The footsteps moved quietly along the hallway, opening the office door, then the living room doors.

The steps were coming toward her.

Closer. Closer.

Adrienne saw the shadow cast from two feet move under the door. Whoever was out there was on the other side of the door, inches from Adrienne's own face.

Adrienne covered her mouth to muffle her breath as the knob started to pull forward. She leaned back, trying to hide in the coats. She had less than a second before she was found out.

Then a cell phone started ringing in another room. Based on how the sound seemed to be echoing off the hard surfaces, it had to be ringing in the kitchen.

Tamarind answered her cell as she entered the front hall full-steam.

"What?" Tamarind snapped.

Whomever had been about to open Adrienne's closet hustled out the back door, unseen by Tamarind, who was clearly pissed. Adrienne let out a sigh of relief.

Tamarind was still huffing into the phone. "Oh my God! I told you, only call me if it is about *me*. None of what you're talking about applies to *me*. So I'm hanging up. Goodbye! *Mommy is busy. Ask Daddy. Call the nanny; that's what I pay her for. Goodbye.*" She hung up. "Ugh. Brats."

Adrienne watched through the crack in the door as Tamarind physically shook off the call, tightened her ponytail, and slapped on a fake smile. Then she exited out the front door.

Adrienne waited twice as long as she had before; then, finally, she lifted the door in its hinges and slowly, silently opened it.

She quickly crossed the foyer, made her way back into the living room, and found the computer that was hooked up to the projector tucked into the tasteful reading nook. She awakened the screen, but the laptop was locked. She tried a couple of passwords—nothing. Not knowing whose computer it was meant no context clues to go off of. And even if she had known whose laptop it was, she couldn't keep the fleet of children shared by the Mom Squad straight, so even the most fruitful area of possible passwords was a blur.

Just then, the door opened. It was Opal, yelling over her shoulder, "Yes, I'll grab it." When she saw Adrienne at the computer, she stopped short. "Do you need something?"

Adrienne found the quickest lie she could: "I just really wanted to check my email."

Opal wasn't amused and wasn't hiding it, "That's my private laptop. Besides, no phones, no email, no posting."

Adrienne knew her time was limited, so she may as well try to get the information she wanted. "Who made the slideshow from earlier? It was really good."

Opal was willing to answer, but her suspicion was still high. "There was an app last year that aggregated photos. I really can't say who took what."

Tamarind bounced in, her ponytail still impossibly full and her butt impossibly high. "Hey, Opal, where did you—" She clocked the tension in the room. "What's up?"

"Nothing," Opal replied quickly, which struck Adrienne as weird. Was Opal covering for Adrienne or for herself?

The slideshow was still going. A photo came onto the projector screen. A dead tree split by lightning, with the sunset coming through its charred branches. It was a perfectly nice photo. Nothing particularly notable. It could have passed without notice, but Tamarind and Opal shared a panicked glance and then slammed the laptop shut.

Their outsize reaction got Adrienne's attention. What was up with these two? First the blackmail files, and now this?

Instead of shutting off the slideshow, closing the program midstream froze the photo of the tree on the screen, half-dissolved but still recognizable. As Tamarind and Opal scrambled, Adrienne stared at it, committing as much to memory as she could.

Finally, Opal pulled the wall plug on the projector. The screen went blank. Adrienne tried to make her face blank as well, to act as if she didn't feel the electricity in the air.

Opal and Tamarind refocused their attention to Adrienne.

Opal wasn't acting nice at all now. "Touching people's private things is a violation of CoMOMunity Guidelines."

"We have to respect each other. Otherwise, our sisterhood of motherhood falls apart," Tamarind agreed.

Opal narrowed her eyes and pulled out her iPad. "Which cabin are you in, again?"

Adrienne opened her mouth, but before any lie came—BAM! The door opened!

Bernice busted in, carrying two bottles of wine, comically stumbling. "OMG! This isn't the bathroom, Ade!"

Adrienne caught on immediately and went full loosey-goosey. "Ohhhh myyyy God. I literally forgot what I was doing!"

Bernice doubled over in a laugh. "Did you not even pee? Ha! Someone needs to slow down on the mommy juice!"

Opal and Tamarind weren't quite buying the drunk-mom routine.

Bernice added another layer to her act. "Wait. Holy cannoli. Tamarind? Opal? You two changed my life!" She bounded forward and gave them both really bouncy hugs that they visibly did not enjoy. "Tamarind, your 'Smoothie to Smoother Thirty-Day Slim-Down Plan' is what got me back in my jeans."

Tamarind took the bait, hook, line, and sinker. "It was one of my most popular Reels. I still get DMs about it."

One down, one to go. Bernice turned to Opal. "And, Opal—the in-app purchase auto coupon finder?"

Opal smirked. "Pretty great, right?"

Bernice waved her arms like a cheerleader trying to signal a rescue plane. "I save two hundred a month."

Adrienne joined in. "Me too."

Bernice turned to Adrienne, and back to fake-buzzed. "Did you try to check your work email again, dork?"

Adrienne put on a sheepish smile. "Maybe."

Bernice laughed. "You are the worst! Guys, tell her she's the worst! But you know, Opal, Tamarind, I am so glad we met, because I really think we could be friends! Like, IRL. Are you ever in Salt Lake? Because, Opal, my book club would absolutely die to have you join! Tamarind, you could lead our pickleball league!"

At this transition from fangirl to clinger, Opal was done with her nonsense. "All right, ladies. Let's go. This is Thea's house. No email, and use the bathrooms in your cabins, please."

As Opal shooed them out, Tamarind called after to Bernice, "Look for my next slim-down plan next month!"

Chapter 15

Mom-Fession

Adrienne and Bernice were still buzzing from their escape as they joined the big tent event that was about to begin. At that moment, Adrienne believed in safety in numbers.

The workstations from McKenna's family-scarecrow event had been pushed to the sides, and each "family" had been posed on the worktables in various tableaux of spooky harmony. It gave the unsettling impression of many more eyes in the room, including those of children, every orange face teetering between witness and judge. Adrienne guided Bernice to seats toward the front, where she could ignore the rows of pumpkins leering at her.

Adrienne asked Bernice, "How did you know to come into Thea's house to find me?"

Bernice gave a little shrug. "I guess when the Elite Moms left but you didn't come out, I felt like maybe something was wrong! Did you get in touch with the police?"

Adrienne shook her head. "But I think I found something more important. This weird tree came up, and both Opal and Tamarind flipped out—practically ripped the projector out of the wall."

"Why?"

Adrienne shrugged. "I don't know. But their reaction makes me think something important happened there. It was a dead tree—split down the middle. Seemed like it was just outside of an oak grove. Do you know where it is on the property?"

Bernice thought for a second, then said, "There's only the one oak grove, by the ropes course."

Adrienne was excited. She had been worried that there could be dozens of groves anywhere on the two-thousand-acre ranch. But before Adrienne could ask more, the Mom Squad came out onto the stage to applause. Then Thea came out, and Adrienne's whispers were drowned out by the Beatlemania-level insanity going on around her.

While the Squad took their spots on the stage, Thea came down to walk among the crowd. This wasn't the Energizer Bunny talk-show-host arrival Adrienne was used to. Thea was more like the bride working the room of her wedding while the band directed people to dance the Macarena. She gave people hugs, checked in with returning moms, and genuinely seemed to want to connect with every woman there. She remembered people's names, their kids' names, their dog's names, and even a couple of hometowns. After a few minutes of this, Thea found an open seat in the middle of the room and asked a shocked woman if she could sit next to her. Then she turned her attention to the stage, a signal that everyone else should do the same. The message was clear: She was one of them. They were just like her.

Opal had the mic and was back to her cool, calm, collected self. "Okay Mini Moms. It's the time we all look forward to. Or dread. It's . . . #MomFession time."

Opal pressed the remote, and the words *#MOMFession* came up on the screen.

Ashleigh held her microphone close and spoke with the tone of a campfire ghost story. "Motherhood isn't perfect. We need a safe space where we can share our worst motherhood moments."

McKenna touched her heart. "Let's get it out here and not on Instagram. No one likes a messy post. It brings us all down."

Ashleigh walked out into the audience. "But it's hard to share. So I think breaking the ice with a speed round is the way to go. Would anyone like to line up? Share in one sentence how they failed this year?"

A group of women sheepishly lined up on the stage.

Adrienne muttered under her breath, "Jesus, this is just like AA."

Yogini Mom from the ropes course was full of sadness. "I had a C-section."

A tall athletic mom with a quavering lip. "I couldn't breastfeed."

A high-strung mom stammered, "I—I had to go back to work . . ." She collapsed into heaving sobs. "And I liked it!"

Each of these revelations was followed by intense support from everyone, and intense eye rolls from Adrienne that she could barely hide. Correction: AA was way better than this.

Ashleigh looked deeply into the crowd. "Wow, everyone. That was a beautiful speed round. Way to get us started. Let's really dig in."

Adrienne couldn't take much more of this, and then realized . . . with everyone in here, this was the perfect time to move around the property unseen. As she started to stand up, she leaned over to Bernice. "Hey, I'm gonna check out the oak grove."

But before Adrienne could even stand upright, a microphone was shoved in front of her face.

Tamarind was there, her eyes hungry. "All right, mom. Time to confess."

The entire room turned their eyes to Adrienne. Adrienne almost tipped over, she was so surprised to be put on the spot. "Oh. No. I really can't."

Ashleigh responded from stage, "You must."

Opal stood next to Ashleigh. "Confessing is how we build trust. Don't you trust us?"

There was no way for her to know for sure, but singling Adrienne out so publicly felt like payback for being on Opal's laptop. Adrienne looked to Bernice. She expected solidarity. She expected Bernice to agree this was insane. A step too far in the ruse. Instead, Bernice's face was pleading. Pleading for Adrienne to say anything to keep up the charade. Because if Adrienne went down, Bernice was tied to her now, and would go down, too.

Adrienne took Tamarind's microphone in her sweaty hand and thought for a second. What on earth could she say that would convince these women that she was one of them? She had never even changed a diaper, let alone raised a child. How was she going to make up a story on the fly that didn't expose her immediately as a fraud?

Then it came to her, stomach churning in its obviousness.

"My worst motherhood moment. Um, wow. How can one even pick? Okay, well. A couple months after my twins were born, my husband and I really needed a break."

As Adrienne retold the story, she remembered the night this all happened. Except it wasn't her and her twins, obviously. It was Chiara.

The story may have been skewed, but the emotions Adrienne was feeling were all way too real. "I didn't feel comfortable with some random person looking after my babies." (This got a murmur of understanding from the group. Strangers equal *bad.*) "So I asked my"—she didn't want to say *sister*—"cousin to come."

Adrienne had arrived at Chiara's house for babysitting duties. She clocked Chiara and her husband exchanging a tentative look as Adrienne shooed them out the door to their date.

Adrienne continued, "My husband wasn't sure. But I told him it was fine. My cousin was a little wild, but she would never put our babies at risk." She took a deep breath. "But when we got home, my cousin was drunk. Passed out, actually. My husband was so mad. But I was madder."

When Adrienne had come to on the couch, Chiara was screaming at her. She had never seen Chiara like that.

"The babies were fine—we had put them to bed before we left. They didn't even know we were gone. I needed a break so bad. I was really at my wit's end; I just needed one night to be myself again." These were the exact words Chiara had been screaming as Adrienne feebly tried to defend herself. The intense regret came back in hot, sickening waves. "And in my desperation, I had trusted her. Over the father of my children. Over my own instincts. I had trusted her. And she broke that trust."

Ashleigh asked, "Did she ever apologize?"

Adrienne shook her head. "No. She never did."

McKenna's anger soaked her voice. "How dare she. How dare she threaten your children."

Adrienne backed off a bit. "I think *threaten* is a strong word."

Moms from the crowd chimed in:

"No it's not."

"I would have called the cops."

"I would have killed her."

Ashleigh looked directly into Adrienne's eyes. "You learned a valuable lesson: you can't trust her."

Adrienne felt bile rise in the corners of her throat. This was true. Chiara had given her so many chances to show up, and Adrienne failed every time. Even these strangers knew it.

Opal said from the stage, "Thank you for your share. Next . . . ?"

Tamarind took the microphone from Adrienne and handed it to Bernice.

Bernice was quiet for a moment. Already near tears, her voice was unsteady when she started. "It's not a moment so much as . . . There are days when I am just so angry. When I got pregnant it felt like my life dissolved in front of my eyes. My job, my projects—I was suddenly invisible. Everyone saw me as this liability. Like they just wished I would hurry up and disappear. That any need I had to try to stay myself, to keep my job, was a burden. The smallest accommodation for me was outrageous. They didn't force me out so much as they made it impossible for me to stay a full person. I was happy to be pregnant. I am happy to be a mother. But I am also so, so angry. I am so angry that I had to slink away from my own life, my own dreams, in order to make this life work in any way."

Adrienne looked around. She expected judgment from the other mothers. But instead, all she saw was recognition. And that unsettled her more.

Bernice was in it now; there was no turning back. And the more she talked, the stronger her voice got. "And now, there's nowhere for me to put that anger. So I carry it around all day. Until it explodes. And who does it explode at? My kids. My innocent kids. My voice just booms out, and I hear it—so harsh. And their little faces are so scared, and they get so, so quiet. And I feel awful. But it's also the only moment of release I get. And the only silence I get—after I explode.

"I want to break. I keep waiting to just *crack*. But I don't. Because if I crack, I will just have to clean up that mess, too. So I keep bending, and bending, and *bending more*. Until I don't even feel human anymore. I don't have a personality. I have to-do lists that if I don't do them, no one does them. I have a fix-it list. I have a shopping list. I have a school list. I am no longer a person; I am just a series of tasks. I love my kids, but that doesn't suddenly make me a good mother every single second. I want to go somewhere and not be asked for a single thing for a *year*. A *year of silence. That is all I want.* I'm already *all alone*. Now I want to actually be alone before I bend one millimeter more. I want to crack open and let this rage out once and for all. Otherwise, I think my rage might eat me alive . . . eat me alive from the inside out."

Bernice stopped talking, and suddenly it was like she came back to herself. Shame seemed to wash over her, and she recoiled from her honesty.

There were several minutes of tense silence.

Then Thea stood up. She was in the dead center of the room, the dead center of everyone. "I need to know: Who feels rage?"

Silently, slowly, tentatively, every single hand went up.

The Squad on the stage took in the sea of hands. None of them looked surprised. They'd expected this.

McKenna was solemn. "Hold it. Own it. It's yours."

"The threats to our family come from all sides," Ashleigh agreed.

Tamarind nodded. "And that rage is natural."

McKenna replied, "It's there to protect our children."

Opal took McKenna's hand. "Our rage is beautiful."

Thea let the silence hang for a few more seconds. The only sound was the slight breeze outside rustling the tent, pulling with it a tumble of dried leaves like strung-up tin cans after a honeymoon car. Then Thea spoke again, but with force. "We need to let the rage out. Otherwise, this mom is right: It will eat us alive. It will make us turn on each other. We need to get this rage out, here, now, where we are safe. Where no one is judging us."

She walked over to McKenna's workstation and rummaged through the drawer until she found a giant pair of scissors. She then started to cut off all the ties that held the walls of the tent up. Within a minute the entire side of the tent had fallen to the ground. The moonlight spilled in. The dust swirled up.

Thea walked out into the moonlight and screamed.

Really fucking screamed.

Not some teen girl in a slasher movie, high pitched and scared.

A scream of bottomless venomous anger.

She turned back to the tent, and somehow, in near unison, the entire summit rose to join her in the field.

And they all started screaming.

They screamed into the night.

They screamed into each other's faces.

They screamed into the dirt.

Adrienne followed them out but moved toward the side. She couldn't see who it was, but someone grabbed one of the husband scarecrows and dragged him to the center. They kicked off the pumpkin head and stomped on it. The pieces of the shattered smile were obliterated as more women ran up to crush every recognizable part of him. Then other moms grabbed the arms and legs and ripped the body apart. They swung the pieces around their heads as they screamed even more.

Then another scarecrow husband was dragged to the center and destroyed. Then another. Then another.

The heads were removed, and the stampede to smash them was vigorous. The bodies were ripped apart faster and faster, into smaller and smaller pieces.

When the scarecrow husbands had been reduced to nothing, the mothers started on the scarecrow versions of themselves. They pulled the clothes off and dressed in the straw-lined shirts. They held their pumpkin self-portraits overhead and howled into them like they were ancient horns, their voices warped in the spheres and shot back out, broken and deep.

But the children scarecrows they left. Those stayed pristine. Rows and rows of fake little children watching their mommies lose their minds in the night. Watching their mommies destroy their unhelpful husbands. Watching their mommies turn their own effigies into a call to action. Hundreds of tiny hollow eyes witnessing a mass unraveling.

Suddenly, Adrienne saw the mothers clearly for the very first time: a group of women pushed so far beyond any breaking point that their fury had no end. She saw their plastered smiles as the tiniest veneer that kept them from violence.

And Adrienne was scared.

In pure animal instinct for self-preservation, she shrank, backing away slowly until she was hidden by a few trees. Years of sketchy drug deals, trips to juvie, junkie second locations—none of those felt as scary as this moment. This rabid pack of Invisalign-wearing Pinterest-crafting Dyson-devoted psychos. These were people who hadn't interacted with wider society in so long that the only rules that counted were the ones they chose. And right now, they chose obliteration.

So Adrienne made the only logical choice she could.

She fucking ran.

Chapter 16

The Car

Adrienne sprinted into her cabin and locked the door behind her. Her breath was ragged from the all-out sprint. She'd just gone from no suspects to every person here was capable of legitimate harm.

She took deep breaths. After a few minutes she peeked out the window. No one had followed her. She was safe.

Adrienne looked at the map of the summit, then looked at the satellite Google Map she had printed out before she came. She circled her cabin and then drew a long line to the ropes course, and more specifically to the oak grove behind it.

She would wait until the middle of the night and then explore when the rest of the summit was asleep, or too drunk to be aware of their surroundings.

After an hour Adrienne started to feel antsy in her little cabin. She needed to steady her nerves and get some fresh air to stay awake. She stepped out onto her tiny stoop to smoke a pre-rolled joint (California Sober). This weekend was bringing up too much shit, and she was struggling to hold it together. But she had to for one more night, and this emergency weed was just the ticket. Heavy on the CBD, low on the THC, she just needed to take the edge off without undercutting her adrenaline completely. The first hit filled her lungs, and she thought, with a laugh, that it was the first deep breath she had taken since she'd arrived. But before she could enjoy it, Adrienne saw Thea. Alone. No Mom Squad in sight. Walking straight toward her.

Thea waved to Adrienne. "I've been looking for you."

Adrienne's stomach dropped.

Thea smiled. "I always introduce myself to new moms. I'm Thea." Adrienne tried to hide her joint, but Thea pointed directly at it. "Do you mind if I . . . ?"

Adrienne was shocked. "Um, of course. Sure. It's your house."

Thea hit the joint like a goddamn pro and, on the inhale, said, "Oh, I don't live here." Long exhale. "I mean, I own it. But this is my stage house. All the TikTok renovations are done here. Instagram family photos. My real house, I don't post anymore."

Adrienne was struggling to make sense of this. "Doesn't that hurt the brand?"

Thea eyed Adrienne. "Why, are you gonna tell them?"

"Definitely not."

"Smart. They'd rip you limb from limb."

Adrienne's eyes practically bugged out in shock. Considering what she had just seen, Thea's joke felt more than a little dangerous.

Thea was matter-of-fact. "You haven't heard? Motherhood makes you insane." She cracked a truly irresistible smile.

Holy shit, was this woman actually . . . cool?

Adrienne felt the tension leave her body. "Okay, so it's not just me."

Thea replied, "No way. Insanity is the only sane reaction to motherhood. You make these tiny precious people, and you love them so much you could die from happiness. You would eat poison to keep them from knowing how hard the world is. So you protect them. Like a good mother. But not too much. You also have to push them into the world. Into the *hard*. Otherwise, you're a bad mother. It doesn't matter what you do, you're doing it wrong. Women are demonized for caring for their children. And they are demonized for not caring for their children. It's torture. You just have to pick the judgment and the failure that is the most acceptable to you."

Adrienne reflected on this. "I hadn't thought about it that way." Seriously. She hadn't. She was seeing this whole thing in a new light. She wasn't a mother now and hoped to never be one. Having her own mother was traumatic enough, and she felt no need to dip her toe back into that deadly current. However, this position had also kept her from ever considering the true interior life of mothers in general, and of Chiara specifically. She added it to the long list of reasons to hate herself.

Thea misread her face as a rebuke of the coMOMunity. She leaned back onto the porch post, "Look, I know this coMOMunity-summit stuff can all seem a little nuts at first. But stay-at-home mothers are a force of nature. And it's specifically because of that that they're preyed upon. Our desire to work, to have money, to keep a sense of our identity, *and* care for our children? It all gets weaponized against us. How many moms do you know that have a cabinet full of essential oils they were supposed to sell? How many got sucked into selling those ugly leggings? Don't even get me started on Mary Kay. The whole world disappeared under our feet, but a pandemic was no excuse for moms. In fact, we were told it was an *opportunity*! For us to do *more. More, more, more.* Always more. I care about these women because they deserve to care for their babies without feeling guilty. Without thinking that being a mother means losing yourself."

Adrienne couldn't help herself; she had to resist Thea a bit longer, push back a bit more. Taking shit on face value wasn't really in her wheelhouse. "And you think posting photos of your bathroom renovation does that?"

"Oh, it doesn't matter what I post," Thea replied. "What people don't get about what I do is that I just look at these women who have become invisible and say, 'I see you.' I reflect back to them their own lives and say, 'I value you, and I value what you do every single day to make your family work.' After being ignored, nothing is more powerful than being really truly seen. They have been told they don't matter, and I am saying to them, 'Yes you do.'"

Adrienne's emotional reaction to Thea's speech was unexpected and unwelcome. The knot in her throat tasted like guilt and regret. These were all the things Chiara had said and that Adrienne had dismissed as silly drama. Adrienne did her best to keep her voice from breaking. "Yes, my sister, she struggled"—she caught herself—"struggles with that all the time."

Thea looked at Adrienne with a deep kindness. "What do you struggle with?"

Adrienne was so tempted to tell Thea why she was really here, but she couldn't quite be that open. Not yet. Instead, she responded with "You know, that woman from earlier—Bernice—she's next door. She's really great. You shouldn't keep women away from you just because they can't afford the Elite Level shit."

Thea was taken aback, but then put it together. "Oh God, one of Opal's ideas, I'm sure. Thanks for the heads-up."

She passed the joint back to Adrienne.

As she walked away, Thea turned back. "My advice about your sister? Tell her she's doing great. Because she is."

Adrienne watched as Thea knocked on Bernice's door and asked to come in. Bernice was floored, and gave Adrienne an *OMG, is this really happening?* look. Adrienne gave her a thumbs-up.

A tiny win amid the shit show.

At long last, it was well nearly 2:00 a.m. Adrienne had dressed in all her darkest clothes and pulled her hair back. She had spent the previous hours sitting on the leather club chair just to the side of her one window, peering out from the edge of her sustainable-linen roman shade. It had been nearly an hour since she saw more than one or two women come back to their cabins for the night, so she hoped that the only people left awake and out on the grounds were the lushes, who wouldn't be looking for her anyway. It was time for her to find the tree that had scared Opal and Tamarind more than a pile of undisclosed gluten. She opened her cabin door and stepped out into the cold October air. The stars were bright, but a low mist had crept in from the unseen Pacific Ocean, blanketing the grass.

Adrienne moved slowly across the main-event areas. She didn't want to be seen, and enough moms were wine-drunk and still screaming Adele lyrics that she had to choose her route carefully to avoid colliding with them. Adrienne specifically recognized Hannah, Maya, Naomi, and Anya in the center of a particularly rowdy group.

The ropes course had taken on an eerie feel in the darkness and the mist. Everything creaked and swayed; logs made low thumps as they collided with each other. Shadows looked like people and then dissolved, only to bloom again in her periphery. Adrienne walked behind the perimeter of the tree line to stay hidden, but also because there were fewer shadows here, fewer things to make her head spin and for her eyes to give sinister intentions to.

She walked for easily forty-five minutes, growing bolder as her frustration rose. She pushed farther out from the tree line, spending less time in the cover of the oak grove. After making several arcs back and forth, she was far enough away from the cabins now that no one was nearby. Hell, she couldn't even hear Adele anymore.

Finally, Adrienne found the dead tree. It was exactly what she'd seen in the photo! No question, this was it! She had a moment of absolute triumph and then . . . an overwhelming feeling of disappointment.

So she found a tree. So what.

Suddenly, this all felt incredibly stupid.

Adrienne walked around it. Nothing of interest to see.

She pushed against it, but it didn't budge. No Pit of Despair hidden in its knots.

Adrienne kicked the tree, at first in the name of investigation, but then she kicked it again. And again. Then all her frustration erupted. She reached into her pocket and took out the mallet from the pumpkin-carving demo. She started beating on the tree. But it was not enough. She threw the mallet over her shoulder, and with her hands, she clawed at the tree like an animal.

The bark ripped under her nails. The wood dug into her palms, leaving splinters nearly an inch long. Dirt mixed with the sweat on her brow and dripped down, filling her eyes, every blink an agony. But she couldn't stop. The last year—Chiara, the unanswered texts, the Missing flyers, the dumb husband, Detective Bautista—it all boiled over, and this dead tree was her target.

She finally grabbed a big piece of the tree's outer ring and ripped it off.

She was sweaty, dirty, and her hands were bleeding. She crumpled to the ground, her rage turning to tears.

But before she could really let the tears go, something in the tree stump caught her eye—something that had been unseen before when the tree was intact.

Adrienne dug carefully, afraid to damage whatever it was. Finally, she unearthed a cracked Apple Watch. The strap was ripped and caked with dried blood.

Adrienne stared at it for a moment in disbelief. She felt like the walls were closing in around her. She knew that was impossible. She was outside, and there were no walls. But the sight of that watch compressed the air out of her chest, and her rib cage hurt from the force of her heart beating inside it.

This was Chiara's watch.

Adrienne ran back to her cabin and double-checked that she had locked the door. She pulled out her laptop, fumbled with a pile of cords from her bag, and after finally finding the right one, she charged up the Apple Watch.

At first, nothing happened; the watch face remained dark. Adrienne worried if it would even work anymore. Her mind spun—if it didn't work, what could she do? Perhaps there was a serial number she could have checked, or an Apple ID.

Then, like a goddamn miracle sent from on high / Palo Alto, the Apple Watch turned on.

It was confirmed: this was Chiara's!

Adrienne felt a weird confluence of emotions—triumph at finding some real proof and then sickened by what that watch was proof of: Chiara had never left here, and someone covered it up.

Adrienne steadied herself. If someone covered it up, maybe even with help from the Squad, then they may be back this year. She tried to think of who Chiara was with in that one photo. All she could remember was a row of blank, blond faces. Besides, in a few short hours, the vast majority of women would be leaving the summit. Elite passes only on the third day. It was clear: Adrienne needed to tell the police what she had found as soon as possible. Ideally before Thea's ranch emptied of 70 percent of the suspect pool.

She looked at the computer—no service, no Wi-Fi. She checked her phone. No service. No Wi-Fi.

Besides, Bautista didn't even know she was here.

She had to get off the property as quickly as possible and bring back help. She zipped the Apple Watch into the inside-breast pocket of her Vuori running jacket and grabbed her keys. No bag, as that could draw attention.

Adrienne walked briskly toward the parking area, keeping her head low. After the oak grove, the artificialness of the ranch was painful. The lights felt so bright, the fake boulders containing Wi-Fi speakers so obvious, the strange pumped-in smell acrid. She was relieved to be leaving this plastic kingdom. Adrienne found her car, but it was stacked in the parking lot, totally blocked in on every side.

She tried her cell phone again, but it still wouldn't work.

She turned around, looking for something, anything.

Then she saw a minivan at the front of the lot. It had a North Utah Knitters Club decal and one of those horrid stick-figure-family stickers on the back—a mom, dad, one older boy, and one set of younger twin boys.

It had to be Bernice's car!

She was so grateful to see her clear next step to freedom and safety. The time for casual was over, so Adrienne sprinted to Bernice's cabin and hammered on the door.

Bernice opened the door, groggy but ready for action, like all good moms. Hypervigilant even when sleeping.

"What's going on? Where did you go?"

"Bernice, Chiara was killed here, and I finally have proof."

Within seconds, Adrienne had caught her up.

Bernice asked the obvious question: "Did you call the police?"

Adrienne shook her head. "Phones are still out of service."

Bernice thought for a second. "Too risky to break into Thea's again. We could Instagram the Apple Watch? Put it up live so there's a record of what you found?"

"As soon as we went live, whoever the murderer is will know we know. And if they are still here, that puts us at risk. Besides, can't go live without a phone and service."

"Of course. Sorry. I've never been involved in a murder cover-up before."

Adrienne smirked. "No Pinterest board for getting blood off your hands?"

Bernice cracked a smile. "Honestly, there probably is."

They shared a tense laugh.

Adrienne knew this was their best and only bet. "I just need to physically go to the police. But my car is blocked in."

Bernice checked her own watch. "Sun will be up soon. Lower-tier moms are packing up; you could sneak out with them in a couple hours."

Adrienne shook her head. "I can't wait. I need Bautista to get here while everyone is still on the property. Can I use your car?"

"Absolutely. I'll drive. You keep trying the cell phone."

"Good idea. I think once we make it over that first ridge, we should have a signal from Ukiah."

Then they heard a noise and froze.

It was someone next door in Adrienne's cabin!

Bernice turned the lights off in her cabin as quickly and as quietly as she could. She grabbed her car keys and then looked to Adrienne to telegraph *What's next?*

Adrienne made a motion to Bernice to follow her. They crept into the bathroom and opened the window. Using the toilet for a boost, they snuck out of the window with the grace of two toddlers trying to climb up a slide. But they made it.

They pressed their backs to the cabin wall and slid away from the stranger still in Adrienne's cabin. Once they'd reached the end of the cabins, there was nothing but fifty yards of open space between them and the parking area. The horizon was turning from navy to gray, and in a few minutes the first rays of dawn would start to reach upward. There was no better time to go than right now. They took one second to get ready, and then they sprinted as fast as they could.

Bernice unlocked the minivan with the key fob, and the security beep ricocheted out in the dark like a cannon. Bernice hopped in the driver's seat and Adrienne took the passenger side.

Bernice pulled out and steered toward the gate, which stood wide open.

They were so close. They shared a look of relief—they were going to make it!

Then BAM!

Opal ran full-force into the side of Bernice's car, slamming her hands on Adrienne's window. Bernice and Adrienne shrieked.

"Get out of the fucking car!" Opal screamed through the glass, her breath fogging up the window with dots of spit.

Opal pulled at the door handle, and as the door opened, she curled her fingers around the frame. Adrienne tried to shut the door again but had to pull it several times, crushing Opal's fingers to get her to let go. Then she yanked it fully shut and locked it.

Adrienne yelled to Bernice, *"Go, go, go!"*

Bernice started to gun it, but the parking lot was tight quarters. She had to make two sharp turns to get on the main drive. Once the gate was directly ahead, she pushed the gas, but she accelerated too quickly and the gravel road made the car fishtail. Bernice slammed on the brakes, which only make the car skid more, and before she could course-correct, the van hit a ditch. The force wrenched the steering wheel from her hands, and she completely lost control of the car.

Adrienne felt a transition into slow motion.

Bernice's scream.

Opal's rage.

The car slamming into the stone pillar marking the edge of the gate.

The last thing Adrienne saw was the dashboard exploding into the airbag.

Then darkness.

Chapter 17

Hayward

Bautista was grateful her shift had been uneventful. After finally closing the Shaw case, she had no energy left for anything. She filed some things. She returned some calls. But the joy of the night shift was leaving messages on work voicemails and being long gone before anyone could call back.

Then Detective Colby, getting coffee by the window, called out across the bullpen, her nasal voice always too loud, "Bautista?"

"Yes?" she answered with a tone that said *Don't make this take long.* Colby had made detective three whole months before Bautista and as such she still liked to pull senior-officer rank. Bautista would normally play ball, but today she really didn't want to be dragged into one of Colby's asinine theories about the mini mall across the street being "a front for something."

"You have that case from last year, right?"

"I have a lot of cases from a lot of years, Colby."

"The mom who cut out on her kids."

"That's not what happened—but yes, that is my case. Gave the last bit of information to the husband a couple of hours ago."

"Hours?"

This conversation was already taking too long.

"That's what I said. Why?"

"Because he is still sitting in his parked car like a real creep."

This got Bautista's pure attention for the first time. "What? He's still here?"

Colby pointed through the window blinds with her coffee stirrer.

Bautista stood up and looked out the window. There he was, the sad, dazed husband. Except he wasn't dazed anymore. He seemed agitated, even from this distance.

Bautista sighed. "Jesus. What now."

Colby sniffed with self-importance. "Need me to help out?"

"If *help out* is code for *get out of your face*, then yes."

Colby forced out a casual "No doubt, no doubt."

From her sharp intake of breath, though, Bautista could tell Colby's ego was bruised and she would pay for her comment.

But that was a problem for later.

Bautista went back to her desk. She didn't have time to deal with the bereaved.

That's what Victim Services is for, she told herself as she settled back down in the too-small office chair with the bum wheel.

But every few minutes or so, she would push her chair back, that wheel squeaking something awful, and check if he was still there. He was there after one hour. Then two hours. Then three hours.

Bautista's curiosity was rising, but she resisted. She had just gotten that case off her desk!

At the end of her shift, the sun pushing up from just below the horizon, Bautista walked to her car. She had checked the visitor parking lot before she had left and was relieved to see the husband was finally gone.

As she pulled out, Bautista felt him before she saw him: Chiara's husband, waving his hands frantically, beckoning her to his car, which he had parked directly across from the officer parking lot. For a second, she considered ignoring him, but she knew that would be a short-term solution. She pulled over.

"Bautista, you have to see this," he said, his eyes wild.

"Sir, what are you still doing here? You should go home."

He shook his head vigorously. "No, no. The sitter's there. This is important. Come with me."

Bautista put on her most compassionate smile, but her teeth were clenched. "Sir, this case is closed now."

"You must come look," he said over his shoulder as he trotted ahead to his car.

Bautista relented, but when she tried to get in the passenger seat, he guided her to the driver's side.

"Please. Trust me," he pleaded.

When Bautista sat down behind the wheel, she didn't see anything particularly amazing. Just your basic midrange Toyota SUV, with the normal amount of kid detritus.

He saw her confusion and then pointed to his car visor. On it, he had clipped a little photo of the twin boys.

"Chiara had this printed for me. She was fanatical about it. She had one, too."

He took out the manila envelope Bautista had given him earlier and spread the photos of Chiara's car all over the dash, the center console, every flat surface he could reach. He lined up each image that showed the visor and, more importantly, that showed Chiara's photo of the babies still clipped to the car. "She would never leave that photo in the car. Never. She took it with her everywhere."

Bautista couldn't follow. "Okay. What exactly are you saying that means?"

Chiara's husband was full of energy now, no longer the docile child from earlier. "I'm saying, she didn't leave the car on her own."

Bautista felt her plan of going home and taking a hot bath evaporate, and she was right. She was exhausted; this family exhausted her. "I believe you, but people who have just driven off a ravine do not act logically. And I really think we need to take your wife's mental state into consideration. By your own account, she wasn't well. What was her last text to you? *A bird can love a fish, but I'm a dirtbag,* something like that?"

Chiara's husband slammed his hands down on the hood of the car. "You aren't listening to me!"

Bautista wasn't rattled, but she was at the end of her patience. She had tried several times to end the conversation nicely, so now it was time to leave the car and not look back.

As Bautista made her move to exit, the husband physically blocked her way.

"Sir, please move," Bautista said through her now visibly gritted teeth, the compassionate smile gone.

"No!" he said, spreading his arms wide. "I'll get arrested if I have to. Arrest me!" he yelled to no one in particular. "Arrest me so you have to listen to me! We have to go there. We have to go to the ranch! Something went horribly wrong there!"

Bautista circled back to her original canned response: "Sir, I want to help you, but we can't demand to search private property based on a photo on a visor. No judge will approve that warrant."

There was a *ping* sound. He looked at his phone, and his jaw dropped. "Oh my God."

Bautista couldn't help herself. "What?"

"If Chiara left that summit in one piece, then why did her Apple Watch just turn on at the McCorckle ranch?"

He held out his phone, showing her the device-locator app and the pulsing dot in the center of Thea's ranch.

Bautista's eyes nearly slid out of her head. "Holy shit."

"There's more. Adrienne is there."

Bautista's brain racked focus, and suddenly she had one more question that she needed answered. "Follow me."

She walked full-steam toward the office with Chiara's husband hot on her heels. As they entered the building, Jarvis was heading out.

"See you tomorrow, boss."

"Jarvis, get in here."

Jarvis's mood lifted. "Are we doing this? Yes! Partners!"

Bautista shot her a look only half as withering as normal. "Shut up before I change my mind."

Jarvis nodded with faux solemnity. "Copy that. So, what's up?"

"Your cousin—he said they found the car yesterday."

"Yes."

"And three other cars had been found down there already?"

"Yes."

"When was the last car found there?"

Jarvis gasped and went to her notepad. She flipped through the tiny pages for what seemed like an hour but was only seconds. "The last car was found there in December."

"If a car was found there in the exact same spot in December, how did Chiara's car from the *previous June* time-jump to now?"

It was the husband's turn to answer. "Unless someone put it there recently."

Bautista cracked a smile. "Did Adrienne say that?"

He smiled back. "You know she did."

There was only one way forward, and that required a warrant.

"Jarvis, find us a judge."

Chapter 18

I'd Rather Be Dead

Adrienne couldn't open her eyes. She would send the thought to her lids, but they wouldn't budge. She tried to move her arm, but it was like lead. She could taste a small trickle of blood coming from her mouth. Or maybe it was dripping down from her head. She felt herself being dragged by her ankles through the dirt, the pebbles getting caught in her hair. No, that had happened earlier, hadn't it? Just the pebbles were still there. She willed herself to sit up, but she knew nothing would happen. Then the darkness took over again.

Sometime later—could have been seconds or hours, she didn't know—she realized she was inside somewhere. The gravel under her body had been replaced with smooth tile. Her entire face throbbed; even breathing hurt. She tried to move, but the slightest physical effort sent a lightning bolt of pain through her head, and she passed out again.

Somewhere in the twilight of her unconsciousness, Adrienne started to relive the last fight she'd had with Chiara before she disappeared. The beginning was always scattered, but the center was clear as day. They were in Chiara's house, and they had been in one of their relatively good patches. Adrienne lay on the bed while Chiara packed her things into little packing cubes her husband had bought her for the occasion. Adrienne noticed that she didn't recognize any of Chiara's clothes anymore. Not so long ago, she'd known every single thing that Chiara wore, right down to her penchant for novelty socks. Now she didn't know a stitch of this new wardrobe. She felt oddly betrayed by this. Offended by every new athleisure legging and no-show ankle sock that Chiara rolled into her (also new) suitcase.

Even though this was the master bedroom, there was kid stuff everywhere. Laundry waiting to be put away had been gathered into various piles like fall leaves that had been raked up and then forgotten. Coffee cups with a thin film of day-old milk littered every surface too high for a baby to reach. This was a house that was barely staying on the rails.

Even with the mess, everything seemed to match, though. Except Adrienne, in her old T-shirt and moto boots. She stuck out like a stray dog at a polo match.

Chiara was already frustrated. "Our childhood was not that bad."

Adrienne was already irate at the minimizing. "What are you talking about? Mom had twins as a single parent and then was basically in a depression for a decade."

Chiara cut to the quick. "Oh God, for once, let's say what this is really about. You're mad that I decided to grow up and have kids. Not everyone wants to be the commitment-phobe weirdo, moving to a new part of the city every year, new job every month, new girlfriend every weekend. Some of us like family."

Adrienne replied quickly—maybe too quickly. "How would you know? We barely had one!"

Chiara couldn't rewrite history with Adrienne, so she adjusted her position. "Fine. Maybe that's true. But I do have one *now*. My own. And if you could be sober for five minutes, you could be a part of it."

That was a low blow, but also completely true.

And that was where this fight, which they had had in various forms a hundred times, took on the flavor of the day.

Adrienne said, voice dripping with derision, "Oh, so it's my fault that you're going on this crazy mommy weekend? Look at these people, Chiara!"

Adrienne took Chiara's phone and swiped through Thea's Instagram.

"What is this stuff? Crafts? Posed photos about #Gratitude? Everything perfect, perfect, perfect? These are the exact same moms who made our mom feel like crap, just with hair extensions and healing crystals. Is this really who you want to be?"

"Maybe! I feel so isolated. No one tells you how isolating it is to have newborns. I'm alone all the time."

Her eyes brimmed with tears, and that was the familiar cue for Adrienne to back off, to make a joke, to build the off-ramp from this fight. She was somehow both the instigator and the peacemaker.

Adrienne cracked a smile. "You're not alone. You're with the babies."

Chiara clocked Adrienne's sly look and then started to laugh. Adrienne laughed. The tension evaporated.

Chiara sighed. "Yup. Two babies. Never away. *Never away.* It's like, wow, get a job already, kid."

"For real. Those babies need to pay some rent."

Chiara pointed to one of her twins, who was gnawing on the side of the Pack 'n Play. "That one? Shit *in* my hand the other day. I'm holding him after the bath, having this sweet moment, and then he shits directly into my hand."

They laughed more.

Chiara said, "Motherhood is wild because you don't know what it's like until you do it. But once you do it, if you don't like it, there's no going back. You're stuck."

"Do you feel stuck?"

Chiara took a second to answer. "Sometimes. I am so happy. But I also feel stuck, and so lonely."

Adrienne went into full peacemaker mode but also couldn't quite drop her point. "I'm sorry I haven't been around. I just don't think these social media mommies are your people."

Chiara pleaded a lost cause. "Then come with me. Make fun of them with me."

Adrienne pretended to consider it, then snarked, "I'd rather be dead."

Chiara threw a pillow at her.

Adrienne caught the pillow on her face and then held it at arm's length. "Oh God, this smells like baby vomit."

Chiara threw another pillow, smiling. "Nope, that's you."

Chiara's husband hated this way that they bounced into intense arguments and bounced out just as quickly. He said it was like watching people play emotional double Dutch with downed power lines. Adrienne detested that he had made this astute observation about her. She was supposed to observe him, and understand him, and reduce him. Not the other way around. But he was right. Adrienne actually considered it their greatest strength. Even if recently, they hadn't been as good as phases past.

Injured but alive, Adrienne finally fully woke up in a laundry room nicer than her apartment (#SageLavender). More specifically, she woke up in the doggy-bathing station. Her neck and head ached, there was a swollen lump above her eye pushing into her vision, and she had to move so very slowly. Any sudden movement sent an ice pick through her temples. After a few minutes she could open her eyes without pain, and a few more minutes later, she could turn her head, taking in every corner of the room, ensuring that she was in fact alone.

Her hands were tied with a sparkly garland that inconveniently had a wire in the center. As her fingers investigated the makeshift restraint, she felt something else: the McKenna pumpkin-carving set was still in her pocket! Careful not to knock over the organic tea tree–oil flea shampoo or the Whisker Love blueberry-facial bottle next to her in the doggy bath, Adrienne wiggled the knife out of her pocket and used it to cut herself free. Even with the garland directly on the knife's edge, it took forever to cut through because of the damn safety blade. #SafetyFirst.

Her hands free, Adrienne checked her chest pocket. She still had the Apple Watch! But the few seconds of charging she had done earlier had run out. The watch was black again. Nevertheless, she zipped it back into her inside pocket for safekeeping.

Adrienne stood slowly, making sure she wouldn't pass out. Once she felt secure on her feet, Adrienne tiptoed to the Dutch door she'd used earlier and looked out. It was dark now. Or maybe it was *still* dark? Adrienne realized she had no idea how long she had been out. Her options were minutes or an entire day. Regardless, night could work in her favor. With any luck, she would be able to get off this mommy-mindfuck property and get to the police under the cover of darkness.

As Adrienne started to turn the knob to the outside door, she remembered the last time she was here, Bernice's sweet, round face helping her find her way into Thea's house.

Bernice.

Where was Bernice?

Adrienne thought back to the car crash—Opal's enraged face, her fists on the window, Bernice's scream. But it had been Adrienne's side of the car that had hit the stone pillar most directly. If Adrienne was okay, then Bernice had to be alive, and most likely somewhere in this house.

The smart thing to do was leave and have the police sort this out. But Adrienne couldn't stomach it. If her leaving now sealed Bernice's death, she would feel completely responsible.

She could not leave without Bernice.

The door from the laundry room to the kitchen was locked. She listened at the door and could hear tense voices on the other side. Adrienne remembered the door was to the side of the room off a small coffee nook, so she knew she could open it a hair and see out of the hinge side to the rest of the kitchen while remaining unseen. Adrienne pressed the safety blade to the lock. After a few seconds she heard a soft click and release of tension in the mechanism. She gingerly lifted the door in its hinges and slowly opened it the smallest amount possible. She gripped the tiny pumpkin-carving blade for protection. The only way this knife was winning in a fight was if the other person had a paper clip, but it made her feel slightly more prepared than being empty-handed nonetheless.

With the door nudged open, she could see the kitchen perfectly. She had expected Opal. She had expected Tamarind. And they were there. But so were the other two members of the Mom Squad. And they were all squabbling like a pit of vipers.

Adrienne got as close as she could without coming out of the shadow. Finally, she saw terrified Bernice in the corner, her mouth bound with a festive seasonal dish towel and more of the sparkly spider garland.

McKenna hissed at Opal, "You said last summit was a one-time thing."

Opal was angry, too. "And it was."

McKenna's tone was a mix of sarcasm and ice. "Hmm. Well, that's funny. Because I count one scared shitless witness in the country-style breakfast nook and a half-dead woman in the laundry room."

Opal replied with an air of positive superiority, "You see half-dead, I see half-alive, so . . ."

McKenna wasn't buying this spin. "Oh. Wow. So we are just going to breeze over *the extremely and entirely dead woman from last year*?!"

The words rang out in Adrienne's ears like a flash bomb: *the dead woman from last year.*

Chiara was dead.

Adrienne wanted to vomit. She wanted to explode. She wanted to dissolve and disappear to avoid the excruciating pain in her heart. Most of all, she wanted to run in there, screaming like a demon, and drown them all in the doggy bath with the blueberry whisker facial. But she waited because she needed to get out alive for anyone to know the truth. It took everything she had to wait. Her hands gripped the doorframe so hard the wood splintered into her fingernails, and she bit down on her own tongue until the faint metallic taste of blood washed over her.

McKenna was still huffing like she was getting screwed out of a Bergdorf's advertised-sale price. "I signed up for one murder. One. Not an annual serial-killer scenario. Unsubscribe, okay?"

Ashleigh was alarmingly serene. "Maybe she doesn't know anything."

Tamarind asked the obvious question: "Which one?"

Ashleigh didn't miss a beat. "The half-dead one in the laundry room."

McKenna was nearly pulling out her perfect auburn hair. "She's the dead lady's sister. What part of her ID did you not read? Or was it the murder collage in her bathroom that you missed? Or maybe you spaced out for the conversation SARA picked up from Cabin 5. Should I play the recording again?"

The SARA speaker in the kitchen pinged on with her perfect robot voice. "Playing flagged recording from Cabin 5 . . ." Adrienne then heard her own recorded voice amplified through the kitchen: "Bernice, Chiara was killed here, and I finally have proof."

All four members of the Squad screamed at the little box, *"No!"*

Adrienne's voice immediately ceased, and the robotic voice cut back in. "Okay, goodbye for now." SARA's light spun and went out.

While she still wasn't into the robot, Adrienne could have kissed that digital spy because it drew her attention to the nook and, more importantly, to her cell phone. All just inside the door where she stood hidden.

Adrienne waited until they weren't looking her way and then ever so gently reached out to grab her phone.

She opened it up—still no service. But then something else on the screen caught her eye. The date. It wasn't still dark from last night. It was the next night. She had been out for twelve hours. That meant the vast majority of the summit was gone, and only the die-hards were left on the property. No easy sneaking out among the crowd for Adrienne and Bernice. She felt ill.

McKenna was the only person who seemed to be fully taking in what was happening. "What are we going to do? I can't kill three people! One, okay; two, maybe. But *three*?"

Tamarind rolled her eyes. "Ugh, I knew you would crack first, McKenna. You have no stamina."

McKenna was livid. "Um, I have *two* sets of twins. You don't know stamina."

Opal was trying to keep her head on straight and, as such, didn't have time for this sideshow. "Will you both shut up? We just need to get through this weekend. Tomorrow we can figure out how to dispose of . . ." She trailed off, and Adrienne saw her eyes calculating how far to push this moment. "Whatever needs to be disposed of."

Tamarind rolled her eyes. "Body. You are talking about disposing of another body. But I vote to not dig another grave. Took my trainer weeks to get the knot out of my shoulder." She tenderly massaged her shoulder muscle.

Ashleigh chimed in with a helpful vibe. "We could compost her! I had to compost my horse once after I shot it. It didn't even smell!" While everyone else's facade was cracking, Ashleigh seemed more herself than ever and, therefore, more unhinged than ever. There was no Actually Sane Ashleigh, and that freaked Adrienne out as much as Tamarind's venom and McKenna's hysteria.

Tamarind, who lived to burst Ashleigh's bubble, rolled her eyes. "We get it! You're rich! You have horses! God, get over it."

Ashleigh was snapped back to earth, and pissed about it. "Is this some whiny one percent thing again? Because I happen to know a lot of nice billionaires, thank you very much."

Tamarind retorted with the tone of a bitchy seventh grader. "Oh, go compost another horse."

McKenna was still pulling at her hair. "Guys! A lost car and a grave was the plan with the first murder. What about this murder? We can't push two cars into the same ravine!"

Tamarind's back was really up now. "I found the last ravine. You find a new ravine."

Adrienne's throat was nearly closed from rage, but she was glad she had stayed hidden. Now she knew for sure.

Chiara's death wasn't an accident.

It was a murder.

And all these bitches were in on it.

Ashleigh was still in la-la land. "We are thinking about this all wrong. We protected our children from a drug user last year, and we protected them from a drug user this year. I feel great about it."

To Adrienne's horror, this point seemed to resonate with the other moms.

Ashleigh continued, "Besides, who can prove she was here? If it didn't happen online, did it even really happen?"

It was Opal's turn to be frustrated. "Yes, you idiot."

McKenna had finally come back to her can-do attitude. "It will all be okay. Teamwork makes the dream work. And we gotta work together, y'all."

Opal was not here for McKenna's rah-rah bullshit. "Cool it with the 'y'all.' We know you're from Philadelphia."

"Spiritually, I am southern," McKenna corrected her.

Tamarind couldn't seem to resist the opening. "So . . . racist?"

McKenna's voice dripped with scorn. "I'm sorry, you are from Orlando. The shitty part. Which is saying a lot, considering it's already Orlando."

Tamarind put on a haughty tone. "I am going to ignore that for now because we need to dig deep."

McKenna wasn't done, though. "Is that what your plastic surgeon said when he shaped your new butt?"

Opal and Ashleigh couldn't help it—they both let out big laughs. McKenna may have been the cattiest of the four, but she was not a liar.

Tamarind gasped. "How dare you."

Ashleigh said, "We all know that's why you missed the Memorial Day BBQ photo shoot."

McKenna was enjoying the pile on. "Swelling not go down in time?"

Tamarind started hurling insults at McKenna, who just kept yelling, "BBL! BBL! BBL!"

Opal was officially over this shit, though. "I've had enough. After this weekend, I am out."

McKenna did not appear to appreciate being dismissed, and had everyone's secrets at the ready. "You're done? No more coMOMunity for Her High Ladyship Opal? Going to go back to your pyramid scheme and the offshore bank account?"

Opal hit the roof immediately, her face turning red with fury. *"The Feds never found anything!"* She was clearly about to mount a defense but then gathered her energy for the problem at hand. "Stop! Stop it! Look, we all have secrets, okay? Tamarind, you're half silicone; I don't care what you tell your followers."

Tamarind gasped.

Opal moved on. "McKenna, your marriage boot camps would probably dry up if it came out that you are divorced."

"It's a trial separation!" McKenna defended herself.

Tamarind winced. "A trial separation for five years? Oh, honey, no."

Opal moved on to her next target. "Ashleigh has like eight nannies she never shows."

McKenna added, "And four homeschool teachers."

Then Tamarind added, "And migrant workers who tend to her orchard."

Ashleigh was completely unfazed by these points. "Technically, I never say I do it all myself."

Lastly, Opal pointed to herself. "And yes, I may or may not have *allegedly* been a part of a multilevel marketing–business *opportunity*. Allegedly. And as fun as this little #MomFession session is . . ." The rest of the Squad winced—no one liked taking the medicine they forced on others. "We have actual problems. Like this mildly injured woman"—she pointed to Bernice—"and the possibly dead woman in the laundry room, and yes, the other very dead woman. So we actually do need to come up with a plan."

McKenna timidly tested an idea again. "I know this wasn't popular before, but I still think maybe we should tell Thea."

Opal slammed her hands down on the kitchen island. "*No.* We talked about this. We are not telling her."

McKenna was desperate, though, and would not be put off. "Why not?"

It was clear to Adrienne that while perhaps these women were capable on their own and in small spheres of influence, in these moments they desperately needed a leader. And Thea was the only person they all respected enough to coalesce behind as a unit.

As McKenna asked Opal for just one good reason to keep Thea in the dark, and Tamarind and Ashleigh started sniping at each other again, Adrienne saw her chance. She jumped out of the shadows, grabbed a comically large kitchen knife from the knife block, and pointed it at the Mom Squad with a confidence she did not feel.

"Stay the fuck away from us!" Adrienne yelled. She pulled Bernice to her feet and yanked the dish towel from her mouth. "Bernice, run!"

Adrienne and Bernice attempted to escape the kitchen but were blocked by one of the two kitchen islands. No matter which way they went, a large marble rectangle stood between them and freedom.

"No one needs two islands!" Adrienne screamed.

McKenna huffed, "How dare you! Thea loves to entertain, and that second island is perfect for catering!"

McKenna, Opal, and Ashleigh grabbed the other three massive chef's knives in the knife block, McKenna coming up as the winner when she saw she had drawn the heavy meat cleaver. Her eyes glinted at the blade. Left without a knife of her own, Tamarind snatched one of the hanging brass pots and a giant baguette.

Opal clocked the bread and rolled her eyes. "Oh Jesus, you and carbs."

Adrienne and Bernice tried to figure out the best way to escape, cowering the long way toward the door as the Mom Squad closed in on them. To slow them down Adrienne grabbed the chairs from the breakfast nook and threw the chairs down between them.

Opal just missed getting hit. "Watch it! Those are discontinued mid-century modern!"

Adrienne couldn't believe that was what Opal was mad about, but she'd work with what she had. She grabbed every chair she could reach. "Fuck you!" (Chair.) "And fuck these chairs!" (Chair.) "And fuck mid-century modern!" (Chair.)

The entire Mom Squad gasped in horror.

Tamarind was scandalized. "Shut your fucking mouth. Mid-century modern is amazing!"

Then, puncturing this blizzard of a nightmare, the swinging door opened, and Thea stood there, framed by the foyer light.

Everyone froze. It was an insane tableau of them holding knives and decorative brass pots, except for Bernice, who held salad tongs, and Tamarind with the bread loaf aloft like a spear.

Thea blinked, unable to take in what she was seeing, every detail more insane than the last. "What the hell is going on?"

Opal jumped in. "Thea, this isn't what it looks like."

But Adrienne wasn't going to let that CEO bitch spin this. She ran to Thea. "Opal is a murderer! She killed my sister! She chased us when we tried to escape! And they are all helping her."

Thea stared at Adrienne and then back at Opal. She was trying to do the impossible math to square this circle. The seconds of silence seemed to stretch for an eternity.

Finally, Bernice let out a terrified plea: "Thea . . . Help . . ."

One look at Bernice's face softened Thea completely. She turned to her Mom Squad. "Opal. How could you? And in my home?" It was a napalm version of *I'm not angry, just disappointed.* Thea took a breath, ready to clean this mess up. "Bernice, come here."

Bernice timidly left Adrienne's side and walked over to Thea like a child reuniting with their mother. Thea pushed Bernice's bangs back and looked at the gash on her forehead. Her body language was so soothing, so maternal. "Are you okay?"

Bernice touched her head, dabbing at the dried blood. "I think so."

"How long have you been here, Bernice?"

"Since dawn," Bernice replied, a slight shake in her voice.

Thea was in full attachment-parenting mode, ready to validate her feelings. "That must have been so scary. I'm so sorry this happened, Bernice." She tipped Bernice's chin up so they were eye to eye. "You have done so well. It really looked like an accident. Just like we planned."

Adrienne felt the thud of her knees buckling and the blood draining from her body. Holy shit, she had been doubled-crossed.

Thea cupped Bernice's face in her hands. "You will be featured in all my fall Stories this year."

Bernice's face lit up with joy and gratitude. "Thank you, Thea. Thank you so much. I have a perfect autumnal palette for you."

Adrienne was equal measures shocked and betrayed. It was her turn to try to square the circle. "You were spying on me the whole time?"

Thea looked at Adrienne with a level of deep compassion that bordered on pity. "Oh, no, Adrienne. You introduced us. Remember?"

Of course Adrienne remembered. The one bright spot of this whole shit show weekend had been Bernice's thrilled face when Thea knocked on her door. Adrienne cringed, remembering her stupid thumbs-up.

Brought down by a mom who couldn't even *say* the word *fuck*.

Thea could read this all over her face. "Yes. You lost sight of your goals. That was a mistake, Adrienne. If you were an actual mother, you wouldn't have made such an obvious error. Moms see the whole board, every contingency. Moms *prioritize*."

Bernice turned to Adrienne, pleading, "I'm so sorry. I really am. I never expected this. It's just all my kids need braces! Do you know how much orthodontic work costs now? Without Thea, we would have to take out a second mortgage!"

Thea was more than Bernice's style icon and online idol—she was also her financial savior. However, suddenly, the mood changed. The Mom Squad giggled in chilling unison.

Thea took a step back from Bernice. "Oh dear. Bernice. Is that why you did this?" She still had the attachment-parenting style tone, but it had become icy—sinister, even. "I hear that you are stressed about money. But I feel betrayed by that. Money should never motivate you." Something she had said earlier in a seminar to unite the moms was now repurposed to push Bernice out. "This is about coMOMunity."

Thea deftly picked up a marble slab from the #RainbowMeals char-CUTE-erie demo and slammed it into the side of Bernice's head.

Bernice's skull cracked with a sick thud, like a watermelon being dropped from a great height onto a concrete patio. She slumped to the ground.

An immediate surge of bile pressed into Adrienne's throat and a high ringing seared in her ears. Her hands went clammy, and her knees felt like they had been hit with a hammer. Bernice was dead.

Adrienne's heart beat so fast she felt like her neck was expanding with each pulse, and the intensity of the sensation reminded her of the obvious: unlike Bernice, she was still alive. For now. As Thea casually put the marble down and the Squad took in the last few seconds, Adrienne saw her moment to act.

She ran, around the second island, out of the kitchen, through the foyer, and out the front door.

The intense rural blackness of the night sky seemed to swallow up everything that wasn't directly in front of her eyes. She was breathing so hard, trying and failing not to panic, that it took her nearly fifty yards of an all-out sprint to realize she was the only sound. She looked for the drunk moms she had left still singing Adele, but they were all gone. It really was day three of the summit.

Adrienne ran toward the event tents, desperate for somewhere to hide. She needed to think. She needed a plan.

She paused by a tree to catch her breath and scan her surroundings. The hay bales caught her eye. Maybe if she could sprint over, stack them, and get behind—

THWAK!

A hunting arrow impaled the tree, millimeters from Adrienne's face, the feathers on the fletching leaving a paper-cut-size slice on her cheek. She jumped back and turned to see where it came from. She saw Ashleigh, who had her hot-pink-camo hunting bow trained on her again, new arrow nocked into the bow string, her white teeth showing in a creepy sneer.

Ashleigh smiled and called out to her target, "Hunting is organic!" She pulled the string back to her lips and said, with love in her heart, "Jesus, be my bow."

THWAK!

Adrienne dropped to the ground. Another arrow hit right where her head had been a second earlier. A few strands of her hair had even been carried by the air and impaled by the arrow. Adrienne ripped those hairs from her head, barely noticing the pain compared to the rest of her battered body.

Ashleigh pouted to heaven. "Not cool, Jesus."

Adrienne sat frozen, her heels slowly digging into the loose dirt but her legs too weak to support her. As she sat, the other members of the Mom Squad joined Ashleigh. They stood in a row like a posed prom photo, except every one of those psychos was both killer Carrie and the mean girl pulling the bucket full of pig blood.

And then the foursome parted, and Thea stood in the center, her golden megaphone from the ropes course in her hand.

Thea cracked her neck and then started box breathing. The Mom Squad instinctively joined her. Tamarind in particular really committed, even going into a Kundalini Pose. Thea ended the breath-work pattern, and they stood staring at Adrienne. Adrienne noticed all the earlier panic in the kitchen was gone. There was not a sliver of doubt on any of their faces. Now that they had Thea's approval, all this carnage wasn't a bug. It was a feature.

The message was clear: kill or be killed.

Thea smiled and then put her golden megaphone to her lips. "Adrienne . . . on your mark. Get set. *Run.*"

Adrienne turned on her heel, scrambled to her feet, and ran deeper into the summit-event areas, frantically looking for a plan, a weapon, an escape. She didn't have her car keys, so that was not an option. After Bernice, she didn't know who to trust, so she couldn't wake anyone. There were no neighbors to run to.

She stopped for a second behind a large bush and listened. Only crickets trilled in the darkness.

Through the leaves, Adrienne watched them split up into four directions, and then chose the fifth option toward the pumpkin-carving tent.

Adrienne ran into the tent to find the tables were each still set with the scarecrow children. The unseeing faces took on the feeling of a funeral mass—everyone seated in rows, waiting for the body to show up.

Because there would be a body. Adrienne just hoped it wasn't hers.

She slid under one of the tables, hidden by the seasonal draping. It was the only good hiding spot, which wasn't saying much when muslin was all that stood between her and certain death. Before she could second-guess this choice or make a break for it, she heard a *tap tap tap*.

Adrienne peeked out of a tiny hole in the tablecloth to see McKenna creeping forward. She still had her cleaver from the kitchen.

McKenna whispered, "Here, kitty, kitty." She tapped her cleaver on the tables and made little kissing noises. "Olly, olly, oxen free . . ."

McKenna *tap tap tapped* her cleaver again.

Adrienne covered her mouth with her hands, trying to muffle her ragged breath.

McKenna twirled between the tables, tapping each one with her cleaver, and then sang loudly, in a voice higher and clearer than Adrienne had expected, "Ring around the rosy . . ." *Tap.* "Sister is so nosy . . ." *Tap.* "Ashes . . . ashes . . ." *Tap.*

This last tap was on Adrienne's table. She willed her heart to stop beating, sure that McKenna could hear it. But McKenna moved on.

"The dead fall down!" McKenna swiftly ducked her head under the draping of the closest table to find . . . no one.

Adrienne was so very close by. She knew if McKenna kept checking tables, she would find her in less than a minute.

McKenna straightened up and started again, tapping the tables as she went. "Ring around the rosy . . ." *Tap.* "Pocket full of posy . . ." *Tap.* "Ashes, ashes . . . I'll chop you down!"

Adrienne waited until McKenna's head was under a table and then threw a pumpkin across the tent to draw McKenna's attention in the opposite direction. She was lucky, and hit a pyramid of pumpkins, which noisily toppled to the ground.

As McKenna followed the sound, Adrienne ran from her hiding spot and grabbed the pumpkins still stacked on her table from earlier. She climbed the lighting rig behind the dais. She thanked whatever god was available for draping the rig in straw mats, as they kept her out of McKenna's view. Now it was time to put her plan into action. Once in position Adrienne threw another pumpkin to draw McKenna to her.

McKenna, who was still checking under tables, heard the new crash. She went toward the front of the tent, not seeing Adrienne above her on the lighting rig.

As McKenna passed underneath, Adrienne seized her moment.

"Gourd yourself on this, motherfucker!"

Adrienne dropped her giant "informal" pumpkin on McKenna's head. McKenna was knocked off-balance, and Adrienne dropped down on top of her. It was inelegant, and they both collapsed to the ground.

They wrestled for a few seconds, McKenna hacking at Adrienne with the cleaver, narrowly missing flesh each time. Finally, Adrienne got her body behind McKenna's and pinned her arms down with her legs.

Adrienne pulled out the pumpkin-carving knife that was still in her pocket and dragged it across McKenna's neck, preparing herself for a spatter of blood.

Except nothing happened.

McKenna snorted. "That safety blade is a real bitch."

Adrienne flipped the blade position in her hand from Slice to Stab and drove it into McKenna's right eye.

McKenna screamed in horror, but this didn't dissuade Adrienne. She pulled the novelty blade from her eye socket and stabbed McKenna in the left eye, then four more times in the chest and stomach. McKenna convulsed for less than a minute, then went still. Dead.

"Sorry about your wife, Tod," Adrienne said, and she almost meant it.

She knew she needed to keep moving; McKenna's death screams had definitely given up her position. She exited the back of the tent and beelined to the oak grove a few feet away, hoping the tress would give her more cover.

As soon as Adrienne got behind the tree line, she stopped. Stopping felt insane, but she needed to know who was where. She couldn't just hope to outrun them all night.

Then she heard Opal whisper, "McKenna?" followed by a small gasp.

From the shadow, Adrienne snuck a look. Opal had found McKenna's body.

Adrienne watched Opal lean down, her face an icy smirk. "Gotta say, Adrienne. Didn't expect you to have it in you! But three against one is still good odds."

Adrienne watched Opal leave the tent and head east, so Adrienne headed west.

In the oak grove, awkwardly running in a crouched position, Adrienne was still looking for a good place to hide out. She saw in disbelief that she was at the firepit where Anya, Maya, Hannah, and Naomi had burned their compromising evidence. Since then, wine bottles had been brought, drank, and left. It all seemed impossible that regular life had been carrying on all this time while she had fallen into a hellscape of murder and death.

Adrienne's head was so turned by this evidence of others enjoying themselves that she accidentally tripped over an extension cord, which pulled twenty-five feet of decorative café lighting off a large tree. Adrienne fell flat on her stomach, and she felt a large rock slam into her hip bone. She wanted to groan in pain, but then she heard a twig snap nearby. From the ground, she saw two figures coming closer. The high ponytail was Tamarind, and the other with the bow was clearly Ashleigh.

Adrienne crawled on her stomach to the only shrub nearby, trying to keep her one hip off the ground. Once she was hidden from view, Adrienne pulled down the side of her pants and saw her hip was already swelling into a giant welt. Then she felt a rush of air, and Tamarind pounced on her like prey.

It was all so similar to the corn maze that Adrienne had a hard time orienting herself for a second. She managed to push Tamarind off her and got to her feet.

They squared off and then attacked with equal fury. Their hand-to-hand combat was surprisingly good. Punches. Jabs. Tamarind even came in with some roundhouse-style kicks that Adrienne just barely dodged.

Tamarind smiled at Adrienne's surprise. "I was an early student of Tae Bo."

Tamarind attempted another Billy Blanks move but lost her footing. As she stumbled, Adrienne grabbed Tamarind's hair and pulled her down to the ground.

"Well, I've bought drugs off sketchy people who tried to scam me. So, same diff." She tried to get her arms around Tamarind's neck, but Tamarind was freakishly strong, considering how scrawny she was. She popped out of Adrienne's grip again and again.

Adrienne heard a stick crack and saw from her vantage point that Ashleigh was methodically making her way toward them, staying low, staying quiet, her bow at the ready. She truly was a huntress.

Adrienne looked around and saw the light behind her, beaming on the ground, making a horizontal spotlight. She had an idea.

Adrienne let Tamarind get out of her grip fully, and they squared off again. Tamarind landed a hard punch in Adrienne's chest; she smiled as she felt the punch truly connect. However, Adrienne was acting more injured than she was, which wasn't hard because the bitch had hit her in the sternum. Adrienne staggered backward toward the light, but not quite into its beam. Tamarind, sensing the opportunity to end this, ran toward Adrienne at top speed.

However, instead of colliding, Adrienne sidestepped Tamarind at the last-possible second.

Tamarind, missing Adrienne completely, ran headfirst into the horizontal spotlight and, more importantly, into Ashleigh's path. Tamarind was backlit, so Ashleigh could only see a staggering figure. She released her arrow, and it impaled Tamarind right in her turquoise Alo Yoga crop top.

Tamarind stared down at the hot-pink fletching and knew exactly what happened. "Ashleigh. You bitch, you shot me!"

Ashleigh looked to heaven again, really annoyed this time. "Oh, come on, Jesus."

But Tamarind was pissed. "Can you wrap up *Chitchat with the Lord* and help me?"

"You know, I don't like your tone."

"Are you serious right now? I don't need your shit, Rapture Barbie."

This was 100 percent the wrong move.

Adrienne watched Ashleigh calmly nock another arrow on her bow, take aim, and hit Tamarind once more, square in the chest. Tamarind fell to the ground, the prey to Ashleigh's predator.

Ashleigh walked over to her kill and sighed. "All that silicone is never going to biodegrade."

But as she savored her friendly fire, Adrienne crept up behind her with a bottle of wine she had grabbed from one of the firepits. She smashed the heavy bottle over Ashleigh's head, the glass shattering into her perfect braid.

As Ashleigh crumpled, blood and wine poured into her eyes, blinding her. Adrienne kicked her on her back and stabbed her in the neck with the broken bottle. For good measure, she turned the bottle, dragging the glass through her skin. Like a spigot, blood started to spurt. She bled out in seconds.

Adrienne kneeled down in Ashleigh's bloody puddle. The tacky wetness immediately soaked her pant legs. She would have loved to kneel away from this spot, but she was so exhausted that even taking a step felt impossible. The blood on her hands was already starting to dry, caking into her nail beds like mud. She wondered what time it was, how much longer she needed to survive until she could hopefully stash away in the back of an unnecessarily large SUV bound for some bland suburb where the biggest scandal was sprinkler usage and flashy mailboxes.

Adrienne felt sick. The cortisol and adrenaline were pumping through her body, making her feel like she could run for miles and never tire. But by the same token, she had never felt more wrung out. Every second of these altercations passed more slowly than an hour, and even when they were over, she felt the physical sensations of the violence reverberating in her skin.

She wanted this to stop. Who could she talk to to make this stop?

Except there was no one to go to. This was not a game where she could call a time-out. There was no fire escape she could flee to.

Had Chiara felt like this? Had she cried out for help? The thought of Chiara in this scenario brought bile back into Adrienne's throat. She retched into the blood puddle.

Behind her, she heard a calm voice say, "What a mess."

Adrienne whipped around to see Opal standing in the spotlight, her kitchen knife glinting. Adrienne scrambled back to her feet and started to run.

The running was incredibly painful. Every bruise and joint seared with each step. But Adrienne wasn't ready to fight again just yet. She needed one minute to steady herself.

Adrienne found herself back on the ropes course. Opal was hot on her heels, and with double the energy Adrienne had left. In fact, Adrienne was exhausted and out of ideas. Taking care of the other three had been flukes. She bobbed and weaved through the logs and tire swings. Finally, she stopped on one side of the cable web, Opal on the other. This was it. This was as good as it was going to get for her. Protection from certain death by a couple of cables. But if death was soon, she needed to know things first.

Adrienne panted, "Are you the one who did it?"

Opal smirked. "What makes you think it was only one of us? We are a coMOMunity."

Opal sprinted toward Adrienne, who continued to duck around the web. Opal tried to stab Adrienne through the cables. She got close a few times and then overcommitted, losing her balance, her weight falling forward. Adrienne grabbed Opal's wrist through the web and yanked it down until Opal dropped the knife, the metal cables grating into her skin. Adrienne kicked the knife away and attempted to make a break for it. But Opal grabbed the back of Adrienne's jacket, swinging her around the side post and face-first into the metal cables.

Adrienne saw Maddie's abandoned hair extensions still tangled up. She couldn't believe it was still there, and then remembered that it wasn't that long ago she had been in this very spot, listening to Beyoncé and hugging strangers. Adrienne ripped the hair out and stuffed it into Opal's mouth.

Opal was disoriented for a second, coughing and pulling the hair from her mouth, strands tangled in her teeth. Adrienne reached through the web, grabbed Opal's hair, and pulled her head through the web. Then, with her hands on the back of Opal's head, Adrienne dropped to the ground with all her body weight. She felt Opal's neck snap on the cables.

Adrienne crawled away before she stood up. She needed some distance. When she finally turned, she saw Opal still tangled in the web, her head at a hideous limp angle, her body pinned up like a discarded marionette.

Adrienne thought back to Opal's answer, that the murder was part of the coMOMunity.

Was it just the Squad acting on their own? Did other moms know? And when had they let Thea know? After Chiara was already dead? Or before . . . ?

She thought back to the Squad's aimless squabbling in the kitchen. They may have murdered Chiara on their own, but there was no way they had successfully covered it up without Thea leading their maniacal energy.

But Adrienne had to know the whole truth.

Thea was the key.

Chapter 19

A Mother's Work Is Never Done

Back on the porch, Thea checked her watch. She hadn't seen any of her Squad in too long. She sighed, her irritation at its consistent low-level hum. She would have to go see what happened herself.

Thea entered the main tent, stepping over piles of spilled pumpkins. In the middle of it all, she found McKenna, her auburn hair matted to her face in blood, the brutalized eye sockets unblinking. Next to her was the pumpkin-carving knife with her own name emblazoned on it.

Thea picked up the knife and turned it over in her fingers. "I told you the carving sets were a bad idea. Specialized seasonal merch isn't multifunctional. And now, if people find out you were stabbed? Ugh, I am going to have to collect all the sets you passed out before they become morbid collectors' items." Thea twirled the knife again until she had it firmly in her grip. She put both hands on the handle, raised the knife over her head, and then brought it down with as much force as she could.

Stab.

Raise.

Stab.

Raise.

Thea's frustration wasn't dissipating, though. She lifted the knife again and then, in a blank-eyed frenzy, stabbed McKenna's torso again and again and again. The lifeless body only responded with deep, unsatisfying thuds.

Finally, Thea felt the knife crack the sternum, like a walnut shell shattering. The knife stayed lodged in the bone, and she took a deep breath.

A release of emotion, but not quite the full catharsis she needed.

Next, Thea found Opal, her prized confidante, strung up like a salami in a novelty deli. She nudged Opal's body, and it slid out of the cables into a sad little heap. Thea started to laugh. This ropes course had been Opal's stupid idea, prattling on about how she had done one once at a corporate retreat with some tech guru she loved to name-drop. Thea had gone along with it to give Opal something to do that was away from Thea's house. Just like her kids: refocus, redirect, reinforce.

Thea listened but heard nothing. No clue about which way to go. The natural inclination would be for Adrienne to head toward the road, so Thea did the same.

As she walked toward the edge of the property, Thea found a cold and pale Ashleigh with a creepy frozen smile. If Thea had cared enough, she might have tried to close her searing blue eyes, but she didn't. She hoped that Ashleigh was happy to have a whole wine-blood thing going on in death.

As she passed Tamarind's bloodied body, Tamarind sputtered up. She wasn't dead!

Thea knelt down next to her. "Tamarind?"

Tamarind's breath was ragged as she looked down at the arrows skewering her. "I think my crop top was so tight it acted as a tourniquet."

Thea felt one emotion only: annoyance. Tamarind couldn't even die conveniently? Thea looked for an easy solution, and there it was. The zipper on the crop top. Thea took the zipper toggle in her hand.

Tamarind's eyes filled with fear. "No, no. I need help. Keep it tight until help comes!"

Thea smiled. "Help isn't coming, sweetie." She casually unzipped Tamarind's crop top. The release of pressure sent a rush of blood, and Tamarind's wounds spurted out several pulses, each splash a little smaller than the last, until the blood soaked the crop top to saturation and Tamarind's eyes went dark.

Thea hadn't believed in the power of the Secret, but tonight was making her reconsider. This mass death was actually quite ideal for her! All her problems solved after months of visualizing! The Mom Squad's brands had become so stale in the last year, both individually and as a group identity. Now she was free.

Having finished her tour of carnage, Thea had a new strategy in mind and headed to the corn maze.

As she cut through the wine-tasting tent, Thea heard glass smash behind her.

She turned to see Adrienne holding the necks of broken bottles in both hands. Blood and mud was caked on her skin, and her clothes were torn. Thea was delighted that her Squad had at least managed to inflict a little damage before failing so spectacularly.

Adrienne's breath was ragged, but her voice was strong. "Tell me what happened."

Thea put on a fake tone of confusion. "What do you mean?"

Adrienne's face flared red. "You know what I mean. My sister. What happened to her?"

Thea smiled her same megawatt smile. "You know, I have always been able to read people. Even when I was little, I was able to anticipate need and therefore exceed expectations. First, it made me the perfect daughter. Then the perfect wife. Finally, and most importantly, it made me the perfect mother. But eventually, that got boring. I mean, how many snacks can you make, you know? So I had to expand. I used these skills to cultivate my Elite Moms. It was fun at first. Like a little fleet of dolls vying for my attention. They poured money into whatever I offered them. I would privately answer their hungry DMs, and at my request, they promised to never tell a soul. They all believed me when

I said they were the only ones I talked to, so desperate to feel special in a world that didn't give two shits about them. They even sent blackmail material to my Squad whenever they asked for it. On my behalf, of course. I never directly asked for it. But it all came from the same place—my ability to anticipate need."

Adrienne's face was flush and her mouth a sneer. "Let me guess: you're an empath."

Thea had to honestly laugh at that. "Oh God, no. Although, many people have tried to say that I am. But knowing what people want and caring about what they want are two very different things. However, in this moment, your needs align with mine. You want information, and I want to share. But mostly, I want to say thank you, Adrienne. Tonight it is you who has exceeded expectations." Thea saw a wave of apprehension on Adrienne's face, and knew she was on the right track. "I was reading a book to my son, Finch. He is obsessed with the ocean now. A welcome change after the truly interminable dinosaur phase and the even more droll outer space era. At night we read a book about a shark and his best friends, the remoras attached to his belly.

"I hate this book. I hate the shark for allowing the suckerfish to cling to his body. And I resent the fictitious remoras beyond any logical measure. After my third dream about being the shark and violently chewing the remoras off my body, the clumsy metaphor could no longer be ignored. The Squad were my remoras. They had so few ideas, their focus so narrow. Nothing innovative, in any respect, for years."

Thea started to slowly circle toward Adrienne, and Adrienne mirrored her movement, keeping their distance the same.

Thea continued, "So you did me a favor tonight. You anticipated my need. Because if McKenna brought up trending llamas one more time, I would have buried her in alpaca shit. And if Opal fumbled one more partnership because she was trying to relive her corporate-titan days, I was going to send the dossier on her MLM to every news organization in the country. Tamarind had been a mistake, but an insipid one. Diet culture is hardly unique, albeit annoying as hell. I mean, Jesus, there's only so many ways to make a smoothie. Ashleigh, however, was becoming a true liability with the covert anti-vaxx pro-life messaging that she thought I didn't see. But I saw it all. Their every mistake, and misstep, and edited post after a commenter called them out. I had no way to elegantly get rid of the Squad without damaging my own brand."

Adrienne was incredulous. "Who the hell cares about some brand?"

Thea raised her hand delicately to her chest. "Many people, Adrienne. Many. The coMOMunity image is all about our sisterhood in motherhood, and that moronic fantasy prints money. So, on I soldiered. Like all mothers do. Make best. Make lemonade. Silver linings. Carry all that social media deadweight and do it with a smile." Thea could sense Adrienne's patience waning and knew it was time to turn the screw. "But this last year had really put me over the edge, Adrienne. Just absolutely endless sniveling from all four of them about committing one measly murder." Thea put on a whiny tone: "'Did we really have to?' 'Why did we all have to help?' 'What if someone finds out?' Blah, blah, blah. The homicide equivalent of *Are we there yet?*" Thea was finally letting out years of frustration, and her voice got harsher as she went on. "How did they not see that protecting their position at the top of the social media heap was the most important thing? How did they not see that it was precisely because of their own pathetic weakness that I had made them all help, so I could play them off each other? Mutually assured prison sentences was the only way to keep those bobbleheads in line." On a dime, Thea's relaxed attitude returned. "But now, looking at their dead bodies, I feel light. Just one last loose end to tidy up, Adrienne. You."

Thea had a rush of pleasure as she watched Adrienne's entire body tense up, prepared to fight to the death.

Instead, Thea gave her a lovely wave and walked into the darkness without looking back.

Chapter 20

An Autumnal Palette

Adrienne stood in the tent, alone and too stunned to move.

Thea just left? What the hell was happening? Was that even real? Had the adrenaline made her hallucinate?

Then Adrienne heard it.

The voice came from every speaker on the property.

Adrienne heard Thea coo, like a mother waking her baby from a long nap, "Elite Moms . . . Elite Moms, wake up . . ."

Adrienne knew this meant Thea was on the corn-maze-observation tower. She walked toward it and then saw every SARA in every cabin purring with light as Thea's voice spread out like summoning.

"Elite Moms. I need you. There is a woman here threatening the security of your children."

From where she stood, Adrienne could see lights in the little cabins flicking on and women slowly coming out the doors to see if this was all some elaborate dream.

Thea's voice came to her from every direction. "The threat—she wants to take all of this away from you. I need your help. I need you to find her."

Adrienne had seconds to react, and for once, the perfect hiding spot was right there. She worked quickly.

In something between a daze and a rabid fever, women walked toward Thea and past McKenna's scarecrow family. The wife form was intact now, and for good reason: Adrienne was inside it, tucked in the chicken wire, the straw fringe covering her face but allowing her a clear view of the Elite Moms. She saw the looks on these women's faces and realized that shit just got a lot harder. There would be no sneaking out in the back of a minivan now.

The Elite Moms gathered at the base of the observation deck, their chins tilted up, taking in Thea's every word.

Thea's voice had slowly risen from cooing mother, and now she was hitting a strong crescendo. "If you bring her to me, I will be so grateful. We need to protect ourselves, protect our children. Whoever eliminates the threat gets to be in my *seasonal Target ad*."

The Elite Moms' hackles went up at the mention of Target, their mecca. They took Thea's orders seriously and fanned out into the grounds of the ranch.

Adrienne knew she had to take out Thea to have any chance. When the Elite Moms had spread out and away but not yet started to circle back, she beelined for the corn maze while still inside the scarecrow. She stopped whenever a group approached, posing, and then moved on. If she wasn't sure her death was imminent, she would have laughed at the pure insanity of this image—a scarecrow running and freezing, running and freezing. But perhaps when you're about to die, the absurd is the freest feeling there is. Finally, Adrienne slid into the cornstalks right before a group of moms passed her. Tucked far enough away that no one could see her, she shimmied out of the scarecrow.

Still on the mic, Thea picked up the iPod, looking for something to motivate her new foot soldiers. After some scrolling, she smiled and turned on the music.

A series of familiar piano chords, and then Adele once again crooned her familiar greeting from the other side.

Adrienne grimaced. "Fucking Adele."

As Adele blared out of every wireless speaker disguised as boulders (#Sonos #SponCon #LinkInBio), the mommies were still on the hunt for Adrienne. She could hear them ripping tents down, overturning garbage cans, breaking down every locked cabin door. Adele was still coming from every direction, the voice of an angel giving those demons a cinematic flair.

Adrienne, hiding in the corn, was surrounded. She kept narrowly missing getting found. She was dodging groups and flashlight beams. She was on the borrowed time between the fatal blow and the fatality.

Adrienne caught a glimpse of Thea tapping her fingers on the railing, clearly annoyed that this was taking so long. Adrienne was shook by this dichotomy. Here she was, her body coursing with terror, sure her own gruesome murder was seconds away, and meanwhile the orchestrator of her demise was *bored.*

Thea turned down Adele and picked up the mic again. "You know, Adrienne, I talked to your sister. Chiara."

Adrienne, who at that second was face down in the dirt, avoiding a flashlight beam, snapped to attention at Chiara's name.

"Your sister told me everything. It wasn't hard. Just had to feed her a bit about my less-than-ideal childhood and how I felt like I needed to be perfect to undo that damage. None of that is true, of course, but I knew your sister would buy it. And out came all her secrets. And yours, too. How hard she tried to be good, but she worried she was just a failure at mothering. And how you were always making the worst choice no matter how much she tried to help you. I told her it wasn't her fault you turned out like this. You had a bad mother."

Adrienne's blood was boiling. But she knew that her rage could mean her death if she didn't take a second to think, to plan. And then she saw something promising out of the corner of her eye—a crate she recognized from earlier—and started to crawl toward it, always keeping Thea in her peripheral view.

Sneaking a peek from between the cornstalks, Adrienne saw Thea press her lips together, and Adrienne realized she was trying to keep from smiling. *Smiling.*

Thea lifted the mic again. "I gotta say, though. As easy as it was to play your sister, you were even easier. You like to think of yourself as the bad girl with the heart of gold, right? The hidden softie. The riser of the downtrodden who can call bullshit when she sees it but play the game when she needs to? So that's who I was for you. I told you little truths to make you feel like you were on the inside. I smoked pot so you would feel like you were getting to know the real me. I called a little bullshit so you could believe you were superior to the women here. And you lapped it up. Because you think you are so much smarter than the rest of us. Well, guess what. You aren't. You're nobody."

Adrienne had reached the crate and said a tiny prayer as she looked inside. There they were: rows of Ball jars, with their specialty wicks, and each one filled to the brim with kerosene. Adrienne carried the crate, balancing it on her bleeding hip but knowing the pain was worth it. She unscrewed jar after jar, pouring the kerosene behind her in a trail at the base of the cornstalks. As Thea cranked up the Adele again, Adrienne was finally done. She flipped open the blowtorch also from the crate and delicately touched the ground with the blue flame.

The kerosene ignited, but more importantly, so did the dry corn. The seven-foot-high husks turned into a wall of flames in seconds.

The line of fire ignited like a fuse, slowly encircling Thea alone in the center.

But right before the two lines joined to seal Thea off, Adrienne stepped through.

It was just the two of them in the center clearing now.

All the other mommies ran toward the fire, but it was too late. They were trapped on the outside. Row after row of corn caught fire, making the walls of flame thicker, wider, impenetrable. Adrienne was relieved her plan had worked. She couldn't take them all on, but she could get to the person responsible for Chiara's death.

Adrienne climbed up to the observation deck and screamed, "Tell me what happened!"

"What makes you think I know?"

"Those sycophants wouldn't do anything without your say-so. Without you telling them exactly what you wanted. Like you would ever relinquish that much control."

A pleased grin spread across Thea's face. "True. They had no imagination. Crafts? Coupons? Calories? Please. I made them from nothing. Built them into something worth having, something worth following. But none of them were even close to me."

"So was it like this?" Adrienne pointed to the frothing moms on the outside of the corn maze. "You made the Squad do it and held yourself back just enough to have deniability."

Thea scoffed. "Wow, you really aren't a mother. All we do is get our hands dirty. If we want something done right, we must do it ourselves. Sure, shooting her with fireworks was a little theatrical. But that wasn't what killed her. No. That would be no fun. She could have lived if she had been able to get the car started. Of course, we had disconnected the battery. Mothers always plan ahead. After we dragged her from the car, I made them each take a turn with the knife. A knife I kept—so they couldn't later snitch on me without snitching on themselves. I even made them all dig the grave. Your sister's death was a real team-building moment for them."

"Why did you care so much about Chiara? Is it just because she went viral? Is that it? Are you that pathetic?"

The word hit a nerve, and Thea was coming close to unhinged as she yelled, "Your sister did it *all wrong*. She wasn't relatable. She wasn't composed. She didn't have text in the photo and in the caption! It wasn't even a Reel! *And yet the algorithm chose her.* And that, I cannot abide. I am lovable. I am easy. I am *aspirational.*"

Adrienne lunged at Thea, but Thea moved away quickly with the ease of a boxer in a ring.

Adrienne overcommitted a few times and almost toppled over the railing.

"Careful, Adrienne. Safety first."

Once they finally collided, the fight was nearly even. Trading punches, kicks, elbows to the stomach, their reach almost identical, so it was hard for either of them to get the upper hand for long. But unlike in the previous fights, Adrienne wasn't in this to survive. She was in this for revenge, whatever it cost her. Even her life. And nothing was more dangerous than that.

Adrienne took punch after punch, but she didn't care because she answered each blow with a harder one. Thea may have looked more composed, but she wanted to live. Adrienne just wanted blood.

The smoke billowed up, making Adrienne's mouth and lungs burn. The heat from the flames rose in powerful waves that blurred Adrienne's eyesight. When the wind shifted just right, Adrienne could see the other mothers prowling below around the outside, screaming for Thea.

For a brief second in the fight, Adrienne seemed to be in control, but Thea twisted expertly, throwing Adrienne into the railing. In a flash, Thea pulled a small paring knife from her back pocket and stabbed Adrienne through the hand and pinned her to the banister.

Adrienne screamed. She could feel the knife nicking her bones and splicing the muscles in her palm.

Thea was sweaty but still somehow dewy. "I admit, I am impressed at your dedication. By the end, Chiara had no such gumption."

Adrienne spit through her bloody mouth. "Don't you say her name."

Thea did her signature pose, one shoulder up, one eye winking. Adrienne had seen her do it while holding kitchen tiles, while arranging flowers, while bonding with babies over birthday cakes. And she did it now as she chirped, "Chiara. Chi-ar-a."

Adrienne screamed, pulled the knife from her hand, and plowed headfirst into Thea's chest, knocking them both toward the edge.

As Thea's body made contact, the banister behind her broke away with a loud crack. Thea was suspended off the edge, her heels barely connecting with the deck as Adrienne held on to her sweater. The cream-merino wool in Adrienne's hand was the only thing keeping Thea up.

Thea looked down at the tractor beneath her, its sharp multi-foot grappler blades extending up like metal jaws. Hitting that was certain death.

Thea turned and stared into Adrienne's eyes, pleading, "No. Wait. Stop. I'm a mother."

Adrienne paused for a half a second before saying, "So was Chiara."

In a rage-fueled shove that felt like an exorcism, Adrienne propelled Thea off the observation tower and onto the heavy farm machinery below.

Adrienne heard a quick succession of slick cuts.

Slice and dice.

Thea's Perfect White Slouchy Sweater blossomed with maroon blood, her body in pieces now. Legs and arms twisted away. A torso without limbs. Appendages scattered. And then, Thea from the neck up, her long chestnut waves of hair spread across the golden hay.

Truly a gorgeous autumnal palette.

Adrienne looked out, and in the distance she saw the flashing lights of emergency vehicles approaching. She vaguely wondered who'd called them. Not that it mattered.

Outside the corn maze, Adrienne saw mothers coming to their senses, getting in their cars and fleeing before the cops thought to stop them. Help was here. But so was reality.

Adrienne climbed down from the observation deck. Bloody. Bruised. Soot and pumpkin guts caked on her face. Scarecrow straw in her hair. Wine and viscera on her clothes. The flames were slowly closing in on her, but there was still a large section of dirt beneath the tower that remained unburnt for now.

She pulled a joint from her pocket. She walked over to the edge of the clearing and lit it from the inferno. Then she went back to the center of the flame-free-for-now area and lay down on the ground.

Smoking deeply, Adrienne pulled out her phone. She went to the album of her and Chiara. She scrolled all the way back. Back through years and years of connection and disconnection.

All the way back to the photo of them in their Wonder Woman costumes. A photo of a photo. A meaningless digital memory of a hard copy Polaroid of a real moment she relived every time her heart beat.

Then Adrienne flipped back one photo more.

The same day, the same Wonder Woman costumes, and between their two little faces was their mom. So much joy and love.

Adrienne lay her head back so she could stare at this moment of pure contentment until she couldn't see anymore, either from smoke or death.

The fire was closing in on her.

Did she want to die? To rest? Adrienne wasn't sure.

Tears rolled down her face, leaving clean tracks on her cheeks where the soot washed away. Big heavy tears that ran into the corners of her mouth and tasted like release.

The emergency lights swirled with the flames and the smoke. Who knew how long it would take them to get to Adrienne. She accepted that they might be too late for her.

None of that mattered.

She had done what she came to do.

For the first time in maybe her entire adult life, Adrienne felt peace.

Epilogue

Summer

Adrienne was surfing.

Badly. So very badly.

But doing well wasn't the point. If she wanted to stick with doing stuff she was good at, she would be sneaking an eighth of psychedelic mushrooms onto a Southwest Airlines flight.

Her sponsor, Lisa, said over and over again whenever she wanted to drink or use, she should connect to "big nature."

She had tried hiking. It was somehow both hard and boring. Pass.

She had tried horseback riding. Her ass hurt for a week after, and plus the horse bit her.

So she was trying surfing.

Well. *Surfing* was generous. It was more, *paddling around small waves and trying not to swallow the entire Pacific Ocean every time her head went underwater*. Which was often. But the mental and physical effort did take her mind off her cravings, which were less and less strong these days and increasingly infrequent.

Mostly, though, she loved being in the ocean because it reminded her that she was, in fact, so small. Chiara's death hadn't swallowed the whole earth, only her heart. And the media circus around Thea's death couldn't pester her for a comment here in the waves.

Immediately after the summit, Adrienne had been in the hospital for over a week. On the second day, and the first time she was conscious for more than five minutes, Adrienne had to give her statement to the local police. A public defender was even present on her behalf, a sign that this case was getting a lot of attention and no one wanted to ruin it on a legal misstep.

As Adrienne talked to the officers, she could tell no one believed her. Not even the public defender. There were shared looks and incredulous notes taken. The longer she talked, the less convinced they were.

When she finished, the officer read through their notebook. "So you're saying Thea McCorckle and her associates killed your sister; covered it up; murdered another woman, who at first was helping them; then they tried to murder you, but you killed all of them in self-defense. And this all happened because Ms. McCorckle needed to protect her *mommy brand*?"

Adrienne found herself oddly defending Thea. "Yes. Why do you keep dismissing her as a 'mommy brand'? She was a multimillionaire. People get killed for a lot less."

The cop looked her dead in the eyes. "How would you know?"

Adrienne stared back, unfazed. "The news."

The cop closed their notebook. "Uh-huh. Okay. Call us when the medications wear off and we can try this again."

The public defender tried to hang around to soften Adrienne up to the idea of a plea deal, but Adrienne told him to go eat a hive of bees, and he left.

Alone in her hospital room, Adrienne thought of Drew in the back seat of the Dodge Charger with all the pills and all the cash. That was Adrienne now. Not a shred of proof to support her story beyond an Apple Watch that could be explained away with no imagination necessary. It had connected to Wi-Fi because it was still linked to the network from the year before. But what did that prove? Nothing. Even Chiara's car magically appearing was being rewritten as she'd abandoned it somewhere and some kids later took it for a joyride. On the other hand, there was a lot of evidence supporting a world where a long-term junkie had cracked after her twin skipped town, and gone on a killing spree, hurting beautiful mothers whose only crime was caring too much.

But Adrienne's story stayed the same no matter how many ways they asked the same questions or attempted to find inconsistencies.

So the cops followed up just to prove her wrong, just to make sure that her trial was speedy, and most of all, to make sure Adrienne was found guilty.

Luckily, the mayhem at the ranch was so widespread, and the risk of wildfires at that time of year so high, that the entire property had been sealed off the night of the corn-maze inferno. Looking around the farmhouse for ways to pin this mess on Adrienne, instead the cops found the murder weapon in Thea's office safe with all the Squad's prints on it. Hard evidence was hard to argue with. That made them chase down the rest of Adrienne's version of events.

Next, it turned out that SARA had recorded the kitchen conversation, too, including Bernice's murder. Apparently, Thea recorded everything that happened in the house, with hours and hours of recordings on servers in the basement, her thirst for blackmail never missing an opportunity. With that, all questions around Adrienne's story disappeared for good, and the paint-by-numbers investigation was completed quickly.

On Adrienne's last day before leaving the hospital, Bautista came to visit. When she walked into the room, Adrienne struggled to sit up straighter, but Bautista made a motion for her to relax.

"I take back everything I said about you," Adrienne croaked, her voice still raspy from the smoke inhalation. "I'm alive because of you."

Bautista gave her a kind look. "It was Chiara's husband, actually."

Adrienne couldn't hide her shock, which sent her into a coughing fit.

Bautista went on as she held the oversize hospital water cup and bendy straw to Adrienne's mouth. "I know what you think of him, but I called every connection I could for a warrant with no luck. He called his neighbor—a former judge himself—and promised him the damn moon to get us in front someone who would listen. Then Chiara's husband was the one who convinced that judge to get us access to the ranch that night. Chiara's husband connected the photo on the visor, the Apple Watch pinging on his phone, and your imminent harm. He's why you're alive."

"I guess I have to call him," Adrienne said.

"He's here."

Adrienne coughed again. "What?"

"He's been here every day. He just stays in the lobby."

Adrienne pushed the tray off her bed. "Bautista, find me a walker."

With tubes and cords trailing after her like tentacles, Adrienne made her way to the elevator and down to the lobby, Bautista keeping her walker steady.

Adrienne saw him immediately, sitting in the middle of the room. His eyes were glazed, but his posture was strong.

"Hey," Adrienne said, trying to convey one million emotions and even more apologies.

He stood up, and without a word, he hugged her.

She hugged him back.

And they cried together for the first time. Their tears were quiet at first, and then quickly they were both sobbing. The emotional dam Adrienne feared had burst at last. For so long, she had wanted him to be angry like her, but now she realized she had needed to be sad with him.

"I'm so sorry," Adrienne said.

"I'm so sorry," he said back.

On that freezing afternoon, everything between them thawed for good.

A week later, cadaver dogs found Chiara buried deep in the oak grove.

Adrienne and Chiara's husband stood at the edge of the ranch, watching the medical examiner's van load the laden gurney, holding each other up long after the taillights had faded.

And now, Adrienne was surfing, fortifying her sobriety with both hands.

Next week, Adrienne was taking her nephews to Mexico (with their dad, of course). They were all going to go back to the beach she and Chiara loved. She would time it so they could all watch the sunrise together.

She would not take a single photo.

Acknowledgments

The author would like to thank the following people for their emotional, professional, and structural support that made this book possible.

Ryan, thank you for throwing your lot in with mine and never looking back. We get where we go together, and I am so excited for wherever we go next. I love you.

My mother, Barney Jean, who set the bar so high and then showed me how to soar over it.

My lovely boisterous family, who always believed even when I didn't.

The brilliant people who cared for my children so I could write, particularly Lena, who saved me.

Liz, Box, Noah, Megha, Selina, Ora, and Emma for their professional guidance.

Christian Capobianco, who provided more than she could ever know.

Lisa, Anastacia, and Natividad for welcoming me to a new era.

Our Los Angeles village of friends, who I will love forever and ever. Meeting you all was winning the ultimate lottery.

Tom Mayer, the gem who continues to tirelessly field my questions.

Alyona and David. I cherish you beyond measure.

Finally, I want to acknowledge my father, who isn't here to see this. I hope somewhere he knows that he ignited the spark when he put my construction paper books next to his on the shelf.

About the Author

Elizabeth Rose Quinn is a novelist and screenwriter. She graduated with a BA in English from UC Berkeley and a master's degree in marriage and family therapy. Born and raised in Berkeley, California, Elizabeth lived in Los Angeles for fifteen years while working in production and writing for television. Her novel *Follow Me* was optioned by Amazon MGM Studios and is currently in production as a feature film. She is married with two children and currently lives in New Mexico. In addition to traveling and exploring nature with her family, Elizabeth loves rolling fresh pasta, swimming in the Pacific Ocean, and looking for rainbows in the desert sunsets.